A Time of Change

Book 4 in the Bovey Tracey Saga

The Continuing Story of
A Town in South Devon
During the Commonwealth
1659 and 1660

Jim Marshall

Front cover image:
General George Monck, first Duke of Albemarle
Sir Peter Lely 1660

ISBN: 978-1-917601-44-3

This one is in memory of my dad.
Born in 1899
A soldier of the First World War
'Up to their necks in mud and bullets.'

CONTENTS

PREFACE vii
CHARACTERS ix
CHAPTER I 1
CHAPTER II..11
CHAPTER III 23
CHAPTER IV 40
CHAPTER V..52
CHAPTER VI 65
CHAPTER VII 75
CHAPTER IX 98
CHAPTER X 115
CHAPTER XI 123
CHAPTER XII...132
CHAPTER XIII 137
CHAPTER XIV 151
CHAPTER XV..160
CHAPTER XVI 166
CHAPTER XVII..173
CHAPTER XVIII...184
CHAPTER XIX 193
CHAPTER XX..202
CHAPTER XXI 218
CHAPTER XXII..227
CHAPTER XXIII...239
AUTHOR'S NOTE...245

PREFACE

Part three of my saga – A Time of Acceptance – ended in 1651. The Battle of Worcester had seen the final major engagement of the Civil War. Charles Stuart (later Charles II) had fled for his life. Parliament was firmly entrenched; Cromwell and the Roundheads were in total control. Things were accepted – generally.

I now ask you to make another leap forward – eight years to the year 1659. Things have changed. Oliver Cromwell, the Iron Man of his age, has died. All the balls of government are once again thrown up in the air. Who will grab them when they descend? Will there be one change, or many changes?

How does this all affect our little band of citizens in far-off Bovey Tracey? News reaches them spasmodically, and after days have elapsed. Have they even the time to spare to consider what it all may mean to them?

There are also changes in Bovey – people come and go. Lives are affected mainly by local happenings. So, not much change there! Plots and counterplots are encountered – and there were many during this period. Did these affect our little band of citizens?

I hope that reading this part of the saga gives you a small amount of the pleasure it gave me in its writing.

Jim Marshall
October 2023

CHARACTERS
Real people in BOLD

<u>The town of Bovey Tracey</u>

John Ramsey	Born 1610	The town baker
Evelyn Ramsey	Born 1612	John's wife
James Ramsey		Born 1609 Apothecary
Avril Ramsey	Born 1612	Apothecary and healer, James' wife
Nell Dawkins	Born 1642	Orphan – adopted by James and Avril
Gil Ramsey	Born 1630	Son of John and Evelyn
Ella Ramsey	Born 1631	Gil's wife – daughter of Abel and Faith Smith
Rosie Ramsey	Born 1647	Their daughter
Jamie Ramsey	Born 1649	Their son
Abel Smith	Born 1609	Blacksmith
Faith Smith	Born 1613	Abel's wife
Simon Smith	Born 1632	Their son
Imelda Smith	Born 1633	Simon's wife – Nee Grubb
Jack Smith	Born 1650	Simon and Imelda's son
Rachel Smith	Born 1651	Their daughter
Dick Allen	Born 1611	Innkeeper
Sal Allen	Born 1613	His wife
Maud Fletcher	Born 1639	May's sister
Simon Dingle	Born 1624	Butcher
Henry Hoggs	Born 1612	Saddler
Primrose Hoggs	Born 1632	Their daughter
Gaston Bessant	Born 1626	Town Bookseller
Glory Bessant	Born 1630	
Isobel Bessant	Born 1648	
Lou Crowley	Born 1613	Widow of Peter Crowley
Felix	Born 1649	Adopted by Lou

| **James Forbes** | Born 1614 | Vicar |
| Ralph Goodes | Born 1620 | Verger – acting churchwarden |

The Parke Estate

Luke Barton	Born 1599	Steward to Sir John
Grace Barton	Born 1604	His wife
Peter Cove	Born 1608	Bailiff of the 'manor'
Laura Cove	Born 1610	His wife
Harry Cove	Born 1630	Their son
Mary Cove	Born 1632	Harry's wife – Nee Ramsey
Will Cove	Born 1652	Elder son of Harry and Mary
Peterkin Cove	Born 1652	His twin
Sam Garvey	Born 1627	Estate servant
Robert Hook	Born 1628	Estate servant
Bernie Wheatcroft	Born 1638	Shepherd
Hob Slater	Born 1636	Orphan adopted by the Coves
May (Fletcher)	Born 1637	Hob's wife
Kitty Slater	Born 1654	Their daughter
Poppy Slater	Born 1656	Their younger daughter

The Brimley Estate

Lady Violette	Born 1586	Widow of Lord Charlton
Luke Farmer	Born 1628	Ex-royalist soldier; Steward
Meg Farmer	Born 1630	His wife
Hal Farmer	Born 1648	Their son
Kit Warden	Born 1627	Gardener; Ex-royalist soldier

Trusham

| Michael Brown | Born 1620 | Hurdle maker |
| Hugh Ratcliffe | Born 1621 | Hurdle maker |

Westminster and elsewhere

| **John Bradshaw** | Born 1602 | MP |
| **Thomas Fairfax** | Born 1612 | Army commander |

Oliver Cromwell	Born 1599	Died 1658
Henry Ireton	Born 1611	Parliamentary officer
Richard Ingoldsby	Born 1617	Parliamentary officer
Sir George Monck	Born 1608	Parliamentary commander
Matthew Kent	Born 1620	Roving Agent for parliament

Stephen DeGruchy	Young lieutenant
Archibald DeGruchy	His uncle – businessman
Francis DeGruchy	Archibald's eldest son
Lionel DeGruchy	Next son (18)
Letty DeGruchy	Daughter
Annette DeGruchy	Francis' wife
Marie DeGruchy	Francis' daughter

CHAPTER I

The last day of March in the year 1659 had brought a cold wind and heavy showers. In the small town of Bovey Tracey, the inhabitants simply shrugged their shoulders and got on with their lives. Living as they did just to the east of Dartmoor, they were very well used to these conditions. Gales and depressions came in from the Atlantic to the west with monotonous regularity. Those who lived up on the moor were a hardy breed.

Inside the church dedicated to Saints Peter, Paul and Thomas, the mood was just about as sombre as the weather outside. A few candles did their flickering best to lift the mood, but they fought a losing battle. The air inside the church was damp, mainly from the soaked clothing of the congregation. That, and the regular coughs and sneezes lowered the mood of depression even further. Adults muttered and children fidgeted. Since they had all gathered inside at ten o'clock, not a word had been spoken – and it was then fifteen minutes past the hour.

In the front pew (gospel side), three parishioners had their heads together, whispering. James Ramsey, Peter Cove and Luke Barton were discussing who should make the address. In truth, they should have decided this well in advance of the service. On a chair to the side sat the Reverend James Forbes. He had been the rector of the church until Parliament had removed him from that office – due to his having been chaplain to Prince Charles – son of the executed Charles I.

Fifteen minutes of deliberation ended when Peter Cove, Bailiff of the Parke Estate, rose and climbed the short steps into the pulpit. In his hand was a sheaf of papers. At once, a sepulchral hush fell upon the congregation as, with a clearing of his throat, Cove made his opening address.

"We have all come together here today to remember those who fell victim to the worst outbreak of the winter fever that any of us can remember. How many more would have we lost had it not been for the wonderful efforts of Avril Ramsey, Mary Cove and Nell Dawkins? Those three, helped by others, must have saved the list of the departed from many more names. It is now just three weeks since the last death. Let us all hope and pray that this is an end to it. I must now read out the names of the many friends and neighbours who we have lost."

He paused for a moment and, a sign of approaching age, perched a pair of spectacles on his nose, then started on the long list.

"Starting right at the top of the village, Zachary Allen, son of Dick and Sal, and brother of Glory. That tavern will never be the same without him. Then we come to Josiah and Alice Grubb. Josiah has been our shoemaker for so many years. What will happen to their business now that they are no longer with us, I have no idea. Then we come to Will and Patience Fletcher. Their daughters May and Maud live on, may the Good Lord be thanked."

May, who had married Hob – once messenger to the Bailiff and now Assistant Bailiff - buried her face in Hob's shoulder and sobbed quietly. Maud, two years May's junior, sat alone and looked lost.

"And then we go right down to the bridge. The whole Gates family, Adam, Olivia and young Kat – all taken from us within a week of each other. Will the mill wheels ever turn again I wonder?"

Once again, he paused as the enormity of a whole family's loss sank in. For some in the congregation it proved just too much – the quiet was split by quiet sobbing. Inexorably, the list went on; wife and daughter of the butcher, wife and son of the saddler, Henri and Eloise Bessant, the Huguenot booksellers. Their son Gaston married to Glory Allen, daughter of the tavernkeepers. The wife and daughter of the Churchwarden, the Sexton and his wife. Finally came the old head gardener of the Brimley Estate – a diminutive chap who in life had been affectionately known as Goliath.

Peter Cove came to the end of his long list, folded it up and placed in back in his pocket. He looked up and around the packed church where many were sitting with tears in their eyes. It had been a horrible winter!

"Let us all now make our own prayers to God for the safe deliverance of all our departed friends. Please, stay as long as you think necessary – we have so much to pray for, not least our own deliverance from this dreadful winter."

He stepped down and joined his wife, son, daughter-in-law, young Hob and his wife May. He closed his eyes and wondered, not for the first time, why so many had been taken from them – and why them?

Reverend James Forbes also closed his eyes. His first thought was almost a side issue. That should satisfy the most ardent of our Puritan Parliament, he mused. A simple service of remembrance, private prayer, and utter silence. No intermediary between God and parishioner – not even a pious sermon!

An hour later, the church had emptied out. Forbes did his usual round of the pews to make sure no possessions had been left behind. Then he left for his cottage, leaving the Churchwarden Ralph Goodes to lock up. Ralph, having lost both wife and son, was in no hurry to leave.

Forbes, sitting alone in his cottage, sat down to a meagre supper of bread, cheese and ale. He also began musing to himself on the same lines as had the Bailiff – why those good people? Having found no answer, he went to bed.

Later that same evening, with the light fading fast at the end of a long and hard winter, the dining table in the Bailiff's large cottage was only just large enough to accommodate all the people gathered around it. At one end sat Peter Cove, Bailiff of the Parke Estate for the previous twenty-four years. At the other end sat his wife, Laura. Normally, all the others would have been sat along the two sides. However, there were just too many, so Laura had two small children perched on stools at either side of her. Peter had another two at his end. On one side sat the Parke Steward, Luke Barton opposite his wife Grace. Filling the other places down the sides were Harry Cove and his wife Mary, and Hob and his wife May.

Laura, who knew what her husband was about to announce, gave him a small nod to signify that it was time and that she agreed with what was to be said. Peter cleared his throat and thus got everyone's attention.

"Twenty-four years I have held the position of Bailiff. You Harry have been my deputy for the last twelve. In a few weeks from now, I shall celebrate my fifty-first year, and on that day, I shall formally hand over the position of Bailiff to you Harry, my son. You are now twenty-eight and have learned more than enough of the business to take over complete responsibility. Your mother and I will still be on hand to offer what help and advice you may require – we shall move into the estate cottage near the gates."

Harry, who had been anticipating such an announcement, but had thought it to be further into the future. He raised his hand to ask a question – a question that his father had anticipated.

"Yes, Harry – it is all agreed and written into a deed. Not only is it approved by those in authority, it is also welcomed by the whole town. You and Mary have been mainstays of this place – you as my deputy and Mary as the town's schoolteacher. I'm sure that Will and Peterkin shall revel in their father's importance!"

The eight-year-old twins, perched on either side of their grandfather, nodded solemnly. Will, twenty minutes older than his twin, never missed an opportunity to exercise his seniority.

"Aye, grandfather. We shall be very important!"

"You, my two brats, shall be exactly as the others in my school – neither favoured nor promoted!" Mary wagged an admonishing finger at her two offspring.

Cove had not finished, noting that Hob and May had worried frowns.

"It has further been agreed that you Hob shall be Harry's Deputy Bailiff. You have lived here nearly all of your life and there is probably nobody who knows the town better than you. Added to which, you have been doing the job for the past two or more years anyway. Harry, once your mother and I have moved to the smaller cottage, the Bailiff's house will be yours and Mary's. I am assuming that Hob, May and their two will still be welcome here?"

Harry looked at Hob and gave a frown of thought.

"Aye, I suppose that would be acceptable," he said, then spoiled it with a huge grin.

Kitty Slater, just five years old, looked at the Bailiff.

"Is my dada really going to be Deputy Bailiff?" she asked.

"Aye, my poppet – he is!"

Kitty looked at Poppy, very nearly three. "Cor!" they said in unison.

Hob had been orphaned shortly after birth and had been taken in by Peter and Laura Cove, brought up as an adopted son. In his younger days he had been recognised as the town's joker, always up to some prank or other. One of his favourites had been placing a dead frog in the bed on the day that Gil and Ella had married. Now twenty-three years old he was a quiet, thoughtful young man. This remarkable transformation had been brought about by May who had been working for Gil and Ella, looking after the chickens, selling the eggs, and sometimes acting as nursemaid to the two children, Rosie and Jamie. Although May would freely admit that she was nowhere near the beauty of her sister Maud, Hob had fallen for her and had started to grow up from that day onwards.

When supper was finished, and the four little ones put to bed, the others sat together in the back parlour sipping at glasses of honey mead.

"Today's service must have been quite a strain on you, May," Laura spoke quietly as she invariably did. "It cannot have been easy for you."

"Nay, it was not at all easy," May replied. "But I had Hob and the children, and all you, of course. I cannot help wondering how Maud coped with it. We have both lost mother and father, but I have my own family for consolation. Maud has nobody at all."

"Dick and Sal at the tavern will not let her grieve alone," Harry was quick to point out. "They lost their son Zachary. Maud has been with them at the tavern now for at least a year. They have to rely heavily on her to help out. Nay – Maud will not lack comfort and a shoulder to lean on!"

Later, Hob lay beside his wife, turned onto one elbow. "Do you feel that Maud needs more than Sal and Dick Allen can give her?"

"When she had mama and papa to go and see every day, she was as right as a penny," May replied. "But now, we are the only family she has left. She dotes on our two and they adore their

Aunt Maud. I am going to have to make the time to involve her more – perhaps ask her to take the children for walks on her day off. Those two, if anyone can, will make her laugh again."

"Please do not take this the wrong way," Hob hesitated. "Maud is probably the prettiest young lady in this town. Why is she not fought over by all the young, unmarried men?"

May looked at her young husband and a slow smile lightened her face.

"Men never notice even the smallest thing!" she almost laughed. "Did you not know that she and Zachary were as close as two people could be without being married?"

"Then, she has lost even more than I imagined," Hob admitted. "Nay – I had not noticed. The poor lass!"

"Maud is certainly very beautiful," May added. "But I know for certain that she and Zachary would have married soon. She always said that she would never marry anyone who she did not love to distraction. Who will fill Zachary's shoes is something that only time will tell."

"And did you make the same vow? Marry only someone you loved to distraction?"

"Yes – and I suppose you will have to do!"

"Thank you for that. Good night, lovely wife."

"Good night, Deputy Bailiff."

"Who would ever have believed such a thing possible?" were Hob's last words before he fell asleep.

"Who indeed! The world has gone completely insane."

That same evening two very unlikely friends met for their weekly discussion of affairs in general over a bottle of Rhenish wine. These two somewhat elderly gentlemen sat in comfortably padded chairs either side of a blazing fire, their feet stretched towards the welcome heat. The Reverend James Forbes, now into his late fifties, had always been a staunch Royalist – had been chaplain to the then Prince Charles, now Charles II of Scotland. Colonel (retired) Lionel Fisher had been the absolute political opposite – a Colonel in Cromwell's New Model Army – until his retirement some three years previously. One of his final tasks had been to lead a small unit to Bovey Tracey and its surrounding villages for the purpose of eliminating an heretical sect that called itself The Vale of Sorrow. Fisher had been attracted to the area by two separate things; one, it was over two hundred miles from Westminster and its machinations; two – it was peaceful, industrious, and was home to many for whom he had formed a great liking. He had bought a large cottage and some grounds towards the neighbouring village of Teigngrace. There, with an elderly housekeeper-cum-cook, he intended to spend his remaining years exploring a place that had slowly wormed itself into his heart – Dartmoor.

"And what has been your latest discovery?" Forbes put his wine glass down on a small side table and regarded his companion with a wry smile.

"Aha! Glad you asked," Fisher returned the smile, knowing full well that the Reverend was gently pulling his leg. "Found myself riding between Yar Tor and Sharp Tor. Place is littered with the remains of ancient hut circles. Consulted the oracle when I got back – soaked to the skin, of course!"

James Ramsey, fifty years old and for many of those years, the town's apothecary, was commonly referred to as The Oracle – his knowledge of ancient history was encyclopaedic.

"And what did James have to add to your knowledge?"

"Said they dated back more than two thousand years. Long after what he referred to as the Stone Age, but hundreds of years before even the Romans came to this country. According to him, the whole of Dartmoor was once forested, but successions of settlers had cleared many parts for grazing and raising hardy crops."

"So, ancient Celtic people?"

"What? Like the Welsh, Cornish and Bretons? Suppose it's possible."

That seemed to end that line of conversation, so the two men settled back and sipped more of the amber wine, then made satisfied grunts.

"Have you any latest news from Westminster?" Forbes ventured, knowing that the old warrior liked to keep abreast of 'happenings' despite his constant claiming to want nothing more to do with what he referred to as the 'goings on'.

"Chappie came to see me the other day – name of Potter – used to be some sort of equerry for someone or other. According to him, Tumbledown Dick is making an even bigger hash of things than usual."

Richard Cromwell, the son of Oliver Cromwell, had taken over the role of Lord Protector of the Commonwealth upon the death of his father in the preceding September. Because of his ineptitude, he had brought upon himself the nickname Tumbledown Dick.

"Is that all an act, do you think?" Forbes probed.

"Could be, I suppose. Can't even think he wanted the job in the first place! On the other hand, could be that he's simply a useless fart!"

Forbes, well used to the somewhat 'barrack-room' language of his friend, merely grinned. "He's got a lot on his plate, nevertheless," he sought to find some middle ground. "Ireland, the Scots, Taxation, pressures from the ultra-puritan wing, not to mention rumblings from abroad."

"Ireland!" Fisher grunted. "May the Good Lord be thanked that I avoided that appalling mess! Nearly ten years past, would you believe! The Irish will never forgive us for Drogheda, not to mention Dublin and other places. Why the hell Cromwell acted as he did is still a mystery to me!"

"It was an unforgiveable massacre, and I do not care who hears me say it!" Forbes growled. "The place had surrendered to Cromwell – yet he proceeded to slaughter hundreds who had laid down their arms. Wicked!"

"Mark my words," Fisher was prone to making pronouncements. "Drogheda will come back to bite us in the arse for many years to come! Like you, James, I hold no candle for Rome or Catholicism, but nobody on God's good earth deserves to be treated like that!"

Forbes waited patiently. His friend was in one of his moods for prediction, and he wanted to find out what was to be the latest forecast.

"Monck!" Fisher muttered, almost to himself. "Monck!"

"Monck?" Forbes muttered back. "What of him? I know he was born hereabouts in Devon, but he is far away in Scotland now, keeping a lid on things there."

"George Monck, a general of considerable ability. I served with him on three occasions. He was ever imperturbable; calm as could be in any crisis. I have had a vague suspicion for many months past that, if anyone is going to alter the shape of England, it will be Monck himself. He is already at daggers drawn with John Lambert – has been for a long time."

"John Lambert – have not heard of him before," Forbes probed.

"You must have done so! John Lambert – one of the more prominent of the Major Generals?"

Forbes, who had certainly heard of the man, took cover behind a wall of innocence, almost goading his friend to expound further.

"It's no secret around Parliament," Fisher grunted. "From all I hear, the man wants to replace the Rump Parliament with a military government!"

"What? A military dictatorship? Surely, such a thing cannot be even contemplated!"

"My dear, innocent Reverend friend. Many things have been contemplated; most have not come to pass. But who is to say when and if a change of mood may take place? Consider our old enemy France. There is growing discontent with their monarchy. Who is to say that eventually this discontent will grow to such proportions that they will do as we did – and take the life of a crowned monarch?"

"But the boy Louis XIV is barely twenty years old! Can you really see the French ousting the Bourbons?"

"Not whilst he has such a pillar of strength as Cardinal Mazarin, shaping him into an absolute monarch. Did you know that he, as the anointed king, actually *owns* every other living soul in France? Not only their beings, also their land, their possessions – all are his by divine right."

"That, I did not know," Forbes said, open mouthed in astonishment. "That is astounding!"

"Astounding but true," Fisher nodded to himself. "Can you see a time when such an abuse of power will cease to be tolerated?"

"Put in those terms, yes, I can. But surely the Bourbons have sufficient strength to outlast what would be insurrection."

"This may sound extremely strange coming from an ex-officer of the Parliamentary forces. But – what would you call the ousting and execution of your own King Charles? Was that not insurrection?"

"I would certainly term it so!" Forbes answered.

"Then, a modern-day precedent has been set, has it not? Now, this Rhennish needs our full attention, would you not agree?"

"With no reluctance whatsoever, I would concur most wholeheartedly!"

CHAPTER II

Rosie had just turned twelve years of age when, during early April, it had been decided to make her the town's May Queen. Needless to say, Rosie was ecstatic.

"Does that mean that I'm the prettiest girl?" she asked, hoping and praying for an affirmative from her parents.

"Actually, no it does not!" Ella grinned at her daughter. "It simply means that it's your turn this year. I had my turn two years before I wed your papa, and I was certainly not the prettiest girl in the town. Primrose and Imelda were much prettier. Imelda still is!"

"Oh no, she is not," Gil shouted from the parlour. "Admittedly she is a very pretty lady, but so are you – and always have been!"

"But papa is *bound* to say that!" Rosie pouted.

"If he knows what is good for him, yes he is," Ella gave a hoot of laughter, very similar to that of her massive father and brother.

"So – I am not the prettiest of all the girls?" Rosie wanted at least some consolation.

"You, my little poppet, are a very pretty young lady and I will slaughter anyone who says differently," Gil came in to give his daughter a pat on her curly head.

"Tommy says that I am pretty," Rosie mumbled.

"And who the hell is this Tommy?" Gil demanded.

"Tommy Franks – he's the youngest of the Franks children from that small farm down past the Heath," Ella probably knew everyone for miles around.

"And do you think he's a handsome lad?" Gil grinned.

"Nay, papa. He's all covered in freckles and has red hair like a curly fox!"

Then he has probably learned to look after himself, Gil thought – learned to wrestle those who call him 'carrots' and 'spotty'. If so, good for him.

It was customary for previous holders of the post of May Queen to 'attend' the current queen, who was obviously much younger that they were. Nell Dawkins, the adopted daughter of James and Avril Ramsey, was seventeen, and had been Queen three years earlier. Maud Fletcher, now nineteen, had been Queen six years before. Both had agreed to 'attend' Rosie during the pageant. Everyone thought that it was just what Maud needed. She had lost her parents and the man everyone thought she would marry. She needed a distraction.

Officially, pageants, fairs, dancing, even music, were all proscribed. Needless to say, in the more remote parts of the country, these strictures were bent – sometimes, out of all recognition. It all depended upon the mindset and the strictness of those nominally in charge - bailiffs, sheriffs, lords of manors. The nearest Bovey Tracey had to such were Peter Cove, Bailiff at Parke (representing the ever absent at Westminster, Sir John), and Lady Violette Charlton at Brimley. Neither of these two were the slightest bit inclined to put a stopper on a harmless pageant.

All that was necessary was for the First of May to dawn fair and most important in South Devon, dry! Rosie, had been awake long before the roosters down in the fenced-off coop had even begun to clear their throats. Her first job on hopping out of her bed was to dash to the window and draw the curtain wide. It was still dark, but she could see that it was not raining. Uttering a quiet prayer of thanks, she hopped back into her bed and tried to compose herself for the day ahead. It did not work – she was far too excited. In the next, very small room, her brother Jamie, eighteen months younger than his sister, slept happily on. He had refused point blank to be a page for his sister. He had refused so vehemently that Ella and Gil had given way as they knew that, had they insisted, the little imp would have found a way to embarrass Rosie. Many were of the opinion that Jamie had started where a now far more mature Hob had left off. If ever a prank was discovered – dead spiders in bowls of milk, slugs found inside newly baked loaves – it was a fair bet that Jamie was either partly or wholly responsible. The only person able to completely subdue him was Mary in her role as schoolteacher. Somehow or other, Jamie would never dream of upsetting Miss Mary, as all her pupils called her.

Desperate to put on the spotless white dress that she would wear for the pageant, Rosie clattered down the stairs and went to look at it as it hung neatly on a peg in the parlour. Every year a new dress was made, and the May Queen of that year allowed to keep it as a fond memento of the occasion. For the past ten years, the dress had been made by Faith Smith, Ella's mother and acknowledged as the best seamstress in the town. Desperate though she was, she knew better than to put her hands on it just in case she left a mark on the pristine surface. Instead, she stood back and admired it. Then, unable to stay still for any longer, she went into the kitchen and started to prepare the porridge for their breakfast.

Ella was not long in coming down as the three roosters finished their morning 'call to arms'. "I swear that they get louder as each day passes!" she grumbled, rubbing sleep out of her eyes. "Ah! Can you not sleep?" she asked Rosie who was busy stirring fresh milk into the large pot of oats. She would finish it off afterwards with a large dollop of honey.

"Too excited, mama," Rosie admitted. Then a thought struck her. "Can we all make sure that Jamie does not put something horrible inside the dress?"

"Have no fear," Ella laughed. "Both your papa and I have threatened Jamie with a dire beating if he attempts anything at all to spoil your day!"

"Aye, that we have," Gil nodded, joining wife and daughter in the kitchen. "Where is the little imp?"

"Still snoring in bed, papa," Rosie answered, giving the porridge a final stir as it thickened properly.

"Then he soon shall not be! He knows full well that he has to feed the hens and collect the eggs." So saying, Gil stamped back up the stairs and was heard tipping his young son out of his bed. Jamie yelled in response, but came galloping down the stairs, tugging on his shirt over his breeches. He said no greeting, but scowled as he gathered up the small sack of grain and seeds. Slamming the door behind him, he went down through the rows of vegetables to the hen enclosure where he filled the small troughs with the feed, topped up the water, then grabbed a large basket and came back into the kitchen with it piled high with warm eggs.

"As soon as you have broken your fast, set up the table outside the front gate and make sure you sell all of them," Ella said, taking a half dozen for the family's use.

Jamie pulled a face, then looked directly at his sister and gave a smirk.

"Jamie's got something horrible planned," Rosie wailed.

"Nay – he's simply trying to get you all panicked," Gil assured her. "He knows full well what will happen should he do anything amiss – don't you, Jamie?"

"Aye, papa. I've promised not to do anything amiss."

"Then stop worrying your sister. It is her special day, and I will not allow her to be upset," Ella waved a finger at her son.

Every small town and village had a slightly different way of celebrating May Day, despite the practice being, if not forbidden, certainly frowned upon. These practices changed over the years as generations also changed. By ten o'clock, a very large crowd had assembled outside the church. Not only the inhabitants of the town itself, but also those from Parke and nearby Brimley. Standing in the lane was a cart with a flat bed, In the centre, facing forward was a large chair covered in yellow cloth – the May Queen's throne. The cart itself, like the patient horse, was festooned with garlands of early Spring flowers. A set of steps stood at the rear of the cart ready for the Queen to ascend.

At a few minutes past the hour, the church doors opened. Nell and Maud, dressed in pale green and with garlands in their hair, came down the steps and stood either side of the cart. Then, alone and quietly shaking, Rosie came down, her hand tucked into the arm of her proud father. Silently, he led Rosie in her immaculate dress to the rear of the cart and held her hand as Rosie climbed the steps to sit on her throne. Lady Violette, that ancient and very grand lady, climbed up behind her, holding a small chaplet of yellow flowers. She stood behind the throne and a hush fell over the waiting crowd.

"Hail, Queen of the May," Lady Violette placed the chaplet on Rosie's head, then handed her a wooden sceptre, also festooned with flowers.

"Hail, Queen of the May," roared the crowd, as Reverend Forbes stood with arms outstretched.

"Let us all bow our heads and thank the Good Lord for our good fortune; pray for good and strong crops to grow in our fields; and that this day may pass in peace and laughter."

He was very careful to refrain from a blessing – as this would certainly be in violation of the laws. He had simply led a crowd in common prayer – and that was perfectly permissible.

After a suitable interval, the town's musicians – trumpets, side drums, flutes – broke out into a jolly march and the procession started all the way down the main street, up into the Parke Estate, then back again to the small square where tables laden with food and drink were laid out ready for a very hungry and merry crowd.

Rosie's 'throne' was placed on a dais and she was escorted there to sit in splendour, her two attendants on small stools at either side of her. A young boy named Felix brought a platter of food and bowed to Rosie as she gracefully accepted it. Felix, a foundling, had been adopted by the widowed Lou Crowley. Felix had been discovered as a tiny baby by Hob when he had been walking along the bank of the River Bovey – abandoned and in a pitiful state. A young woman's body had been found the next day, at a fair distance from the baby. Nobody had ever discovered whether that young woman had been the mother – or what had transpired.

Rosie ate demurely – a source of wonder for her mother who was watching for any sign of mischief from Jamie. Ella, remembering her time as May Queen, relived her experiences through her daughter. Ella was a very contented mother.

A long way from these festivities, a quiet meeting was held in a small room in a private house not far from Westminster. Five days after the May Day celebrations, on the 6th of May, yet another momentous change was taking place. Six years earlier, Oliver Cromwell had dismissed the remainder of the Long Parliament – the remainder of which was referred to as the Rump Parliament. He had been declared Lord Protector of the Commonwealth – and had ruled as such with the support of his New Model Army.

Then, on the 3rd of September 1658, Cromwell had died – ironically on the seventh anniversary of the Battle of Worcester, the battle which had seen the end of Prince Charles' ambitions. Cromwell's son Richard – Tumbledown Dick – had replaced him and had reinstated the Rump Parliament. It was generally recognised that this was, to say the very best, a shambles. He had referred to it as the Third Protectorate Parliament.

Two men sat at a small table in the equally small room. Both were quiet for a while as each fought for the words to say. Matthew Kent had been a parliamentary agent for some years and had spent some time in the West Country seeking out possible troublemakers. He had spent a considerable time in Bovey Tracey, a little town he had come to admire. Now approaching his thirty-fifth year, he was contemplating a return there. He was also contemplating his resignation from parliament's service.

His companion was far older. Canon Rigby had long retired from positions within the Anglican Church. Renowned as one possessing encyclopaedic knowledge on matters both clerical and political, Kent had sought him out on numerous occasions for a deeper insight into matters that he was investigating. The two had struck a chord with one another. Neither felt inhibited to utter to the other thoughts that they would probably be well advised not to utter in public.

And now, all had changed yet again. The army under Major General John Lambert had summarily removed Richard Cromwell from office. Somehow or other, the Rump had been reinstalled. William Lenthal as Speaker stated that 'this be a Commonwealth without a king, a single person, or House of Lords'.

"And what are we all to make of this, eh?" old Cannon Rigby raised bushy eyebrows at his young companion.

"The Lord only knows," Kent replied, looking totally mystified. "Heaven knows, Tumbledown Dick was inept – to say the very least. But what is anyone to make of the mess we now find ourselves in?"

"One thing I know for sure," Rigby muttered. "Monck will not take very kindly to Lambert's actions. However, what he will do about it – what he is *able* to do about it – is another matter altogether."

Kent was thoughtful for a moment. "That declaration is intriguing," he said slowly. "Commonwealth – well yes, that is plain and straightforward. As is the bit that states without a king or House of Lords. But what is intended by the words, 'a single person'? Does that imply that all decisions are made by a Committee, that there no single person shall be accountable? That is either a shrewd move, or one of abject cowardice!"

"Lenthal would not have uttered those words without the agreement and foreknowledge of the majority. He is Speaker, not the leader. So, who originated the words? Lambert? Probably does not possess the imagination!" Rigby grunted.

"You have a poor opinion of Lambert, then?"

"Not of his military prowess! He has proved that often enough. Despite what I just said, perhaps he *was* the one to come up with the phrase. Maybe he has enough self-knowledge to know that a committee of some sort *is* needed. Then again, perhaps I was right in my original statement – that he is not anywhere near imaginative enough. Bless me! I'm dithering in my old age!"

Kent looked wryly amused at that statement. "If there is anyone less likely to dither, I have yet to meet him," he gave the old Cannon a grin.

"Kind of you to say so – but this situation has left me doubting my own words and even my own mind. First, we have a king who will not listen to his Parliament. Then we have a Parliament which does not trust its king. Then we have years of war and strife, far too many lives lost – and for what? Extreme views prevail and a king loses his head. Suddenly, we are a Commonwealth, then a Commonwealth with a Lord Protector. The Military is in control until the Lord Protector dies, leaving a rather inept son in charge of things. Now we have military rule again, albeit with a Parliament. No, I tell you this most solemnly – things simply cannot go on like this. The good people of England know not who is in control from one day to the next!"

Kent simply had to butt in at that point. "From my everlasting travels around this country – especially down into the West Country – the good people of England have but one major concern – how to ensure they have the crops and food to sustain life. Everything else, believe me, is secondary to that concern!"

"I suppose you must be right," Rigby acknowledged. "I have lived far too long in the cities and tend to forget that the vast majority live in the small towns and villages. A poor harvest and a wave of sickness is of immediate concern to them. What happens far away in Westminster must appear almost trivial by comparison."

"What happens in the countryside is of importance to those in the cities," Kent argued. "City dwellers do not grow their own crops. From all that I have seen over the years, poverty in the city is far worse than poverty in the countryside. At least poor villagers have some means of access to food, no matter of poor quality. But to return to your summary – what do you see as the likely outcome of all this?"

Rigby gave a bark of laughter and regarded his young friend with a frown, then a big smile. "Ha! You would put me to the test, would you? I see two possible outcomes. The first is that things remain as they are – a Commonwealth governed by a Parliament answerable to the Army. The second is that it all collapses into a heap of nothingness, and Charles is invited back, but with severely restricted powers."

"Of the two, I have a distinct preference for the second of your visions," Kent said. "It would mean a return to the practices of an organised Church of England, and some pleasures allowed for the people who have been denied them for so many years."

"Music!" breathed the old Cannon. "How I have missed the music. William Byrd and Thomas Tallis – both dead many years ago. But their music can set hearts rejoicing. I long to hear it again."

"Then, for the sake of your heart, let us pray for your second vision to become a reality!"

Three days afterwards, back in Bovey Tracey, James Ramsey closed and locked the door to the apothecary shop just after five o'clock. Not that they were ever truly closed! At any time of the day or night, there might be a call for help from anyone in the town, or in the outlying villages. James, the apothecary for the past twenty-two years, was often called out for broken bones, stitching cuts, and any variety of emergencies. The nearest physician was in Newton Abbot – a man much given to the practise of letting blood. This was anathema to James' wife Avril, someone who was called upon for sickness, fever, any illness really. Her belief that blood was best kept inside the body was shared by her husband and her one-time apprentice Mary.

Between them, they had tended the many victims of the recent winter fever, and it was due to their combined efforts that the death toll had been far lower than many other towns. Nell, very nearly seventeen years age, had been adopted when she was four. Her mother had died giving birth to her. Her father, buried in Bovey Tracey churchyard, had died following an accident when he, his father and daughter had visited the small town back in 1646. The small family were travelling tinkers, mending pots, pans, kettles etc. On the death of Nell's father, her grandfather had simply abandoned her as 'being of no use to me'. James and Avril, childless, had not hesitated and had given the little girl a loving and caring home.

For the past six or seven years, Nell had taken over from Mary as apprentice in the shop – Mary taking over the newly found school. Avril had almost given up trying to teach Nell anymore – she recognised that the girl was now fully competent to attend and treat any patient that came along.

"Another day done, we hope," James muttered as the last shutter was put into place. "May we have yet another evening and night of peace."

"Amen to that!" Avril nodded, putting away the pestle and mortar, cleaned after crushing cloves of garlic with mint.

"I shall attend to any call this evening," Nell volunteered, coming into the shop from where she had been preparing supper. "I know the last night call was three days past, but I am quite happy to attend."

"First of all, my dear young lady, we sit down to supper and discuss your coming birthday. It is only one month away. What would you like in the way of a celebration?"

They went into the back parlour and sat down to a simple supper of fresh bread, bacon and then an apple pudding.

"I should like what we always have – simply a large family gathering with a meal and some mead."

"Ours is indeed a large family!" James grinned. "My brother the baker and his wife. His son Gil, his wife and their two children. Gil's sister Mary and her husband and two twins. Gil's wife Ella's family, the Smiths and their son, his wife and children. That means that we shall gather in the tavern as none of our homes is large enough to accommodate the lot of us!"

"And is there any special guest you would like to ask?" Avril probed.

"No – I can think of no one," Nell replied, missing completely the point of the question. Avril looked at James and they shared a look. Why the young men for miles around were not clamouring for Nell's company was strange to say the least.

Strange, but Avril had a shrewd idea why Nell kept them all at arm's length. Nell knew only too well that her own birth had been the cause of her birth mother's death. Although Nell attended births, helped the mothers during labour, Avril knew that Nell was mortally afraid of being in the same position as her departed mother. Therefore, she kept men at a distance. Nevertheless, Avril lived in hope that Nell would find happiness with some good man – eventually.

Changing the subject with his normal tact, James let out a secret that he and Avril had kept from Nell.

"On the day of your birth, Avril and I have devised a present for you that we both know will be received with joy. I am not able to declare you an official apothecary – I do not have that power. But what I can do is to hand you a Certificate of Competence – competence to act as apothecary with full access to any resource you may need. Mary will draw it up on a proper parchment and both Avril and I will sign and seal it."

Nell was silent for a moment as this sank in. Then a tear trickled down her face.

"There could never be a more welcome present," she managed. "I give you my word that I shall never let you down, nor I hope, any patient who may come my way. Thank you so very much."

"No more than you deserve," Avril added. "Also, James and I have found a jewel for you. I shall say no more about it but keep it for you to discover on the day."

The birthstone for April was a diamond, the most iconic of all precious stones. Avril had discovered a pendant necklace on a thin, gold chain when she had last been in Exeter. The diamond was set into a gold surround. It was plain and simple, just what Nell would have chosen for herself.

Despite it being quite dark, Nell donned her warm cloak after supper and let herself out. Neither James nor Avril questioned this. They knew full well where she was going.

After walking quietly up the main street, Nell let herself into the small churchyard and made for the far side where her father's grave was situated. Nell visited it every week, leaving flowers whenever she could find suitable blooms. She sat down on the low wall at the head of the grave.

"Hello, dada," she said. "I have wonderful news to tell you."

For the next fifteen minutes, she regaled her father with the news. Finally, blowing a kiss at the headstone, she walked quietly back home, let herself into the shop, locked up behind her and went quietly to bed.

One pair of eyes had seen Nell come and go. Reverend Forbes was so used to seeing Nell visit her father's grave that it no longer registered – until that particular evening. Nell made a habit of visiting during daylight hours; to see her passing into the churchyard after dark was very unusual. Forbes wondered what special message she had passed to her departed father – for it was bound to be special at that time of night. He returned his attention to his visitor.

Colonel Fisher was looking unusually tense that evening. News had eventually filtered down to Devon of the latest momentous happenings in far off Westminster.

"Only one good thing has come from all this," he growled into his ale mug, "the end of Richard Cromwell. Not that I've anything particular against the chap – he was just not cut out for the job."

James Forbes uncannily latched onto the point made days earlier by his ecclesiastical colleague, Canon Rigby.

"No single person," he mused aloud. "What is that supposed to mean, I wonder? If not one single person, then how many – and more to the point, which persons?"

"Haven't the slightest notion, old friend," Fisher admitted. "But is the statement supposed to reassure us that the idea of a Lord Protector is dead and buried? The whole idea makes no sense whatsoever. You can only ever have one man making decisions in a battle – there is not the time for conferences! There simply has to be someone in charge. Collective decision making cannot work!"

"There speaks the old soldier," Forbes gently ribbed his friend. "Speaking for myself, I see nothing wrong in collective decision making. Less chance of the extreme view being adopted."

"No, cannot agree!" Fisher came back strongly. "Need someone at the helm all the time. When things go right, he gets the praise. When it all goes wrong, you shoot the blighter and appoint another. Every entity in the world needs a figurehead, someone who is held accountable. That's what Charles Stuart could never get into his thick head – thought he was accountable to God and to God alone. Forgot all about the people he was supposed to head!"

"What about this rumour that Monck is decidedly unhappy with the actions that Lambert has taken?" Forbes wondered.

"One excellent soldier taking exception to the actions of another excellent soldier? Twas ever so, and I'm profoundly glad that I am no longer a part of it! If Monck really *does* take strong exception to it, then we can expect even more strife. What I fear most is Lambert's impatience with a civilian Parliament. Should he decide it is not to his liking, he may well reintroduce some sort of military rule – and that is something that Monck will never tolerate. No, old friend, I see nothing settled coming out of all this. What was it that Will Shakespeare said in one of his pieces? Things bad begun make worse themselves by ill – or something to that effect. Could be prophetic if you ask me!"

CHAPTER III

The summer had been fairly good on the whole – enough sun to ripen the crops, yet just enough rain to keep things on an even keel. The whole of the West Country heaved a collective sigh of relief as the last of the grain was stored away safely. Gil and Ella also were happy as their vegetables were still growing and producing a good enough yield to keep the money rolling in. Rosie, aided on occasion by a reluctant Jamie, looked after the still growing flock of hens. Not only did they sell eggs, they also sold pullets to Simon Dingle, the butcher. All in all, Bovey Tracey was a moderately happy and contented little town.

It was not until the 20th of September that a travel weary Matthew Kent rode into the town and made immediately for the tavern. The last time he had been in the town had been eight years previously. He was both surprised and relieved to see that very little had changed. Now, just short of his fortieth year, he faced a future that was at long last his own to devise. Two things had prompted his leaving Westminster. The first was the ever-changing situation with both Parliament and the Army. One seemed never to know from one day to the next who was 'king of the castle'. Being a man of rigid self-discipline, he could no longer stomach the uncertainty, the lack of continuity. The second reason was the fact that he longed to be his own master. Working for a Parliament that was as unstable as quicksilver had brought him to realise that he trusted the judgement of one person only – himself. Perhaps, he mused, old Canon Rigby had sound judgement, but he viewed the world from a different perspective to Kent.

"By all the saints in heaven," Dick Allen gasped as Kent opened the door to the large taproom. "Tis Master Kent returned again. Welcome, Master Kent. What brings you here this time? Not more trouble I hope!"

"Not this time," Kent grinned. "No troubles of which I am aware. This time I come for good. I have at last summoned the courage to resign my position and to seek a life of comfort and ease far away from the convoluted mess in Westminster."

"Then you will be made very welcome here," Allen extended a hand which was grasped and shaken. "Are you in need of lodging?"

"Aye, that I am. Until I can find a place to buy – and I know not where or what – I would very much appreciate a room here, plus of course, the excellent fare and superb ale."

"Sal!" Dick called over his shoulder. "Come here and see who is arrived to join our community."

Sal, now in her mid-forties, came bustling from the kitchens where she had been supervising her cooks in the preparation of the evening supper.

"Bless my soul – tis Master Kent!" she said. "You be very welcome here."

"What has been happening here since I left?" Kent asked. Then could have bitten his tongue when the sorry tale unfolded.

"Last winter was cruel to us," Sal was on the verge of tears. "The winter fever took our Zachary from us, along with far too many others. For many a month this town was in mourning from the losses."

"Then I mourn your loss. He was a grand lad."

"Someone else mourns him apart from us," Dick added. "Young Maud Fletcher and our Zachary were as good as betrothed. She still mourns him and will seek no other."

"And what of the delightful Glory?" Kent hoped that this was not the doorway to another tale of woe.

"Our daughter is not what she was, and that's a fact. She is long married to Gaston Bessant and now aids him at the bookshop. The elder Bessants were also taken last winter."

"As if they had not enough sorrow in their lives!" Sal remarked. The Bessant family of father, mother, and son were Huguenots who had escaped the vicious killings in their native France and had settled in Bovey Tracey – and had been welcomed.

"But you are tired from your journey, and would no doubt welcome a mug of ale," Dick remembered that he was a tavern keeper and 'mine host'.

"Indeed, I would," Kent dropped his two saddle bags at a nearby table and sat down with a sigh of relief. His horse was safe enough in the stables behind the tavern. The ostler and his lad had been there for years and knew their business. Kent at last allowed himself to relax.

However, his peace was not to last much longer. The hour approached when the tavern started to fill up with the evening's customers – a few of whom would also partake of the supper on offer. One of those to arrive was an old lady accompanied by a much younger man. Kent glanced up and, with a broad smile, sprang to his feet.

"Lady Violette," he gave the smallest of bows knowing that this indomitable old lady did not stand on unnecessary ceremony.

"Master Kent – or do my old eyes deceive me?" she came towards him as he pulled out a chair for her at his table.

"Your eyes, I suspect, are as keen as the youngest falcon," Kent grinned. "And who is this hovering at your elbow?"

"This fellow hovering as you put it, Is Kit Warden. He is now my head gardener and a friend of my steward. Both steward and all the staff seem to believe that, should I be left to travel any distance further than ten yards, I shall collapse from sheer exhaustion – therefore, must be accompanied wherever I go."

"I leave you in capable hands, my lady," Warden gave Kent a smile. "I shall be on hand for your return journey." So saying, he wandered over to the taps to get himself a mug of ale.

"Bah, piffle and balderdash!" the old lady, now well into her seventies grunted as she straightened her skirts under the table. "I come here one evening every week to keep my finger on the pulse. I cannot abide not knowing what is happening. I am still perfectly capable of undertaking a journey of a mere two miles without a nursemaid!"

Lady Violette Charlton, long widowed, had taken the Brimley Estate many years before and had returned it to its former glory. Her untiring efforts had yielded as well kept an estate as Parke with its myriad servants.

"And what brings you here again, Master Kent? Not more trouble I hope?"

"No trouble at all," Kent replied, pouring Lady Violette a glass of wine from the small ewer that had been left on his table.

"Simply a wish to escape from the madness of Westminster and a life of peace and quiet down here far from the tumult and disorder."

"So, you have left your post for good?"

"Aye, and with a glad heart. What I shall do now that I am here I have yet to determine. But having saved a fairly generous salary for many years, I can take my time and find somewhere to my liking, perhaps a small business that takes my fancy."

"After the ravages wrought on the countryside last winter, there are many opportunities for a man of means."

"Aye – I heard that the winter fever was severe. I was sorry indeed to learn of the losses."

"My old head gardener was also taken – hence the promotion of young Warden. You may remember him – Garside, his name was. But better known as Goliath because of his small stature."

"That, I do. The losses you mention would probably be of farmers, would they not? I am not at all sure that I would know what to do with a farm! But pray tell me what else has happened."

"First and foremost, in my mind is the school. I am its patron. Young Mary is married to Harry Cove – now Bailiff in his father's stead. No, they were not taken. Both his parents retired. Mary, bless her, has twin boys, now seven years of age, and a couple of rascals! You will remember young Hob – that rapscallion messenger. Well, you never saw a change like it. He is deputy bailiff now and married to young May Fletcher. They have two little girls – quite sweet angels, or so they appear. Hob is now the model father and man of business."

"I would never have thought that possible," Kent laughed. "I hope that Peter Cove is still hereabouts. He and I got on very well."

"He and Laura live in a smaller cottage on the estate. I'm sure they would welcome a visit."

"I shall be most happy to do so."

Kent enjoyed his first evening back in the small town. There were many happy memories stored away in his brain. Yes, he decided as he lay down to sleep in his comfortable room; yes, I am glad I have come here.

The fickle climate of the West Country turned a somersault the next day. Down came a thick mist – rolling down from the moor. Not only a mist, but a damp one as well. Up on the moor, it would have been almost impenetrable and very miserable. Down in the Bovey valley, it was just a damp mist that beaded clothes with moisture and chilled the body underneath.

Jamie Ramsey, the latest in a long line of practical jokers, was soon to celebrate his tenth birthday. His mother, Ella, was sister to Simon Smith, both the children of the huge blacksmith Abel Smith. Jamie and his cousin Jack, the son of Simon and Immelda, had teamed up some years before. Jack was nearly a year younger than Jamie and followed Jamie's lead in most things. That morning, the two of them were rummaging around in the yard behind the smithy. It was a veritable cornucopia of delights for two young boys. Discarded lengths of iron, old tubs, broken tools, broken wheel hoops, the list was endless. The yard ended at a low fence where the two lads were poking around looking for anything that could be used in their next game.

Jamie climbed up onto an old ploughshare that had years before been discarded as beyond economic repair. Balanced precariously atop the thick and rusty coulter, he peered around. He really wanted to find something he could use to poke down rabbit holes – something long and bendable. Frustrated, he almost was on the point of giving up when he espied something far more interesting on the far side of the low fence – something that glistened with the beads of moisture that were covering most surfaces.

"Jack," he called down to his cousin who was searching under a pile of old and bent sheets of tin. "Jack – there's something sparkling in the field. Got to go and see what it might be."

"We have to get back to school," Jack reminded him. "Dinner is almost over, and we do not want to be late for the afternoon lesson – it's going to be history, and I'm interested in the tale of when the Romans were here."

"Aye, I know that!" Jamie retorted, jumping down from his perch. He scuttled along the fence to where there were two loose boards, squeezed through and scampered back to where he had seen the object. In the thick and tangled grass on the far side of the fence he stopped, and his mouth gaped wide in astonishment.

"Jack – climb up and see what I've found," he shouted. Jack, having seen his more adventurous cousin do so, climbed cautiously onto the old plough. He peered down at his friend on the other side of the fence. Then, his mouth gaped wide. Jamie was brandishing a short sword – and not any sword. Its hilt was decorated with twisted golden wire – and it was this that had caught Jamie's eye.

"Who would throw such a sword away?" Jack gasped. "It is worth a lot of money surely!"

Jamie was certainly an adventurous and mischievous lad but even he knew that he could not keep such an object.

"I wonder if it is from that battle that happened here before we were born?" Jamie muttered.

"Nay – cannot be. Look at the blade! It is hardly marked with rust at all – and it looks very sharp!"

Jamie tested one edge with his thumb and nodded. Indeed, it was sharp and almost unmarked. "Then it must have been thrown here recently. What prize idiot would do such a thing?"

He was just on the point of turning back towards the loose boards when his eye was caught by something else. A few paces further on was a thick blackthorn bush that spread along the fence, about six feet in height. Just at the very base nearest to Jamie, and hard against the fence so as to be almost hidden behind the bush was a large, black leather shoe. The buckle was what had caught his eye. He knelt down on the wet, long grass and peered behind the bush. And then he went deathly pale.

"Jack," he faltered. "Jack – there be a shoe by the bush and there be a leg in the shoe!"

That was far too much for Jack to swallow. His immediate thought was that his cousin was up to another of his japes. He went down to the hole, squirmed through and came to join Jamie.

"Yet another of your japes?" he snorted.

"Nay – not a jape at all. Look for yourself!"

Jack let out a yell and stood up shaking. "There be a body behind there!" he quavered.

"Aye – I told you so!" Even in the midst of the worst nightmare he had ever experienced, Jamie could not resist pressing home his point. And then he started to think a bit more clearly.

"Jack – we both must go and get your father and grandfather. I'll bring the sword to show them."

Jack said nothing, turned on his heel and ran back towards the hole, squirrelled through and ran like the wind for the smithy. His father and grandfather were busy at the anvil shaping a piece of iron to be set atop an ornamental gate.

Simon looked up and regarded his panting son.

"Jack – what's amiss? You look as if you had seen a ghost."

Just as Jack was about to speak, Jamie arrived, sword in hand.

"Satan's bollocks!" Abel shouted. "Put that thing down. Where did you find it, you lummock?"

"Father, grandpapa – you must come. Jamie and I have found a dead body. The sword was within a few feet of it." Jack at last had found his tongue.

Simon regarded his nephew with suspicion. "Jamie, if this be another of your pranks, I shall make certain sure that your father tans your backside until you will have to stand in school for the rest of the term!"

"Nay, Uncle Simon. Tis exactly as Jack said. There indeed be a body. Please come and see for yourself."

Simon looked closely at his son and saw nothing but the frightened face of a scared young lad. He believed him.

"Jamie – put down that sword on the bench over there. Then you and Jack take us to where you say there is a dead body."

"We are going to need a billhook or an axe to get the thorn bush away – oh – and a wrench to remove boards from the fence," Jamie had been giving the expedition some thought.

Suitably armed, the four marched to the back fence where Simon made short work enlarging the hole. A few minutes later, they were all gazing down at the shod foot that stuck out from behind the dense blackthorn. Abel hooked the axe over one of the branches and heaved it down to the ground for Simon to sever it with the billhook. It was a long task. Jamie. minding carefully the wicked needle-like thorns, pulled each severed branch away into a large pile. Jack just stood there gazing fearfully as first a leg, then another doubled at the knee, finally a torso, two arms and a head. Four pair of eyes gazed down at the exposed body.

"Gentry!" Abel muttered. "See the fine tunic, breeches and hose. Those shoes are not a countryman's shoes!"

"What say you, father? He looks to be about thirty years of age," Simon ventured a guess.

"Aye – that would be my guess also. But I have never set eyes upon him. We had better leave him exactly as he is and raise the bailiff. I wonder what young Harry will make of all this?" Abel snorted.

Simon turned to his son. "Jack – go and get that sword and put it back exactly where you found it. Then you and Jamie run as fast as you like and fetch Bailiff."

"Afore you go, have either of you lads any notion who he may be?" Abel asked.

The answer came in the form of two shaken heads. Jack was soon back with the sword, which Jamie replaced in the long grass where he had first spotted it. Then the two lads hared off down the village and into the Parke grounds. It was Hob who answered their frantic knocking.

"What causes you to attempt to break down the door?" he asked, regarding two young faces bathed in sweat.

"We need Master Bailiff. There be a dead body behind the smithy," Jamie managed to gasp out.

"And I have just seen pigs flying over the moor!" Hob immediately jumped to the conclusion that Jamie was up to his tricks.

"Nay – honestly!" Jack gasped in his turn. "My father and grandfather sent us post haste to get Master Bailiff."

"Stay there and get your breath. I'll fetch Master Harry," Hob sort of believed Jack.

"What is all this about a dead body?" Harry Cove came to the door, following his deputy. "Believe me, if this be some prank, I shall administer a very severe beating!"

"Tis no prank, on my honour!" Jack stuttered. "The body lays behind the smithy and my father and grandfather are guarding over it."

Harry Cove was a very methodical young man. He was close to thirty years of age, being seven years older than his deputy Hob. Harry went back to his small office, put paper, pen and ink into a satchel and bade the two lads lead the way.

Arrived at the remains of the blackthorn, Harry and Hob gazed down at the body in their turn.

"I know not who he may be," Harry said. He cast a look at Hob. If anyone in the town knew people, Hob did. Hob, however, shook his head. They were shown the sword.

"Master Smith – could you and Simon lift him clear of the fence so that we may lay him out and see how he came to his death," he asked.

That took the large pair just two minutes. The body lay on its back, eyes firmly shut. The man had dark brown hair, worn fashionably long down to a lace collar. The features were at rest – a thin nose above full lips. The tunic was of burgundy cloth, interlaced with silver thread.

"Whoever he be, his clothes cost a pretty penny," Hob observed. "But there is no sword belt, baldric or scabbard. So, who owns that sword? Also, our man has no dagger or poniard that I can see."

"There is also no blood anywhere on his front. Let us see whether there be any on his back." Harry rolled the body over, then back again.

"No blood, no rents in the tunic, no hole where a bullet might have entered. He certainly did not place himself in there, so how came he to be here?"

Hob knelt at the side of the body and pulled down the fine lace collar.

"Look here – he has been strangled. There is deep bruising about the throat." Hob pulled open one eyelid. "Also, the eyes are covered in little burst vessels. Aye – he has been strangled and placed here."

Harry had been busy making a sketch of the bush, the fence, the smithy, and the positions of both body and sword. He then turned to Abel.

"Master Smith – may I impose further on you and Simon? We need a large board to carry him to the church where he may be laid out in the side chapel. Then I must summon all in the town to see whether or not he is recognised."

About an hour later, with the body laid out and covered in the church, Harry Cove went back to the estate and immediately sought out his father.

"I hear that you have an unknown corpse on your hands," Peter Cove gave his son a grimace of sympathy.

"Aye, father, I certainly have. And it is on that very subject that I need your help and advice. What in the name of all that is holy am I supposed to do? Do I get it identified first? Do I send to Exeter to advise the Sheriff? Do I call down the army of angels from heaven?"

Peter regarded his son with wry amusement.

"Harry, my boy. Sit down and we'll have a mug of ale. That is always the first step in matters of this kind!"

Jamie, being ten years old, had been given the job before school to help his father's parents in the bakery. His job was to trundle the small cart around the town delivering bread to the many customers. In return for this service, he received quite a generous weekly handful of coins. John and Evelyn, not getting any younger, were delighted to get whatever help they could. Their fond hope was that their grandson would eventually take over the bakery. Whether or not that would satisfy the irrepressible lad was another matter altogether!

Jack was nearly a year younger than his cousin, but also had a part-time job. Hob, when a much younger lad, had been Peter Cove's messenger. Now, as deputy bailiff, he simply had no time for this and it had been Hob's own suggestion that Harry employ Jack before school and afterwards. Harry had seen that this was quite a good idea, Jack being a quiet and very responsible boy. It was Jack therefore who sped around the town with the summons for all people to attend the church at the end of the workday.

At his father's suggestion, Harry had penned a long letter to the Sheriff in Exeter, describing in detail what had occurred, and the steps that he was taking. Two of the servants on the Parke estate had been parliamentary soldiers – they had ceased to be so some years before and had proved excellent employees. One was Sam Garvey, the other was Robert Hook – nicknamed Haddock because of his facial similarity to that fish. Harry went to see the steward, Luke Barton, to ask if one of them could be spared to deliver the letter to Rougemont. Needless to say, Haddock being the more adventurous, volunteered like a shot and was soon mounted on a fast gelding and alternating between a trot and a canter towards the county town.

On receiving the news that the church was being used as temporary morgue, Reverend Forbes hurried to see the body for himself. He did not recognise the man. However, he sent word to his friend Colonel Fisher – who also could not recall having ever seen the chap. The two repaired to Forbes' study and, without a word to one another, broached a new bottle of fine wine.

"No chance of self-murder," Forbes grunted. "Unless he has managed to find a way to strangle himself with his bare hands!"

"The bruises on the throat correspond exactly with two thumbs and eight fingers," Fisher agreed. "That beggars the question of how it came about. No other injuries anywhere. So, was he drugged beforehand, or did he meekly submit to his own strangulation?"

"We shall perhaps know more when James Ramsey has carried out a thorough examination. I would trust that man's judgement way ahead of that drunken sawbones from Newton Abbot!"

James accompanied by Nell, were at that very moment carrying out their detailed examination. Starting at the head and working systematically down to the big toes, they could find absolutely no indication of any other injury. No contusion on the head, no sign of even the slightest puncture mark anywhere on the body. Their final thought was to prise open the mouth, already stiff from rigor. Nell, whose eyesight was by far the better, used a small wooden spatula to move and flatten the tongue.

"No bitten tongue, no bitten cheek, no bruising where something has been forced into the mouth," she announced, straightening up with a puzzled expression. "But – there is just the faintest smell of something bitter."

James bent down and sniffed. Then he stood up and the two of them shared a look.

"Aconite?" they both queried as one. Some years before, aconite had been used to end the lives of two people who had been found in the field behind the church. That had been proved to be a case of collaborative self-murder.

Nell rummaged in her bag and came up with a cotton swab. Using a pair of long-handled tweezers, she poked the swab deep into the throat, swished it around and brought it out again. The same smell was there, stronger.

"Seems like he was poisoned, drugged into a stupor before being strangled. But why go to all the trouble of carting the poor fellow to that field behind the smithy – and then concealing it behind a dense bush?" James wondered.

The two covered the body up again and went to find Harry to report their findings. It never occurred to Harry for one moment to doubt the findings; James, and now Nell, were recognised as experts in the field of human anatomy and what happened to a body.

"So, deliberate poisoning, then strangulation, then transported, then concealed," he scratched his head. "Who is he, where did he come from, where was he killed, who did this, and was it just one killer? What I sorely need is a message from Heaven!"

"And who owns that sword, and why was it simply left there?" James added to his woes.

"Aye, thank you for that," Harry gave a rueful grin. "Let us hope that the Sheriff sends someone down here who is more used to dealing with mysteries of this kind. And now I suppose I have to muster all and sundry past the body – just in case someone actually *does* recognise the man. I'm willing to bet a month's stipend that nobody hereabouts will put a name to him!"

Harry was proved absolutely correct. Over one hundred and ninety people peered at that face. None could even hazard a guess as to his identity.

Later that evening, Harry placed the whole mystery before Mary. He had the greatest respect for his young wife's intelligence. But Mary expressed her own complete bafflement. It was a somewhat troubled Bailiff who went to bed that night.

Robert Hook had returned the same night, having delivered the letter into the hands of the Sheriff's clerk. When told that it contained details of an unexplained murder, the clerk had promised that he would bring it to the Sheriff's attention the very next morning. Hook had ridden back, stabled his horse after a feed and a rub-down, then had simply gone to bed.

Mary woke up a few moments before Harry, having had an idea that might help in the investigation.

"Harry, why do I not get young Rosie to go and look that that young man, at his face and clothes? You know how excellent she is at capturing a likeness; she could draw the man before his features disappear into a death mask. Then there will be something to show to others when he has been buried."

"That is one of the reasons that I asked you to marry me," Harry gave her a grin and a morning kiss. "That keen intellect!"

Some few years before, Rosie had astounded everyone by producing a lifelike drawing of a person. She had been very young at the time – young enough for the smaller-minded inhabitants to suspect witchcraft at work. Since then, she had kept her talent to those who recognised it for what it was – a talent of some magnitude.

Now twelve years old, she readily agreed to do as asked. Excused from school that morning, she went with her Uncle Harry to the church. Rosie asked that the cover be removed completely, swallowing nervously at what would be revealed.

She gazed for some minutes at the body, then started to look more closely.

"He rides a horse quite a lot," she muttered to herself.

"And what have you seen that tells you that?" Harry enquired.

"See the insides of his breeches – all shiny. Also, he rides in shoes sometimes instead of boots. The shoes have grooves worn under the instep and at the insides where he had put his feet into stirrups."

Harry regarded his young niece. "That was well observed. Now, is there anything else you need to see?"

"Can I peep at his open eyes? I need to see what colour they are, whether I need to draw them dark or light."

Harry swallowed a bit but put a thumb to one eyelid and prised it open. The pupil was very dark. "I do not know whether that will help or not," he said. "Perhaps all eyes go very dark after death. You will need to ask your great uncle James."

"That I do not know," James replied when Rosie asked the question.

"Aha, but I do," Avril laughed. "All eyes lose colour after death. But I have no notion whether they darken slowly or quickly. You had better err on the side of caution and show him with slightly dark eyes."

Rosie went home and sat at the parlour table with her paper, pens and ink. Gil and Ella gave her peace and quiet so that she could concentrate – uttering threats to Jamie that, should he disturb his sister, all sweetmeats would be withdrawn for a month – at the very least.

By the time dinner was ready, Rosie had completed her picture. It showed a young man standing at the side of a horse. The likeness to the dead man was unmistakable. He was looking straight out of the picture at the viewer, one hand casually in a pocket, the other over the horse's neck.

Harry, who came to collect it, was astounded.

"That is truly remarkable," he whistled. "I have seen your work before, Rosie – but this is superb. Thank you so much!"

Rosie blushed happily at this fulsome praise as Harry took the picture back to his office to show Mary, Hob, his father and mother, and anyone else who happened to be around. All said it was a wonderful likeness.

That afternoon, a visitor arrived from Exeter. He banged on the door of the Bailiff's house, and it was Hob again who answered the summons. He opened the door and then gave a cry of pleasure.

"Captain Larkin!"

"Nay, young man – Colonel now! And how fares the young Hob?"

"Deputy Bailiff now!" Hob said, growing an inch taller.

"Then Master Peter Cove has promoted you, has he?"

"Not Master Peter. Master Harry his son be bailiff now. Are you sent from Exeter?"

"Aye, indeed I am. I hear that you have an unexplained murder victim."

Hob led him to Harry's small office and opened the door. "Look who has come in answer to your summons," he chortled.

"Ye Gods – I never thought to have the pleasure of your company again," Harry sprang up with hand extended. "Come and sit and I shall tell you what we know so far. I must say that it is good to have a friendly face here again!"

Larkin, then a Captain, had been in Bovey a few years previously when the self-murders and the fanatical sect had been investigated. He had also been there some years before that as a Sergeant. He was known to most in the town and respected for his quiet, polite manners.

Hob acted as steward and fetched three mugs of ale, then joined the discussion as Harry relayed to Larkin all the information that they had unearthed to date. Finally, he passed across the picture of the young man. Larkin looked long and hard at it, then shook his head.

"I have never to my knowledge set eyes on this fellow. He has the look of a young officer, but I could well be mistaken."

"Aye, I see what you mean – he does have the look," Harry nodded. "But on a lighter note, if you intend to stay with us at the tavern, you will find another old acquaintance there, Matthew Kent. He has retired from Government service and come to live hereabouts. Also, a Colonel Fisher has come – he is living near to Teigngrace."

"I shall certainly enjoy meeting Kent again – a most able and amiable man. Fisher I have heard of – I take it he is just as forthright in his comments as he used to be?"

"Oh, indeed. He has palled up with our Reverend. They have regular meetings where they discuss world affairs over bottles of excellent wine."

"Anyway, to business. I suppose I should start with viewing the body, the site where it was found, and have a chat with whoever it was who found it."

"Then I shall let Hob give you the tour. I have to settle a dispute between two smallholders down on the Heath – both claiming rights to apiece of ground that mice would shun!"

"I wish you joy," Larkin grinned at him as Hob prepared to lead the way up to the church.

Hob walked over to the bier and pulled back the cover, exposing the face of the dead man. Larkin looked hard at it, then gave a shrug.

"It is as I said – I have never seen him before. In that, I believe I am not alone?"

"Nay, Colonel – nobody in the town recognises him," Hob agreed sadly.

Larkin was about to turn away when he caught sight of the short sword.

"Is that the sword that was found nearby?" he asked, picking it up and examining the intricately wound hilt and pommel.

"Aye – it was just a few feet from the body."

"Then, this is something that I certainly *do* recognise. There is a young officer in my regiment by the name of DeGruchy. He has a personal short sword that could easily be this one's twin. However, this man is not him! I need to have a message sent post haste to Exeter so that young DeGruchy may be brought here. It is very possible that he could put a name to the fellow. Swords like this are usually given to family members, or to near relatives."

"Then it looks like Haddock is in for another journey," Hob laughed. He knew that Hook would jump at the chance.

The next morning, armed with a letter of authority from Larkin, Hook again rode to Rougemont. He was back in mid-afternoon with a young officer who was somewhat perturbed at the reason for his summons.

The first thing he did was to produce his own sword and lay it beside the one that had been found. They were identical as they lay on the Bailiff's table. The young man swallowed and admitted that he now needed to see the body. Instead, Harry produced the picture and watched DeGruchy's face turn white.

"That is my cousin Francis, or it could indeed be his twin – although he does not have a twin," he gulped. "I have to see the body and the clothes he is wearing to be absolutely sure."

That evening, Harry, Hob, Larkin and DeGruchy sat in the Bailiff's office, having had a hurried supper.

"I now have to relate all that I know about my cousin Francis," DeGruchy said, having recovered somewhat from confirming the identity of his relative.

The other three sat back and relaxed.

"I have just received some information," Colonel Fisher put down his wine glass with a grunt of satisfaction. "Came via a chap on his way to Bodmin - of all places. Seems that Lambert is set on removing parliament altogether and replacing it with rule by the army. Whether or not he does so, is open to some question. What I do know is this – Monck will take violent exception to such a move. Our troubles are not over by a long chalk!"

Reverend James Forbes regarded his friend with consternation.

"Surely, he cannot even consider such a move?" he gaped.

"Lambert is just about hot-headed enough to do so. Although I for one, sincerely hope better judgement prevails," Fisher growled.

"And when has better judgement prevailed these last years?" Forbes queried.

CHAPTER IV

The previous evening's meeting in the bailiff's office resumed the next morning. Just as the young officer had been about to start his narrative, there had come a furious knocking at the door. It seemed that a noisy altercation was taking place between two of the cottagers down on the Heath. With a sigh, Harry and Hob had mounted their horses and had gone to attend to it. Apparently, it had all started when one man accused his neighbour of stealing one of his chickens.

Harry and Hob had weighed in and had managed to separate the two, who had stood a few feet apart spitting invective at one another. It was only when Harry threatened them both with hefty fines that tempers cooled. It finally collapsed in red faces when another from further down the Heath came to intervene holding a protesting chicken. She had found it pecking at her patch of grass.

Paul Larkin was young for his rank. He was still 'feeling his way' with his small regiment. Not that he doubted his ability – far from it. He had seen many an action and knew that he had acquitted himself well and had commanded a much smaller group than a regiment with care and precision. He arrived with young DeGruchy, the two having spent a comfortable night in Dick Allen's tavern.

Hob had made sure that a large jug of ale was ready to wet whistles. He was all agog to hear the tale, still young enough to revel in the adventures of others.

"My family lives in Wiltshire, as I'm sure the Colonel knows," DeGruchy began anew. "My father inherited a small manor with some farms. However, before he inherited the estate, we all lived until I was twelve in London. My father has a brother – Archibald DeGruchy. He is a very successful businessman, importing fine wines from all over the continent, and returning there with his ships laden with fine English wool fleeces. Uncle Archie has three children, Francis who is much my age, Lionel who is just eighteen, and little Letty who is fifteen. Uncle always hoped that Francis would learn the business so that, when the time came, he would take it over completely. But he reckoned without Francis' fierce streak of independence. Francis once told me in strictest confidence that his ambition was to become, as he called it, a soldier of fortune. He would learn all the arts of swordplay, pistol shooting, fast riding and whatever he deemed necessary. Then he would simply take ship to either The Netherlands or France and offer his services to whomsoever needed them. By so doing, he believed he would be able to amass a small fortune and then buy for himself a life of leisure. He declared that a few years of hardship would yield far greater riches that what he termed 'a miserable trading business'. I was well old enough by then to realise what it was he was seeking – a life of thrills and adventure, rather than what he saw as years of crushing boredom. But as he had sworn me to secrecy, I kept this all to myself. Given how it has all ended, I shall curse myself forever for that decision; Francis could well be alive and bored today had I spoken out!"

"You would have immediately lost the friendship and respect of your cousin had you done so," Colonel Larkin interrupted.

"Aye, sir, that I would! But now his death lies heavily on my conscience. I should have been brave enough to do what now turns out to have been the right thing."

"And have you any knowledge of his activities when you and your immediate family moved to Wiltshire?" Harry prompted.

"Yes Colonel, and again I have to apologise for the fact that I again kept this to myself. I heard nothing at all for years – that is until two months ago when a letter arrived at the barracks addressed to me. It bore a seal that I immediately recognised – Francis' own, a copy of his father's. Thinking that, after all this time, my cousin was about to regale me with his adventures, I was surprised indeed to find that the letter was written in a very neat, small hand – far removed from the inelegant scrawl that Francis had adopted. I have kept it with me and, with your permission, I shall read it to you."

He delved into an inside pocket and withdrew two folded sheets of paper, one of which still bore the two broken halves of the small seal. He took a breath and commenced.

"To a cousin by marriage whom I have never met, greetings. I must first introduce myself. My name is Annette DeGruchy and I am the wife of your own cousin Francis. I write to you in some agony of indecision for I have not heard from Francis for the past three months. We met at the church of Saint Jean Baptiste four years past. I had been with my friend as a guest at her marriage. Francis was what you would call a groomsman – a dear friend of the bridegroom. Three months later we were married and living in the region of Paris that is called Montparnasse. Francis had obtained a lease to the top floor of a nice house, and it is from there that I am writing. Slowly, over that first year, I came to learn from him what his life had been like before we met. He had served some lord in Germany, another in Spain, but had eventually taken employment with a Seigneur, a distant relative of the Bourbons. He had fought several small battles before being, as I then believed, paid off handsomely for his services. That happened just nine months ago. Since then, we lived quietly together and have been blessed with a child, a sweet angel we have named Marie. Then, two days before he disappeared, we received a visitor. He and Francis remained closeted together for some hours in deep conversation. I was not introduced to this person, who left without even the courtesy of a farewell. Two days later, Francis kissed me goodbye and said he would be returning in a week as he had been entrusted with a very important mission. I thought no more about it until ten days had passed without a word from him. Deeply concerned, I went to his bureau and started to look through his papers. Imagine my dismay when I found some bearing the imprimatur of a certain Abbe Justin. He, as some of us in France are aware, is the leader of a violent group that is dedicated to the violent overthrow of any regime in Europe that is not dedicated to Rome. Therefore, I implore you, should you hear from my husband, impress upon him the void that he has left here in Paris – and to return as soon as he may. I will always be your loving cousin by marriage, Annette (with a small kiss from little Marie)."

Stephen DeGruchy folded the letter and returned it to his pocket. There followed a long silence as each of the other three digested what they had been told. Harry was the first to break the silence.

"Are we to infer from all that that your cousin was on some sort of mission from these people, those who seek to undermine our own country?"

"I can put no other interpretation on her writing," DeGruchy replied. "I wrote back to Annette but couched my words in seemingly innocuous phases – that I was happy to make her acquaintance and that I would be happy to comply with her simple request. I have yet to receive anything further."

"Hmmm," the Colonel frowned. "This indeed puts an entirely different light upon the finding of the body. If he were indeed on some sort of mission, then who was his contact here – for he must have had one! What was he doing anywhere near this small town – as he must have been somewhere hereabouts. Why was it necessary to kill him? And, having done so, why was it necessary to conceal the body? Surely, there are more secure ways of concealing a dead body! The area is certainly not short of fast-flowing rivers, deep old mine shafts, caves."

"I am only too glad Colonel that this is your mission and not mine – for I would not have the faintest idea where to start!" Harry gave a look of sympathy to Larkin.

"I, on the contrary, have some small ideas how I may proceed," Larkin said quietly. "First, I must seek leave of absence from my regiment. I shall also require you, DeGruchy, to accompany me as this is far nearer to your kin that it is to anyone else's. We must travel as soon as possible to London where I know many whose advice and knowledge may be of great help."

"The only help I can offer is to start travelling around the neighbouring villages to see whether anyone recognises the man," Harry said, somewhat reluctantly as he and Hob had more than enough to keep them occupied.

"That would be a great help," Larkin accepted it gratefully. "Knowing where he was, perhaps who he was in contact with, would be of real value."

The small meeting broke up at that point. Larkin and DeGruchy went to the tavern for a quick dinner, then a ride first to Exeter. They would then both undertake the two or three-day ride to Westminster.

Harry and Hob ate a quick dinner and then Hob volunteered to ride out with the picture. It would take him some days to cover all the villages and small towns from Moretonhamstead in the north, Ashburton in the west, Chudleigh in the east, and Newton Abbot in the south. Hob was not daunted by this – he loved riding about the countryside.

As he had expected, his travels took Hob three days. His last port of call on what had been days of fruitless journeys had been the small town of Chudleigh, to the east of Bovey Tracey. Having spent a whole morning there asking every shopkeeper and person he could find, he at last gave up and was on his slow way back when he was overtaken by a man riding a very tired looking horse. The man was swarthy, had a large cudgel hanging from a strap about the pommel, and a fierce expression on his face. Hob had been about to call a greeting when the angry face made him think twice. The rider slowly gained distance and was also heading for Bovey Tracey.

Hob dismissed the man from mind and continued on his leisurely way, thinking over all the denials and blank looks he had received when shown the picture of the young man now known to be Francis DeGruchy. Where in the name of hell had he come from to be dumped unceremoniously behind a blackthorn bush miles from where he had originated? He could think of only one other possibility – that he had not travelled anywhere near far enough. He, with Harry's agreement, had deliberately not gone to Newton Abbot, despite this town being far nearer than others he had visited. The people who safeguarded law and order in that town were known to be a prickly lot, never happy to have their 'patch' invaded by anyone who they saw as 'damned outsiders'. Hob knew that he would now have to prevail upon his boss to change his mind.

All that was put to one side as he rode into Bovey Tracey to be confronted by a large crowd milling about in the main street outside the church. He dismounted and pushed his way through the throng to where, in the centre, he found Harry standing hands on hips between two sets of contestants. He was not really surprised that one of these was the angry man who had passed him on the road. He was being constrained by Simon Smith. Abel, Simon's father was constraining the other contestants –

Matt Crowley and Herb Grindley. Harry's voice was being drowned out by that of the angry man.

"Eight years they have lied!" he bellowed, red in the face and struggling uselessly against the might of Simon's muscles. "Eight years of falsehood and trickery!"

Matt and Herb had, eight years previously, been for a short time soldiers in service to Prince Charles. They had ended up at Worcester where they had witnessed the final defeat by Cromwell's army. They had also unknowingly witnessed the flight of Charles that had ended up for a while in a priest's hole in Boscobel House. On their very circuitous way back they had devised a plan to start in business making barrels. The angry man came from Taunton and was the largest maker of barrels for many a mile. Thinking to clear any obstacles to their prospective business, Matt and Herb had ridden to Taunton, had seen the man, and had spun a tale that they were from Ilfracombe – a very large distance from Taunton and thus no threat to the man's business. It had taken the word of a travelling tinker to appraise the man of the truth – Matt and Herb were operating in Bovey Tracey, Matt's home town.

The man had his cudgel in one hand, a hand that was engulfed in the much larger one of his captor. Simon was heard to speak fairly quietly to the man, saying that, should he not immediately drop the cudgel, he could say goodbye to the integrity of the bones in his hand. The man was too far gone in fury to take any heed of that warning. Matt and Herb for their part were shouting that they had every right to operate their business anywhere they chose. They had had the good sense to sell their completed barrels far away on the south coast, in Brixham, Plymouth, even as far as Saltash in Cornwall. Their business had thrived in the intervening years, and the two were very popular members of the town's community.

Harry had had more than enough. He drew in a large breath and bellowed for silence. Simon, using his free hand, clamped it over the man's mouth, favouring him with a glare that dared him to take a bite. Slowly, the hubbub subsided.

"That is better," Harry declared. "Now – who are you and why have you come here disturbing our peace?"

Simon, at a nod from Harry, removed his hand from the man's mouth.

"I am here to ensure that these two vermin take no more bread from the mouths of my family and my workers. They lied to me and have started a business in direct competition to my own – a business I inherited from my own father some twenty years past!"

Harry turned to Matt and Herb. "And is there any truth in what is alleged?"

Matt had the grace to look a trifle ashamed. "Aye, Master Bailiff – what he says is substantially true. All those years past, we travelled to Taunton and spoke with this man, hoping to learn how he operated. So as not to antagonise him, we pretended that we would start our own business in Ilfracombe – so far from him that he could have no objection."

"Lies! Lies!" roared the man.

"Indeed, it would seem that you were misled somewhat," Harry observed. "However, there is no reason why they cannot operate here. My own father as Bailiff at the time granted them permission to begin. The estate steward granted them a lease of the old barn where they might start. All I can see is that you fear competition!"

"We are no competition to him," Herb broke in. "We sell many miles from his area – mainly in Plymouth, where he has never ventured."

"Then I see no reason for your journey here," Harry faced the man. "Your own business would seem to be under no threat from theirs. So, I suggest that you mount your horse and start upon your journey back whence you came."

"I shall have justice," the man stated almost quietly. "Even if it takes me weeks. I shall put these two out of business by any means I may contrive."

"I hear what you say," Harry came back at him, equally quietly, but everyone in the crowd strained to hear. "So, let me make it plain to you. If you or any agent of yours attempts violence against these two – or against their business – I shall make it *my* business to stop you and hand you over to the Sheriff. I trust I make myself plain?"

"You shall never catch me! I *shall* have my justice!"

"You have received my warning. Now – be on your way and do not let me catch sight of you here again."

Simon, at Harry's nod, released the man, but first deprived him of his cudgel by the simple means of squeezing the man's fingers eliciting a yelp of pain. He turned a furious face to Harry and then at Matt and Herb.

"You have been warned," he hissed, mounting his horse and walking it slowly back towards Chudleigh.

Abel stood aside from his two. "Any sign of trouble, come quickly and let Simon and me know," he offered.

Lou Crowley, Matt's mother came towards her son, little Felix trotting after her. Felix, a foundling, had been 'adopted' by Lou those eight years before, making her life far more tolerable following the death of her husband.

"Take a care," she said to her son. "That man was in earnest!"

"Aye, mother, that we know. We shall watch out very carefully."

And then, at long last, Hob was able to report to his boss the absolutely negative results of his peregrinations.

"Oh well, it was a forlorn hope at best. I agree with you that we shall have to approach Newton Abbot and perhaps Teignmouth and Torquay. That will require thought and a cart load of tact."

Larkin and DeGruchy had taken their time over the journey to the capital. They had stopped overnight in Westminster then, on the twenty-sixth, had taken the short ride into the city itself and had made for the import and export business of DeGruchy's uncle. It was necessary for them to ride right through the city and out at its eastern gate to where Archibald DeGruchy had his business down on the wharves.

Archibald, a rotund figure, well dressed and in obvious command, was standing at the dockside supervising the unloading of a cargo. He looked up at the approach of the two figures and his face broke into a broad smile of welcome as he recognised his nephew.

"Stephen, my boy. What brings you here – and in the company of a senior officer, unless my eyes deceive me?"

"Uncle, let me present my Colonel, Colonel Larkin. Colonel, my Uncle Archibald DeGruchy."

The polite and formal introduction was sealed with firm handshakes. And then it was time for the bad news.

"Uncle, we have travelled here from Devon with very bad news. Francis has been found murdered."

The older man looked immediately ten years older. He went to a bollard and sat down upon it. He looked up at Stephen and Larkin with a look of immense sadness.

"How and why?" he managed to ask.

"This is hardly the place for such a conversation," Larkin interposed. "Is there somewhere more private where we may confer?"

Without speaking, Archibald led the way into his large warehouse, up a set of stairs at the side and into a large and very functional office. He waved to two chairs facing a large desk and slumped into his own chair.

"And now please tell me all that you know," he almost implored. "I have not set eyes upon my son for some years now and have had in that time just one letter in which he said he was in the employment of some German or other."

As was proper, Larkin left all the explanations to Stephen – as a part of that family. Stephen related all that they knew about the finding of the body and that its arrival at its final resting place behind a bush was still a complete mystery. The old man was literally astounded when Stephen handed him the letter from Annette – even more so when he learned that he had a granddaughter named Marie. He handed the letter back and sat back looking utterly defeated.

"I had no notion of his marriage, nor of the birth of his daughter. So – who in the name of heaven is this Abbe Justin – and how does he even come to affect the life of my son?"

"All of this we have yet to discover," Larkin took over now that the familial details were completed. "Our first duty was to appraise you of the news. That we have now done and can concentrate on finding out how, why, when, and where your son met his death. I have been specifically charged with this task, but it would seem that you sir as completely in the dark as we. Is there any chance that either of your other two children may be privy to their brother's movements?"

"I sincerely doubt that." Archibald seemed to have recovered somewhat from the initial shock. "Lionel works with me here in the business and is as open and honest as any young man I have ever encountered. He would not have been able to keep any such knowledge to himself. Letty on the other hand, is a quiet and very reserved young lady. I shall have her brought here with Lionel so that we may jointly question them. I have no doubts about Lionel and you Colonel as a stranger will be able to cast an unbiased eye upon Letty."

Larkin and Stephen then excused themselves, partly to give the old man time to digest the news in private and partly to find dinner at a tavern until the other two children arrived. Needless to say, their talk over a dish of beef pie and vegetables was all about the seeming secrecy with which Francis had conducted his life.

They arrived back at the warehouse soon after the two children had responded to the summons. The first thing that impressed both soldiers was the family similarity between the two and their departed elder brother. Lionel was about the same size as Francis had been, whilst Letty was a quiet and reserved much smaller version. Both had obviously been crying. Larkin was at his most sympathetic.

"Please believe me when I say that under normal circumstances I would not intrude upon your grieving. But as no doubt your father has told you, your brother Francis' life has been taken from him – and it is our duty to find out the why and the wherefore. I'm sure that you can appreciate that time is of the essence here."

"Will you read out the letter for us, cousin?" Lionel asked Stephen. "Believe me, I had absolutely no idea Francis had taken a wife, nor that we now had a little niece."

Stephen again withdrew the letter and slowly read it out in its entirety. This time, Archibald was able to hear it out without any outward sign of emotion. Not so Lionel or Letty. Lionel stared open mouthed as Stephen drew to a close. Letty showed no emotion whatsoever – or none that either Stephen or Larkin could see as she looked down at the floor between her feet. Lionel was the first to speak.

"It has all come as a great shock to me," he admitted, wiping a stray tear away with the back of his hand. "Whatever he has been doing, where he has been, for whom he has worked – I have known absolutely nothing!"

"And what of your sister?" Larkin enquired. "Did you have knowledge of any of this?"

"Please be so good as to give the Colonel an answer," her father commanded.

Letty looked up and faced Larkin defiantly. "No – I had absolutely no knowledge whatsoever of this marriage or the child," she said quietly.

"But what of the other matters? Where he has been; what he has been doing; for whom?" Larkin pressed.

He received a rebellious look that did not evade her father.

"Letty – kindly do not prevaricate. If you know anything at all, now is the time to say. In fact, I order you to do so!"

Letty gave a sigh and seemed to deflate. "Then I have to admit that I received a letter from Francis just one year ago. He was very brief and told me that he had been received into the Catholic Church and was a guest at some place in France run by Jesuits."

"Dear God in Heaven," her father exploded. "And did you not think this was information that you should properly have divulged to your father? And what of before that letter?"

"I can only apologise, father. Francis swore me to secrecy. And no – I received nothing before that letter and nothing since."

"Jesuits? Abbe Justin? It would appear at first glance that your son was somehow involved in their secret work," Larkin mused aloud.

"I would agree that, at first glance, such would appear to be the case," Archibald nodded. "But is it not equally possible that he was being used to infiltrate, to act as spy against them?"

"Yes, Master DeGruchy – such is equally possible. I shall not know until I have made very extensive enquiries. And to do so, I shall need to seek out those in Whitehall who may be able to shed more light upon the matter," Larkin stated.

"May I ask one favour of you, Colonel – that you allow my nephew Stephen leave of absence to travel to Paris and offer a place here with us to his widow and child? I cannot abide the thought that we shall remain in ignorance of them, nor that she believes we have no place in our hearts for her."

"In all conscience, I could do no other," Larkin agreed at once. "You must travel there and back as a civilian – that is for your own safety."

"And I shall provide more than adequate funds for your journey," added his uncle.

"Then I shall be very happy to undertake the mission," Stephen DeGruchy looked almost delighted that he was to be entrusted with such an adventurous task.

Larkin took his leave, again expressing his sincere condolences to the family. He rode back through London and onwards to Westminster, determined to ferret out anyone who could aid him in his task. But first, he needed the necessary authority.

CHAPTER V

Mary's life was not made any easier by the fact that two of the children in her school were her own twins, Will and Peterkin. The boys, aged seven, were always up to something, plotting in whispers when they should have been paying attention. In desperation, Mary had shifted the lads; Will now sat on the left of the front row whilst Peterkin sat on the right of the middle row. Somehow or other – and Mary suspected what was centuries later to become known as telepathy. Others, being more spiritual, suspected the influence of Lucifer himself.

However, the twins were not her biggest concern; that 'privileged' position was occupied by Jamie Ramsey. Jamie was Mary's nephew, in that he was Gil's son and Mary was Gil's sister. Jamie could always be relied upon to interrupt with questions. Some of these were indeed very pertinent. Some on the other hand were merely *im*pertinent. Jamie's sister Rosie, now an advanced twelve years of age, had finished with school the previous year. She was literate, numerate, and an accomplished artist. She was also in sole charge of the big flock of chickens on the smallholding.

That morning, the last day of September, the twins were unusually subdued. But they always were, Mary thought, when the subject for the lesson was a reading from the bible. Not so Jamie! Up shot his hand. Mary supressed a groan and nodded to him.

"Please, Miss Mary, what does it mean when it says that God gave man dominion over the beasts of the field?"

During the reign nearly ninety years previously of Mary – always now referred to as Bloody Mary – every child was exposed to Latin, the language of every church service – not that one in a hundred had understood one word of it! Mary had studied that old language as she was as ever curious about everything.

"Is it the word dominion that you do not understand?" she enquired. She received a vigorous nod in reply.

"Then I shall have to explain. The word dominion means lordship, ownership, control."

Jamie immediately spotted an avenue he could exploit.

"But if man is given ownership of the beasts, why do I not own any beasts? I am a man!"

Mary knew full well that, unless she put a stop to it, Jamie would exploit this for the remainder of the lesson.

"First things first, Jamie. You are not yet a man!" that elicited titters of amusement from the rest of the class. "Secondly, you have misinterpreted the words completely. What the bible is telling us is that God put mankind over the beasts, the birds, the fish – he meant us to be his greatest creation. He sets us on a higher plane than other creatures."

"So, I am of more importance than a sheep?" Jamie tried hard to inject a sincere note into his question, although inwardly he was struggling hard not to laugh.

"Well," Mary put on a thoughtful face. "Let us all consider that proposition, shall we? Let us consider a sheep – it gives us wool with which we can spin and make the clothes that keep us warm. It can provide milk that we can turn into cheese. It can provide us with delicious meat that we can eat to maintain our health and strength. What can you provide us with, Jamie?"

"Silly question!" That came from a rather pugnacious lad from one of the farms on The Heath. Jamie favoured the lad with a scowl. He looked for support from Jack. Jack found great interest in his fingernails and resolutely declined to be drawn into supporting his lifelong friend. Sometimes, Jack found Jamie a bit of a trial!

"But I am a part of mankind," Jamie fought a rearguard action. "I am above the animals, so I should have some of my own!"

That gave Mary the opportunity to end that once and for all.

"Then you should go home after school and *demand* that Rosie gives you some of the chickens. Do you believe for one moment that she will agree? I suspect that she will probably box your ears!"

And that really did cause a gale of laughter – they could all imagine Rosie's reaction to such a demand from her little brother. And then came the sound of the bell for the end of the lesson. Lou Crowley, with little Felix, lived in the rooms above the schoolroom and as a part of her agreement, kept the place clean and tidy and rang the bell as necessary. Mary gave a sigh of relief.

"Class dismissed. Home for dinner and back here at one o'clock!"

Mary gathered the twins and walked with them back to their home in Parke. Over a quiet meal, she again pondered what she had been teaching that morning. More and more she found herself at odds with the whole concept of Creation and Dominion. She knew that she was regarded as a 'clever' person and knew that she thought deeply about things. Why, she had often wondered, were women regarded throughout history as somehow inferior to men. She had many years previously believed she had the answer to that one – and it came from the very book from which her morning's text had been taken. According to the very first part of it, God had first created *man* in *His* own image and likeness. Therefore, God was a man! Then, almost as an afterthought, God had created woman, using a rib stolen from the man to build upon. Mary, from her deep knowledge of human anatomy, knew this to be a load of rubbish – men and women had the same number of ribs! And then somehow, the woman had proved herself unworthy of the man by yielding to temptation, thereby leading the man into everlasting sin. Women were weak, were untrustworthy, were temptresses. Had God made a catastrophic mistake? Or had He simply made another version of a human being who quickly displayed simple human weakness? That latter possibility sat far easier with Mary. And that had led to all sorts of inner turmoil. Voicing any of that aloud would have resulted in her being labelled a heretic!

Now twenty-seven years old, Mary had come to terms with her turmoil. She taught what was expected and knew she was being hypocritical. She had learned to live with that. But she also knew that she was very lucky – she had married a young man who respected her, listened to her, sought her opinions and advice – and not many women in her experience were so lucky.

Hob rode the five miles into Newton Abbot armed with the picture, a small parcel of bread and cheese, and a leather flask of ale. His first port of call was to the church of Saint Lawrence. He had a note in his pocket that he had elicited from Reverend Forbes. He left his horse loosely tied to a picket fence and went in search of the rector.

Having read the brief note, the rector gave Hob a sympathetic glance.

"I take it you have heard of the phrase 'needle in a haystack'? That, I fear, is what you are embarked upon – a very long search. What brings you here?"

Hob then started on a long explanation of his searches so far, how wide-ranging they had been, and how damnably frustrating it had all been.

"Then all I can recommend is that you visit each and every tavern in the town - and be warned, there are many of them! Forget about the landlords and landladies – question the serving wenches and the ale drawers. They see everyone; they remember everyone. And may the Good Lord assist your efforts Believe me, you may well need it!"

Having visited nine taverns, Hob remembered those words. He had manfully refrained from supping ale in each tavern, thus keeping a moderately clear head. Without a shred of hope, he pushed open the door of the tenth tavern, the one situated on the road that led eventually to Coombe. It was by then mid-afternoon, and the place was very sparsely populated. Three old men sat huddled together playing some game or other that consisted of moving metal discs around a chequered board. The one serving girl in attendance looked up at the newcomer and immediately lifted a mug from the table and went to draw ale. Why not, Hob thought – I damned well deserve one!

And then he fell into his usual routine. He spread the picture on a dry part of the table and asked the girl if she had ever seen the man before.

"Not for some days, now," came the very unexpected and very welcome reply. "He stayed here for three days, met with some men from the town every evening, then simply disappeared. His belongings are in the storeroom as he never came back to collect them."

Hob could hardly contain his excitement. At long last, he breathed.

"Then I shall have to speak with the landlord as the man in question was found days past in Bovey Tracey. He had been murdered and it is my task to discover whence he came, who he met. I shall have to see these belongings as they may shed some further light on his movements."

Hob rode back to Bovey Tracey late that afternoon with three sheets of paper covered in his notes. He could not wait until he could tell what he had found out. However, that had to wait as it was determined that Colonel Larkin also needed to be present – and he was expected back the next day.

The first day of October saw yet another change in the weather – warm sunshine and an almost cloudless sky. Hob had been busy gathering together every conceivable interested party for his report. Colonel Larkin also had information to relay, and it was right that he would report first as his was the earliest to be learned. The large main hall in Parke was the only place large enough to accommodate the number of people. Larkin, Harry, Hob, Peter Cove, Matthew Kent, Luke Barton – all were sitting around the large table.

First to speak was Larkin, who relayed all he had learned in London about the DeGruchy family, and that young Stephen had set off for Paris to invite the widow and her child to come and live with the family. And then it was Hob's turn. He spread his notes on the table before him and started.

"Francis DeGruchy arrived at the Three Tuns in Newton Abbot on the evening of the fifteenth of September. He paid for a week's lodging in advance and was allocated a small room on the top floor of the tavern. According to the landlord, he was a quiet and polite young man, well dressed and with two fairly large saddle bags. His horse, a mottled grey, was stabled at the tavern. It is still there, being cared for by the ostler who has taken quite a shine to the animal. On the evening of the sixteenth, the day after his arrival, he took supper at the tavern, having ridden out after dinner – nobody knew where he had been. Three men unknown to anyone at the tavern joined Francis at supper. They sat at a table in the far corner and conversed for over an hour in very quiet voices. The performance was repeated the next day – Francis rode out in the afternoon and met with the same three men that evening. The next day, the seventeenth, there was a slight change – Francis remained in his room all afternoon, but again met with the three men for supper. Then, on the eighteenth of September, the maid took up a tray of breakfast to his room, only to find Francis absent. His belongings were all there, including the two saddle bags. The bed had been slept in, but of Francis himself there was no sign. When he had not made an appearance for supper, the landlord removed the belongings, packed into the bags, and put them safely into the storeroom. The serving staff were adamant that the three men did not make an appearance that evening – and have not been seen since. I questioned everyone as carefully as I could as to the appearance of these three individuals. All I could elicit was that they were all in their thirties or forties, were well and soberly dressed in black, that they arrived and left on horseback, and that nobody had ever seen them before."

Everybody sat back to digest this narrative. Kent was the first to speak. He had been making his own notes and turned them so that everyone could see. There was a straight line with dates appended above the line and facts written beneath.

"So – he arrives on the fifteenth, goes riding somewhere in the afternoon of the sixteenth, meets three men that evening. The seventeenth is a repeat performance. But on the eighteenth, he goes missing and the men are not seen again. We then jump three days to the twenty-first when his body is discovered about five miles from his lodging. Do any of his belongings shed any further light on him or his movements?"

"Nary a one," Hob grunted. "Changes of clothing, a pocket bible, a spare eating knife, not one shred of paper. If we had not already known his name, he would be completely anonymous."

"And none of the staff recognised the men?"

"They were all adamant that they had never seen them before. And given the fact that the Three Tuns is a very popular tavern, that probably means that they were from somewhere a fair distance away."

"Does any of this take us even the smallest step further forward?" Larkin asked.

Harry then spoke for the first time. "I consulted Avril Ramsey about the state of the body. She examined it very closely and also the place where it had been found. She was of the opinion that Francis had been killed at least twenty-four hours prior to its discovery, given the state of rigour and the weather conditions."

Kent made another note on his timeline. "So – killed sometime on the twentieth, strangled after being drugged senseless, carted to the field and dumped. But why was his sword, a sword instantly recognised by his cousin, left for all to see? It makes no sense whatsoever. A body killed elsewhere, all signs of identity removed, but a clear indication of identity left close by."

"The immediate need is for the identity and purpose of these three men be discovered. Has anyone any idea how this may be accomplished?" Larkin asked.

That was met with a deafening silence – nobody had the slightest clue how this could be done. Kent himself summed it up.

"Three men, middle years, soberly dressed, arrive and leave on horseback. That suggests that they travel no more than twenty miles or so. What towns and villages lie within a twenty-mile radius of Newton Abbot? I suspect over fifty! Is such a search even feasible?"

Lady Violette Charlton was not feeling at all well. Being made of very stern stuff, she had been up since sunrise as was her usual routine. She had hardly touched her breakfast, and that set a small alarm bell ringing inside the head of Meg Farmer, her cook and wife of her steward Luke.

"That is not at all like her ladyship, she muttered as the plate of eggs and new bread returned hardly touched. But she had a very busy morning and thought no more about it. Not so Lady Violette; she knew that all was not well. At the age of seventy-three she knew full well that she had passed the normal life expectancy of women of her social class. She had, she admitted to herself, been waiting for some such to happen for many a past month. I wonder what it is, she muttered to herself, sipping a glass of weak ale. Then, giving herself a good shake, she went into her study to attend to a pile of correspondence.

By dinner time, she knew that something was seriously amiss – her chest was tight, and breathing had become painful; also, there was pain above her heart, into her left shoulder and down her left arm. "Heart!" she muttered, eyeing her plate of stew with revulsion. "Damned stupid thing. I suppose I should consult the oracle!" She rang the bell that always stood beside her plate.

"My Lady?" Luke Farmer answered promptly.

"I need you to send for Avril Ramsey. There is a matter that I must consult with her."

Luke made his little bow and withdrew to the kitchen. "Lady needs Avril Ramsey," he reported to his wife.

"Aye, no wonder. She ate almost nothing this morning," Meg replied. "Shall you send young Hal?"

The lad in question looked up from his place at the kitchen table. Hal, their son and now eleven years old, had come galloping in from school just fifteen minutes earlier and was busy shovelling spoons of stew into his ever-hungry mouth.

"Aye – he's as fast now as Hob ever was."

Within another five minutes, Hal had managed to empty his large bowl and was on his way, running all the way past Parke, up the main street, past the silent mill, and arrived at the apothecary's shop. He was hardly out of breath.

"Mistress Ramsey, Lady Violette needs to see you – urgent like, my father said."

"Then tell Lady Violette that Nell and I shall be there as soon as we can make it," Avril gave the lad's mass of curls a pat, much to Hal's disgust. He made his way slowly back to school, duty done.

Nell meanwhile, had collected the two ponies that they used for their longer visits. Avril had packed a small bag with what she almost knew she would need. She had been expecting a call like this for some time. The two were at Lady Violette's bedside by two o'clock. Violette relayed all her symptoms – which were slowly getting worse.

Both Avril and Nell knew precisely what they were dealing with – a very old lady whose heart was slowly giving up. They also knew that, when the muscles around the heart finally went into spasm, the pain would be almost unbearable. Avril cocked an eyebrow at young Nell.

"A weak concoction of belladonna to ease the stress on the heart?" Nell queried.

"Absolutely right," Avril managed a smile at her young deputy.

"Stop conferring as I were a piece of the furniture," the old lady demanded. "Tell me in simple terms what is amiss – as if I had not a good idea already!"

"You heart is in a weakened state," Avril never hid the truth from this patient. "It is slowly failing and there is absolutely nothing we can do to reverse it. All we can do is to ease the strain and perhaps dull your senses with poppy so that you are not so aware of the pain."

"Damn that!" was the stern reply. "I shall need all my senses for what must be done! By all means relieve the stress on my old heart if you are able - but send me to sleep and I shall curse you from beyond the grave!"

"We would not dare to incur your wrath, from either side of the grave, would we Nell?"

"No, indeed, we would not. Lady Violette's wrath is to be avoided at all costs!" Nell managed a smile at the patient who was sitting propped up on pillows.

"Then, bless you both. Give me this belladonna stuff and then please do me another small favour if you will. I understand that Master Kent is in the town again. I would be very obliged if you could get a message to him and say that I would appreciate a visit this evening. I shall still be alive then, shall I not?"

"I shall do my very best to make sure that you are," Avril crossed her fingers behind her back. "Nell, would you travel back now and see if you can locate Master Kent?"

When Nell had gone, Avril prepared the mixture obtained from the nightshade plant. Used in the wrong proportions, it was a killer. Used in small quantities, it was firmly believed to be useful for relaxing stressed muscles, especially those around the heart. Avril stayed with her patient for a full hour to ensure that it worked as she wanted. Lady Violette slowly managed to relax to the point where Avril believed it safe to go down to the kitchen. There, she instructed Meg how to mix the correct quantities. "One dose every four hours," she told the young woman who was in some distress at the condition of the old lady, a mistress who everyone had come to admire and respect since she had bought the estate over ten years previously. Avril took leave of her patient and rode slowly back home.

Matthew Kent was both intrigued and somewhat apprehensive as he sat at Lady Violette's bedside early that evening. Intrigued as to the purpose of his being almost summoned; apprehensive as he digested the information that young Nell had imparted about the old lady's health.

"You are no doubt intrigued as to why I have asked you to come to see me," Lady Violette opened the conversation as she sat propped up by numerous pillows. She is a mind-reader, thought Kent! He could immediately see the pain lines etched upon that old and kindly face. Nell, he thought, had not exaggerated.

"I have wondered," he admitted, trying to inject a light tone into what he could see was some effort by the lady.

"Then, let me enlighten you. But first, I have in the past been doing some investigation of my own. This may cause you some righteous indignation that I should even contemplate enquiring into you and your antecedents. But please bear with me as there is a point to all of this."

She laid back to recover her breath. Kent held his peace. He was even more intrigued.

"Now," she was able to continue after a few breaths. "I have discovered that you are thirty-eight years old, are unmarried and unattached – as far as I can tell; that you have been for some years a peripatetic investigator for Parliament; that you are sober, very reliable, and totally honest. No – do not blush! I speak only what others report and that I have myself observed. Incidentally, why a handsome man of your years has remained unattached is a mystery to me. However, I am now going to enlighten you as to my situation."

Again, there was a pause for breath. This time, she sipped from a glass containing the belladonna concoction.

"I was married when I was very young to Lord Charles Charlton. We lived in some style not that far from Westminster. Unfortunately, we were never blessed with children – and that is to my own everlasting sorrow. My husband died some twenty years past, leaving me all alone in a large house with a host of servants who had been with us for as long as I can remember. After only a year, I became heartily sick and tired of the hustle and bustle, the intrigues and the plots surrounding the Court of the late king. My husband was the only child of a very distant relative of the Courtenay family – very prominent in this county. I am therefore no blood relation to any of them. I was also an only child of parents who were both only children. Therefore, I have absolutely no kin of whom I am aware."

Kent was starting to have the funniest feeling that all of this was not only germane to the issue, but of vital importance. He again waited as the old lady took another sip and further breaths.

"I bought this small estate back in 1642 – or was it 1643? I brought with me only my long serving steward and personal maid. During these years I have endeavoured to bring the place back to what it should be. I think you might agree that I have done a fair job?"

"Indeed – it is in fine condition and is a great credit to you," Kent spoke only the truth – Brimley *was* a fine, though small, estate.

"Both steward and maid perished some years back during a very bad winter. I have been very well served since by Luke Farmer and his wife Meg, plus the others who work in the house and grounds. The three small farms attached to the estate are fruitful and well managed. Those farms provide more than sufficient funds to cater for the upkeep of the house and grounds. So, that is my current situation. In another few moments, we shall be joined by both steward and cook, also by a lawyer from Ashburton. All will be here to witness my will and testament – including your good self."

Yet another pause, this one much longer than those previously. It was obviously taking a great effort on her behalf. At the same time, Kent was wondering why he had been singled out to bear witness when there were many residents in the town who were far better known to her – the bailiff and the Parke estate steward for instance.

The three arrived in the bedroom together – Luke Farmer having admitted the lawyer, one Hector Anstruther to whom Kent took an immediate dislike. Large, very fat, sweating from the effort required to climb sixteen stairs, he gave Lady Violette a cursory bow before almost collapsing into a chair. Luke and Meg Farmer hovered by the door until summoned to attend closer.

"I trust that you have brought both copies," the old lady said to what was presumably her local lawyer.

Two sets of papers were produced from a bulging satchel. Lady Violette kept one for herself and handed the other to Kent.

"Please read it aloud so that everyone here may hear and understand," she said quietly to him. Kent peered at the formal writing, took a deep breath and commenced.

"This is the last will and testament of me Violette Anne Charlton. I declare myself to be of sound mind and I defy anyone to say to the contrary. Having no kin nearer to me than cousins many times removed, I make these dispositions freely and of my own devising. To my very faithful steward and cook, Luke and Meg Farmer, the sum of one hundred pounds each. To each remaining member of my staff, the sum of twenty-five pounds. To the trustees of the town school, the sum necessary to purchase outright the freehold of the school premises. To the orphan Nell Dawkins and to the foundling known as Felix Crowley the sum of fifty pounds each. The total remainder of my estate, being comprised of Brimley Manor, its grounds and attached farms, and any sums of cash remaining after the above bequeaths have been satisfied, I leave all to the care of Mary Cove, wife of the Parke Bailiff. To ensure that the terms of this will and testament are followed faithfully to the letter, I hereby appoint Matthew Kent as executor. I recognition of his service, he will upon signing this document receive the sum of two hundred pounds. Given on the first day of October in the year of Our Lord 1659, by my signature. To be witnessed in one another's presence by Hector Anstruther, Luke Farmer and Meg Farmer."

Kent gazed at the old lady with awe, folded the paper and handed it back into her skeletal hand.

"Have no doubt that I shall carry out the duties of executor to the letter," he said, receiving a smile and a nod in reply.

Anstruther witnessed the lady's signatures, appended his own, took one copy and an envelope no doubt containing his fee. With a glower at Kent, and a respectful nod to Lady Violette, he huffed and puffed his way out of the room. Luke and Meg had signed but stood almost rooted to the spot. Meg characteristically, was the first to speak.

"That is a very generous and unexpected gift, My Lady."

"Nonsense – well deserved and fully merited. Off you go and bring me up another glass of that weird concoction. I shall sleep tonight."

That left Kent still gazing down on this remarkable old lady.

"Tomorrow, Master Kent, please bring Mary to see me. I would like to be the one to break the news to her. You can spin a story that I need to consult her about some school matter."

Later that night, Kent was unable to drop off in his bed at the tavern. Another very remarkable lady – this one much younger – was going to be a rich landowner, and it would be up to him to see that all the deeds of transfer were properly in order. But for that to happen, one very remarkable lady had to die. From all he had been able to observe, that day – or even hour – was not that far off. And that made him very sad.

CHAPTER VI

The next day, the second of October, Fisher and Forbes broke with tradition – or rather, Colonel Fisher broke with tradition. Having risen early, he found himself at something of a loose end, so he went riding. Being in the open air, riding through gorgeous countryside, always lightened his mood. It also gave him the opportunity to think. The result of this mounted cogitation was that he rode to the top of Bovey Tracey and stopped at the smithy. Abel, who was alone in the forge that morning, looked up and recognised the old soldier.

"The Lord's blessings be on you this fine day, Colonel," he hailed, tossing a large piece of iron rod onto the fiercely burning flames.

"And to you, Master Smith. I have a boon to ask of you."

Abel, never a one to waste words, simply raised one bushy eyebrow.

"I find myself plagued with far too much time on my hands," Fisher launched into an explanation. "For someone such as myself used to the daily tasks of command, this has proved more than irksome. Therefore, I have decided to make better use of those hours. I would be grateful to you Master Smith if you would teach me the rudiments of your craft so that I may myself set up a much smaller version of all this and make things of which I may eventually take some pride."

Abel regarded the bluff Colonel with amazement. His first thought was that the old man wanted a mere hobby. But at second glance at the resolute features, decided that the man was in deadly earnest.

"I shall of course recompense you for your time," Fisher added as a further incentive.

"That shall not be necessary, Colonel. If it would suit you, I shall do as I did years past with Simon. He came and watched for days on end, then started on a simple task before repeating days of watching. That will cost me nothing. I shall be only too pleased to tell you what I am doing, why I do it that way, how I do it. I shall also be happy to answer the questions you may wish to put."

"Excellent! I could wish for no better instructor! May I attend you on the morrow when you might make a start?"

Abel thought that it would all be rather a nice way to spend his days. He was immensely proud of his work and the reputation he enjoyed. Fisher bade him a good day and crossed the road to the church and his friend James Forbes.

"You are going to do what?" Forbes regarded his friend with amazement.

"Learn a useful craft, indulge myself in honest labour. What is so remarkable about that?"

"Well, nothing, I suppose," Forbes smiled. "So, how about celebrating your new-found occupation with a mug of Sal Allen's finest ale?"

The two settled down in Forbes' garden, Fisher on a wooden bench and Forbes on a low wall covered in plants – his favourite camomile bench. Fisher then broached a subject that was, for all he knew, unknown to the Reverend.

"Tell me, James – have you ever heard of The Sealed Knot?"

Forbes' expression indicated that he had not.

"Then, pray let me enlighten you. The Sealed Knot was and is a sort of secret organisation that Charles started up back in '53. Whilst in his exile, in between begetting numerous children upon all and sundry, he sent messages to sympathisers both in England and Scotland. Some of these members we got to know and may be known to you also. Sir William Crompton, Sir Henry Villiers, Henry Hastings, Lady Tollemache, Baron Maynard?"

"Certainly, I have heard of both Villiers and Maynard," Forbes nodded.

"There have been at least two small uprisings, the last of which was quietly put down by Lambert himself – at a place called Winnington Bridge. And that was only two months ago!"

"That I most certainly did not know," Forbes admitted.

"It all goes to show that there is continued and growing unrest with what is being done in Parliament – or perhaps I should say, what is being utterly mismanaged. I have been of the opinion for some months now that the day when Charles rides through

London to be reinstated cannot be far off. Lambert has stretched patience too far. Monck is making more and more noise against Lambert. It simply cannot go on. So, tell me, James. You were Charles' chaplain and knew him well. What sort of ruler would he make?"

Forbes hung his head and peered into his ale.

"I fear, a very poor one," he said quietly. "He is far too interested in his own pleasures. Some would call him a hedonist and to be brutally honest, they have it right. It would be pleasure first, country second."

"But yet you would wish him back?"

"Under certain circumstances, yes. Let me explain. I have always known that young Charles is almost the direct opposite of his father. He is as frivolous as his father was serious. I can see no possibility of the return of a crowned king unless he be circumscribed by a set of rules governing what is his to decide and what is Parliament's. Given what I know of young Charles, these circumscriptions would be absolutely necessary."

"Then you are also minded that there is an end to the notion of divine right?"

"That may sound strange coming from such as me – but yes. Given that the only possible occupant of that throne is young Charles, he has to be set about with limits to his authority."

"And do you see him taking those responsibilities seriously?"

"When the mood takes him, yes. At other times he would want to be surrounded by laughter, fun and games."

"A figurehead, in other words?"

"At times, yes."

"And what of his younger brother James?"

"A far more serious young man – and a very capable commander. If there is trouble afoot, be sure that James will be sent to deal with it."

"But perhaps none of this may come about," Fisher brought that conversation to a halt.

Mary was deeply concerned for the health of her sponsor and friend, Lady Violette. When she was contacted on her way home to dinner with the twins, she became even more concerned. Kent relayed the message faithfully – that Violette wanted to speak to Mary on school matters. Sensing sone urgency in his tone, she left the twins in the care of May, Harry and Hob being out and about some estate business.

Collecting her own pony from the stables, she accompanied Kent on the short ride to Brimley. During that ride, she endeavoured to pump Kent for information about Lady Violette's state of health. She had heard from Avril that all was not well.

"It would seem that there is some trouble with her heart. Your Aunt Avril saw her twice yesterday and prescribed some concoction or other. It seems to have brought benefit to the old lady."

Mary, from her years with Avril, immediately thought to herself, 'belladonna'. The deadly nightshade plant was not named by accident. It *was* deadly, but not in the hands of a skilled apothecary. Used in very small quantities, it had been used for centuries to ease pain and some other conditions. It was also a relaxant.

It came as no surprise therefore that Mary found Lady Violette looking drawn but quite relaxed as she sat propped up by a multitude of pillows. Meg, who had been attending to her, gave Mary and Kent a smile of welcome and slid unobtrusively from the room. Violette looked warmly at Mary and patted the bed for her to come and sit.

"Thank you, Master Kent. Please make yourself comfortable as well. Now, I have something of importance to tell you, Mary. I wish that you promise me to hear me out before you utter any comment."

Somewhat bewildered, Mary nodded her consent.

Violette took a sip from her glass before commencing her well-prepared speech. "I have spent the last few weeks drawing up and finalising my will – no, do not look like that! I am an old lady, and this is prudent as I'm sure you would agree. This latest trouble with my heart has made the effort even more germane. Yesterday, I signed it and had it witnessed. I have appointed Matthew Kent as my executor as he is probably the most honest person I have encountered. I have made specific bequests – monetary rewards to my excellent staff and so forth. I have also made a sum of money available to the school trustees, one of which you are, Mary. That sum will purchase outright the freehold of the premises."

Mary, as she had promised, said nothing; her face however, betrayed what she was thinking – that this was a superb gift and would ensure that the school remained functioning for the future. Violette then reached for Mary's hand before continuing.

"I have been here in Brimley for just over sixteen years. In those years I have endeavoured to return this place back into what it undoubtedly was before being allowed to decay. I truly believe that I have been successful. During two terrible winters I have watched your Aunt Avril and you, then young Nell, work yourselves into exhaustion combatting the horrible disease that carried off far too many good folk. Why did I then propose you for the role of schoolmistress? I can answer that in one word – integrity. I have seen many young people come and go throughout my long life, but you have never wavered. You sought knowledge from your earliest years and used that knowledge to help and support others who were not blessed with your God-given gifts. Mary my dear, when I have gone, the entire Brimley estate will become yours. No – do not start remonstrating with me. My mind is made up and is as clear as a bell. However, the law being what it is – bloody disgraceful – it would be immediately become the property of your husband. I know that Harry would never usurp his rights, he is also made of good and honest stuff. So, what I have done is to make you legal custodian of the estate for the length of your lifetime. I know that you will guard it and nurture it as I would have done. Live here, put in a manager, if you choose. Use its proceeds to do good. I know that I leave it in the very safest, trustworthy hands."

Mary sat as if poleaxed. Whatever she had imagined her summons to be it most certainly was not what she had just been told. She simply sat on the bed with her mouth open.

"I have given Lady Violette my word that I shall be on hand to help and facilitate whatever you decide," Kent added, seeing that the void needed to be filled somehow or other. "There is of course, the question of the right of ownership of the estate. Being its legal custodian does not imply ownership. Therefore, the terms of the agreement making you custodian also contains instructions as to the estate's eventual destiny."

Lady Violette managed a secret smile. "That miserable lawyer who was here yesterday, has drawn up this agreement – and to my specific instructions. The freehold ownership of the Brimley estate upon my death is to be transferred into a trust. You, Mary and you, Master Kent are appointed trustees, with Mary being appointed as custodian. The trust is an open-ended affair. There are no named beneficiaries. Whosoever you choose to replace you as trustees is something I leave confidently in your capable hands."

Mary at long last found her voice. "I'm now worried stiff that I may not be capable of what you ask," she faltered. "It is something that I never even dreamed a possibility. I also hope that my duties as custodian do not commence for some considerable time. The whole place will never be the same without you!"

"Stuff and nonsense! Let me ask you a simple question – do you honestly believe you are unable to act as the custodian?"

"Honestly? Yes, I do. But I shall feel an awful weight of responsibility!"

"Then that is precisely why I have appointed Matthew to share some of the burden. You also have good and reliable relatives to whom you can go for advice. You will not be alone in this – everyone I know hereabouts will be more than willing to assist you whenever you feel the need to ask. Now – back to your children and impart more knowledge into their heads. Come back to confer with me whenever you feel the need. I somehow seem to know that this stupid heart of mine is not yet on the point of total collapse!"

Impulsively, Mary leaned forward to kiss the old, wrinkled cheek. She did not trust herself to speak any further. Kent, with his own farewell, joined her as they left the large mansion to ride back to the town.

"Well? Now you know," Kent gave her a sideways smile.

"Aye, now I know," Mary returned the smile. "I have much to think about. The first thing I must do is to relate all of this to Harry. He will be as astounded as I am."

"I know your husband quite well," Kent grinned. "He will have as much faith in you as Violette does. In my humble opinion, Lady Violette has made a very wise and well-informed decision."

Mary rode on quietly, her thoughts turned inwards. "Dear God, I urgently need all the help You can spare," she muttered to herself. "That is not the only news I have for Harry."

Matthew Kent had another matter pressing on his mind – the murder of Francis DeGruchy. Later that day, he called upon Harry and Hob. With Larkin also in attendance, the four made some sort of start on furthering the investigation.

"My only recommendation is that we visit this tavern, the Three Tuns, and start questioning those people who frequent the place. I think it highly unlikely that nobody can give us some indication of the men who spoke to young Francis – especially the serving girls. In my experience, they are the most likely to have information as they are probably the most inquisitive people on this planet. They watch, they observe."

"For my part, I can think of no other course of action," Harry nodded. "After all – Francis can tell us no more than we already know. Neither can that young sister of his. Until – or even if – his wife and child arrive here, his doings in France remain a mystery. I would agree that tracing these mysterious men is of great importance."

"Not to mention the somewhat sinister Abbe Justin," Kent reminded them. "What part does he play in all this? Was Francis doing his bidding? If so, what was that bidding? If not, was Francis acting as some sort of agent for those working against the Abbe's interests? If that was indeed the case, there is little or no chance of us learning his role. Mouths in Westminster will certainly be sewn tightly shut."

Hob sat quietly absorbing all this. He was still young enough to feel a thrill to be part of a possible espionage endeavour. As he had nothing to add, he remained prudently silent.

"Who amongst us is best suited to question the serving girls, and who best suited to question the customers?" Larkin asked. "My known rank precludes me from either task. I would be seen as an official inquisitor – and nothing on this earth shuts mouths quicker than questions from a senior officer!"

"I can undertake the job of questioning the customers," Kent offered. "I have no status anymore. I am unknown to all of them."

"And there is nobody better suited to probing the brains of the serving girls than Hob," Harry gave huis deputy a broad grin. "Good looking young man, friendly grin. None better!"

"Then I pray you keep my part secret from May," Hob insisted. "She would certainly not understand!"

Mary quite deliberately said nothing at all to her family until her twins and May's two children were tucked up in bed. And then she asked Hob if he would kindly go and ask Peter and Laura Cove to come and join them. Later, with a fire crackling away, Peter, Laura, Harry, Mary, Hob and May all sat together, the five looking at Mary for the reason for the summons.

"Today, I received some very exceptional news," she started with an almost guilty expression. "As you know, Lady Violette is seriously ill. Aunt Avril does not expect her to last more than a few more days."

"She will be a sad loss," Laura spoke for them all. "What she has brought about at Brimley, what she has done for this town and especially the school, is quite remarkable."

"I was asked to go to see her this morning. Believe me, I had no idea why I was required. It seems that she has spent some time recently making and perfecting her will. She has made Matthew Kent her executor."

"And a wise choice, if you ask me," Peter Cove interrupted. "Despite his allegiance to Parliament, I have always found him to be as straight and honest as any man I have ever met."

"How do you know all this?" Harry looked at his wife with a hint of misgiving.

"Believe me, Harry – I had absolutely no idea in my head why I had been summoned. It seemed that she wanted me to be aware of the contents of her will. As you know, I have been very close to her, what with her close association and support for the school. It was the school that I believed she wanted to discuss. And in part, it was. I was made aware of the entire contents of the will, and I must now tell you what I discovered."

"Should not this be kept until the will is presented formally by the executor after she has passed?" Laura asked.

"Under normal circumstances yes, it should. But if you bear with me for a while, you will learn that these circumstances are far from normal. She has left very generous amounts to her servants. That would be expected of her anyway. She has also bequeathed a sum of money to the trustees of the school so that the freehold of the premises may be purchased – making the school immune from any monetary liabilities."

"That is indeed very generous," Peter Cove allowed. "But - so like her!"

"Then she turned her attention to the Brimley Estate. She explained that she has absolutely no kin nearer to her than a very distant cousin at least three or four times removed. She has set up an open-ended trust that has Master Kent and me as trustees. She has also appointed me as custodian of the entire estate until such time as Master Kent and I jointly agree to appoint a beneficiary or beneficiaries."

That was met with a stunned silence. Again, Harry was the first to speak.

"But what does this all mean? Are you obliged to live there as the custodian?"

"No, Harry it does not – or I am as sure as I can be that is not the case. In any case, my place is here with you, and I would not ever want to be anywhere else!"

"Just checking," Harry gave her a wink and a broad grin. "But how can you act as custodian without actually living there?"

"Ah – I have had an idea on that score," Mary had indeed been thinking very deeply about her new responsibilities. "Matthew Kent has stated that he desires to live hereabouts and has made no secret of the fact that he is seeking a suitable house. What better than one of the trustees takes up residence there? As custodian, all I shall have to do is to ensure that the place runs smoothly, make decisions as and when necessary. For the legal side of things, I have my revered father-in-law; for the running of the house itself, who better to advise me than Peter Cove? And for the three small farms and the grounds, I have my brother and Ella."

"Thank you for the vote of confidence," Peter Cove laughed. "But have you broached this with Master Kent?"

"No, I have not. But you may rest assured that I shall do so tomorrow."

As they were settling into bed that night, Mary turned to Harry, leaning up upon one elbow.

"There is a further reason for my wishing above all things to remain here with you," she said quietly. "In the not too distant future, the twins will have a baby brother or sister to keep them amused."

For once, Harry was too stunned to reply. Stunned and very happy. And I'm only just getting used to being called Master Bailiff, he mused.

CHAPTER VII

Hob and Kent deliberately started out in mid-morning for the short ride to Newton Abbot and the Three Tuns. They knew that the tavern staff would be extremely busy until the morning chores were completed. Hob planned to be one of the very first of the morning's customers, hoping thereby to get the serving girls mostly to himself. Kent would wait until the dinner hour was close to ending, thus catching the regulars supping their ale after eating. It almost worked out that way.

Hob had about an hour before the girls would be rushed off their feet. He sat down at a corner table and asked for a mug of ale. The girl who took his order and returned with a mug of ale was inclined to linger and chat with the young man.

"You be not from hereabouts then?" she asked.

"Nay – I seldom come here. I'm from Bovey," Hob gave her one of his most ingratiating grins, using the name Bovey instead of the more correct Bovey Tracey.

"Be that where that body were found?"

"Aye – and nobody any the wiser how it got there. My friend and I are trying to discover the identity of the three gents he were seen with in this very tavern."

"I heard summat about that, men here asking questions. I never saw the young gent myself, but I can ask the other girls for you. Some were questioned afore, but there are two here today who were not."

That was yet another thing that did not happen as stated; the two girls, hearing that a rather good-looking young man was seeking information, arrived at Hob's small table together. Hob looked up and saw two young faces looking down at him. He had never seen them before, so was obliged to start afresh, showing them the picture and telling them why he was seeking information.

One of the girls who introduced herself as Maddy, glanced at the picture and simply shook her head.

"Aye, I saw him here, but never did I see him with others. He
sat alone."

"I saw him with three gentlemen on two evenings," the other
girl said slowly, looking closely at the picture. Hob's pulse
quickened a little.

"Can you describe these three? And what made you say they
were gentlemen?"

"Cos I knows they be!" came the assertion. "Well, at least, I
knows one of them be. My brother married and went to live in
Stoke last summer. I sometimes go there with my father on a day
off. One of those gents lives close by in a house by the rectory."

Hob knew that Stoke was the shortened name for the little
village of Stokeinteignhead, past Coomeinteignhead and on the
road that led to Shaldon. That small village was situated on the
west bank of the mouth of the Teign; the town of Teignmouth
was situated on the east bank.

"And do you happen to know this man's name?" Hob was
hardly daring to trust his luck.

"Nay – he be a close man. Hugh, that's my brother, says he
has no dealings with any in Stoke – just stays in his house or his
garden. House be weird – all black and shut in."

Hob also knew that 'close' meant secretive. But he now had a
very fruitful lead and had to get to Kent to share the news.
Thanking the girl, whose name happened to be Lily, Hob downed
the rest of his ale and hurried out to meet up with Kent.

"That is indeed welcome news. See what a handsome young
man may achieve!"

"And I still would not want May to learn of it. Not that she is
jealous, but least said, soonest mended," Hob grinned. "Anyway,
Master Kent, what do we now do with this information?"

"For a start, my name is Matthew. Master Kent is far too
formal for friends. I suggest that I also delve into the business
with the locals after dinner. You never know, I may be able to add
more to the story. Then we go home again and share all this with
the others. And then a plan may emerge.

The two spent the rest of the morning walking around the
town, down to the church of St. Lawrence and back. They gazed
into shops, stopped at stalls. Hob purchased three lengths of fine
ribbon. One was in deep red for his wife May. The other two were

yellow and blue, one for each of their daughters. Kitty – just five and Poppy nearly three, never had enough ribbons to braid through their hair.

Sitting apart back in the tavern, they ordered the set dinner. It happened to be pork with a side dish of parsnips and cabbage. It was extremely well cooked. Lily made it a point to ensure that she was the one to serve Hob – even more reason why his mission be kept from his young wife!

Kent meanwhile, started conversations with as many of the locals as he could manage. Armed with the new information, he probed as innocently as he could.

"Aye," one man admitted. "That miserable bugger I do know. Comes in here now and again with two more of his kind – three of the longest faces I have ever set eyes upon! My son is a carter and often goes down that way. I go with him sometimes to lend a hand if the load is a heavy one to manage. I have seen him in his garden tending his plants. What they are I know not. What his name is, I have not the slightest idea. Nor do I know the other two. But I did hear tell that one of them hails from Maidencombe."

And that, despite strenuous efforts, was as much as Kent was able to glean. They made their leisurely way back to Parke, happy that their mission had yielded some result.

Matthew Kent arrived back at Bovey Tracey with Hob in the mid-afternoon, eager to relate their new information to the others. Harry and Larkin were very keen to get going the very next day – to ride the twelve miles to Stoke and drag information out of the man who had been identified by two witnesses at the tavern.

"And what makes you suppose he will divulge any information?" a rather sceptical Harry grunted.

"Oh, he gets no choice in the matter!" Larkin replied. "I shall take a couple of my soldiers with me. We utter not a word, grab the man, throw him over a horse and take him to Exeter. Then, when he is confronted with a dungeon cell, I start asking him questions. If he proves reluctant, we offer him some encouragement."

"But what if this man has powerful friends?" Harry asked. "When my father was engaged in the search for the members of that sect, one of the senior members had very influential friends!"

"Availed him nothing in the end," Kent chuckled. "His so-called friends deserted him faster than rats leave a sinking ship. As far as I know, he is still languishing in a cell somewhere."

"What sort of encouragement would you be talking about?" Hob was keen to know the details.

"To start with, just a rough going-over. That, plus the promise of a week in a dank dungeon, usually does the trick. He has been identified by two completely independent witnesses. The man knows something, and he *will* tell us!"

"I wonder who he is?" Hob mused.

"He could be the Duke of Somewhere, for all I care," Larkin grinned. "He has information – and I *will* get it out of him.!"

That evening after supper, Mary rode up to the tavern to speak with Kent. She was a trifle apprehensive to outline her plan to him but knew that it needed to be done as soon as possible. She had ridden to Brimley before supper to find that Lady Violette was just a little bit weaker. It was readily apparent that the old lady had not much longer to live.

Kent, summoned down from his room by one of the serving girls, found Mary waiting for him in the back parlour.

"Is this to be the first meeting of the trustees?" he asked, holding out a chair for Mary. He sat down opposite her and cocked his head to one side.

"I suppose it is," Mary admitted. "Please would you allow me to outline a plan that occurred to me, one that needs us both to be in absolute agreement?"

"Certainly. I have been engaged on other business today, but I know we need to make some sort of plans for the not-too-distant future. How is the dear old soul?"

"Fading away slowly, I'm sorry to say. I know that Aunt Avril would agree with me. When I saw her earlier, Lady Violette was just that bit weaker. It cannot be long now."

"Then I for one will mourn the passing of a truly wonderful lady," Kent nodded.

"When I told my family about the terms of the will and of the trust, they were naturally somewhat taken aback. Harry, bless him, was worried that I would want to move into the manor myself to act as custodian in situ. There is no way that I would do any such thing. My place is by his side - and I would not want to be anywhere else. But the estate certainly needs someone there to keep it running. The steward and his wife, Luke and Meg, are excellent – but it is hardly fair to place the onus upon them. It then occurred to me that you are looking for a property. What more fitting than you should take up residence there?"

Kent stared at her open-mouthed in astonishment.

"Believe me, that had never occurred to me!" he replied. "In one sense, it certainly answers two problems – my need for a house and the estate's need for a supervisor. But there is another way of looking at it – and one that perhaps has not occurred to you. How would it be viewed if one of the trustees took advantage of his appointment and secured for himself a very comfortable house? I have no knowledge of the law regarding trusts – but I would not be in the least bit comfortable if I should be viewed as taking undue advantage."

Mary sat back and digested that.

"Oh – you are right. That had certainly not occurred to me. And I suppose you are right. But where does that leave us. I am supposed to be the estate's custodian. How may I carry out that function properly if I am neither there myself nor have anyone there as my eyes and ears?"

Kent sat back and gave her a big grin.

"You, Mary Cove, have the answer available to you – and not a hundred miles from you. Your father-in-law and mother-in-law presently live in a small cottage. Who better to take day to day management than those two who have spent many years in virtual charge of the management of law and order for the entire Parke estate?"

It was Mary's turn to gaze open-mouthed.

"By all that is wonderful, that would indeed be a perfect answer. But would they even consider it, having just shaken off the mantle of responsibility – only to don yet another?"

"But they would only be acting on your behalf, and for a much smaller affair than a whole town and estate. Why do you not put it to them? If anyone could persuade them, it is you."

"You credit me with far more persuasive powers than I know I possess," Mary laughed. "However, you are certainly right – I can only put it to them. If they are definitely against the idea, then we shall have to think again. Every decision we make must be unanimously agreed. It can never be that we start in motion something that one of us is not happy with."

"We still have, the Good Lord permitting, some days left to us before either of us has to start acting our roles."

"Then, I shall make it my task to set the idea before Peter and Laura. Perhaps we could meet again tomorrow evening and I can tell you my success - or abject failure."

The proposed expedition to Stokeinteignhead did not happen the next day. Lashing winds and torrential rain put a stop to that! Colonel Larkin, who fancied himself an expert of West Country weather declared that it was set for at least three days. May, who had lived there all her life, was the one most people turned to for a forecast. She could never explain how she did it, but her prognostications were seldom far off the mark. According to her, the storm would probably blow itself out over the next twelve hours.

Mary braved the storm to go to the school only to find that her two were the only ones who had turned up. Sighing, she turned them around again and got back home soaked to the skin.

"No school today, then?" Harry gave her a grin.

"That's one of the reasons I married you," Mary glared at him. "That incisive wit and penetrating observations!" Having sent her seven-year-old twins up to their room to get out of their soaked garments, dry off, then put on dry clothes, she dashed upstairs to do the same herself. She was back downstairs some fifteen minutes later to set the boys the task of reading a short chapter from an account of the adventures of Sir Lancelot – then to write a short essay with their thoughts.

Shortly afterwards, Peter and Laura Cove came in, shaking water from their waterproof capes. It was too good an opportunity to miss – Mary asked them to accompany her into the small parlour as she had something she wished to discuss with them. She had briefed Harry the night before and was mighty relieved when he was very enthusiastic about the idea.

"Well, and what are we supposed to discuss?" Laura gave her daughter in law a hug and a kiss on her cheek. They all sat down around the small log fire which was sending out a comforting heat.

"You will recall that I have been tasked with the custodianship of Brimley – along with Matthew Kent as my co-trustee?"

"And you have discovered a difficulty in carrying out that somewhat onerous duty, I suppose?" Peter Cove gave her a broad grin. "Laura and I knew that there would be snags!"

"The main snag, as you put it, is my position here. I am Harry's wife and the twins' mother. My place is here with them – and there is nowhere I would rather be. Therefore, my moving into Brimley as its live-in custodian is not even a possibility. My first thought was for Matthew to take up residence, and we discussed it at some length yesterday. He pointed out that there was one large snag with that idea! Whilst it would be perfectly proper for me as custodian to take up residence – which I have already said I shall not and could not do – for him to do so could well be regarded as an abuse of his status as a trustee; it might even be unlawful."

"I think that Peter and I would certainly agree with all those points," Laura nodded. "So, how may all this be resolved?"

Mary mentally girded her loins for the plan she was proposing.

"There *is* a way," she began. "The first thing as custodian I must do is to entrust the house and estate to someone, or some people, of unimpeachable integrity. To do anything else would be a breach of my duties. How would it suit you both to move into Brimley? It would ensure you a retirement of comfort and ease, rather than having to fend for yourselves in the cottage. There is nobody in this town or in Brimley who would raise the slightest objection – you have been the mainstay of the town for many years and are regarded with respect and absolute trust."

"And who instructed you in the subtle art of flattery?" Laura laughed. "Yes – we know we enjoy the trust of most people hereabouts. But you gird us about with the mantle of sainthood!"

Mary coloured and shrank back into her chair. "Believe me, I did not mean any disrespect," she managed.

"Mary, we both know what you were trying to do, and we take no offence whatsoever," Peter reached across to grab Mary's hand is his. "But just for once, we are slightly ahead of you. The snags that you so correctly identified occurred to both of us as well. Had you not made the proposal, we would have done so ourselves!"

Mary sat up straighter. "Do you mean that my and Matthew's clever plan was anticipated? Do you both really want to make the move? This is the best outcome I could ever have envisaged. It also solves my one major problem. How could I be blessed with such wonderful parents in law?"

"The blessing is mutual!" Laura said in all seriousness. "Believe it or not, Harry was overjoyed when you and that other lad declared yourselves merely friends. He came straight to us and was in a dither about approaching you. Both Peter and I told him that he would be the biggest fool in Christendom if he did not take a chance to state his case. That he did is the best day's work he ever accomplished. He gained the perfect wife, and we gained the daughter in law in a million."

"And now who is using the subtle art of flattery?" Mary burst out laughing, mainly as a release of the tension she had been under. "Dear Violette is not going to last much longer. Despite the awful weather, I must ride there and tell her that her home and estate are going to be in the safest of hands."

Harry got to hear of Mary's proposed short trip and immediately said he would come with her. By the time dinner was over, the rain had become a deluge, turning the roads and lanes into torrents.

"I simply have to go," Mary insisted. "For all I know, she might have already died and me none the wiser. Matthew must also attend every day as he is her executor. I said that I would bring news so that, if necessary, he can visit after supper."

By the time the two were ready to leave, they looked completely different. Both were wearing stout boots, their clothes swamped in massive waterproof capes, their heads enveloped in wide-brimmed leather hats.

"Sorry, old girl," Mary apologised to her mare as they splashed their way out of the estate and onto the Brimley lane. The mare gave a snort in reply, blowing out nostrils filled with rainwater. Mary sensed disapproval in the snort.

Kit Warden, long-time soldier friend of the steward Luke Farmer, dashed out to take their horses and shelter them in the dry stables with hay. He set a lad to drying and brushing the soaked mounts.

Luke himself led Mary and Harry up to Violette's bedroom. Just before opening the door, he turned and said softly, "she is much the same, but just a little weaker each day."

"I am neither deaf nor dead!" came a voice from within. "Luke Farmer – kindly show whoever stands without into the room so that they may see for themselves that neither condition yet prevails!"

Luke grinned at Mary and opened the door for the pair to enter. Violette was, as before, sitting propped up against pillows. Mary could see at once that the breathing was just that little more laboured. A skeletal hand was placed over the old lady's heart, almost as if seeking confirmation for its owner that it was still beating.

"You bring me the honour of a visit from our esteemed bailiff," she reached out her other hand for Mary to grasp gently. Harry gave a smile in return and took a seat in the window so that Mary could get Violette's full attention.

Mary wasted no time in preliminaries – she knew they would be brushed aside. Instead, she plunged straight into her account of the new arrangements. To her surprise and relief, Lady Violette gave her a smile as she finished.

"With Master Kent as my executor and trustee, with you as trustee and custodian, and now Peter and Laura Cove as the new occupants, I am as well served as anyone could be. It is an excellent solution. I am absolutely sure that they will carry on my work here. So, cease that frowning Mary dear, and rest assured that I am more than content."

Mary barely was able to supress a sign of relief. Somehow or other, she would make the time to carry out her duties as custodian, schoolteacher, mother, and bailiff's wife. After all, she reasoned, with Harry's parents actually looking after the place, her duties would be only an occasional visit and a report to the trustees – of which she was one.

Violette raised her free hand and made another effort. "Luke Farmer, I know you are skulking without. Come in here!"

The door opened and Luke came to stand at the foot of the bed. "You shouted, my lady,"

"Indeed, I shouted! Now, I have something to tell you that you need to pass on to each member of the staff. Master Kent and Mary Cove are my trustees. The retired bailiff and his wife, Peter and Laura Cove, will take up residence here when I am no more. I want you to relay that to the staff and also my personal assurance that each and every one of them is secure in post. I make this a stipulation!"

"There would never be any doubt about that," Mary confirmed.

"Then I shall do so at once, my lady," Both Mary and Harry could see the look of utter relief on the steward's face as he hurried out.

"Now to another matter," Violette continued. "That Hector Anstruther, the lawyer I hired to draw up the will, may well attempt to impose his pennyworth. He is a mere functionary. He simply drew up my will to my precise instructions. Matthew is my executor, and you are my trustees."

Mary grinned at her. "If necessary, I shall get my cousin Simon to sit on him whilst Matthew reminds him of his true position. Do you really expect that he will attempt to interfere?"

"The man is a competent lawyer and an obnoxious individual, full of a sense of his own importance. So, yes, he may well."

"Fear not – Simon sitting upon him will soon empty out that sense of importance."

"He will probably sue for assault!"

"Using who as witnesses? Everyone else present will be struck both blind and deaf. Now, onto Matthew himself. I have no doubt he will come to visit you this evening. Is there any message I may give him?"

"No, no message. I intend to be here a few more days yet. So, be on your way. I am sure your children need you as much as do I."

By the time Mary and Harry had returned home, the rain had almost stopped, and the wind had dropped to a mere breeze. After shedding their protective gear, Mary and Harry found the larger parlour filled with four children and a hassled May.

"What you forecast has indeed happened," Harry told May. "You are indeed fey!"

"What does fey mean?" Kitty demanded.

"What does fey mean?" Poppy immediately echoed her elder sister's question.

Harry regarded the five- and three-year-old girls. "Fey means that your mama is at one with the pixies, knows what they know."

"Is mama a pixie, then?" Kitty looked at May in awe.

"Nay – your mama is far too big to be a pixie! Pixies are tiny, like fairies, but wise in the ways of the moor and the weather."

"Then how does mama know what the pixies know?"

"You shall have to ask her!"

"Thank you for that, Master Bailiff!" May favoured Harry with a big grin.

"Does mama know the pixies' magic?" Poppy was agog and standing on tiptoes.

Mary was always at pains to tell the older children in her school that magic was really advanced trickery, but never to the young ones. The look of awe of those little faces was priceless – and she let it remain so until they were old enough to understand.

Will, elder than his twin by a few minutes, was on the point of airing his superior knowledge until a glance from his mother stopped him in his tracks. Mary would not take kindly to the little ones being wrenched away from their dreams!

Peterkin, the other twin, was not so observant. "There is no such – "

"Whatever you were going to say, do not!" Mary ordered. Will gave his brother a nudge. The two were almost identical in appearance, but widely different in temperament. Will was impulsive; Peterkin was slow and deliberate. It led to endless rows and wrestling matches.

"My mama is a pixie," little Poppy danced around the room, not in the least understanding that neither pixies nor magic existed. May gave a sigh of resignation.

CHAPTER VIII

"Are we sure which man we are after?" Paul Larkin asked as he and Kent rode side by side through the small village of Combeinteignhead.

The aftermath of the previous day's rainstorm had played havoc with the lanes, many still almost awash with the muddy water coloured deep rusty red – typical of South Devon.

"Yes, I am sure – or at least, I have a very good description and an accurate location of the house," Kent replied.

"Still just want us to grab the bugger, sir?" queried the taller of the two troopers riding just behind his colonel.

"Seems the easiest thing to do. Give him the scare of his life. Make hm wonder what is coming next," Larkin replied. "Grab him, rope his hands behind his back, thrust a gag in his mouth and them sling him on the spare horse. And take no notice of anything he says – that is if you give him time to say anything!"

Kent was not at all sure that he was comfortable with these shock tactics. If they were happening to him, he would indeed be very apprehensive as to his immediate future. However, he bowed to superior military knowledge. After all, they desperately needed answers and these tactics might just get them.

"Rough him up a bit as well, sir?" the shorter of the troopers asked.

"No – and that will make him wonder all the more!"

"Pity," both Larkin and Kent heard the man mutter.

After another couple of miles along the twisting lane, the next village came into view. Away to their left they could see the slowly widening path of the river Teign as it made its way to the very wide mouth between Shalford and Teignmouth. Kent had never been down this side of the river before and assumed that there would be a ferry between the two places as there was certainly no bridge.

They passed the tavern, walking their horses very slowly. Already, many village faces were peering out of doors and windows, not at all sure what to make of a very senior army officer, two heavily armed troopers, and a smart gentleman riding through their village.

Kent stopped and pointed at a larger than average cottage on the right. It was exactly as it had been described to him. And to cap it, a man answering the precise description was picking apples from a tree in the front garden. Larkin looked at Kent, who nodded emphatically. Larkin turned to his men. "Go," he ordered very quietly.

It was over in less than a minute. One moment, the man was picking apples, the next he was struggling between two troopers, being bound and gagged, dragged out and literally thrown onto the spare horse. And then inevitably, someone intervened.

"Hoi, whoever you are, you can't be a'doing that here!" a portly man came waddling out of the next house. "I am the head man here and I say you release him immediately!"

"Head man?" the taller trooper gave him a big grin. "Then poke that head between your legs and kiss your arse goodbye. And then get out of the bloody way!"

Larkin wheeled his horse about, then set off at a smart trot. Kent came next, then the tall trooper leading the spare horse by its rein. The shorter trooper gave the village a cheery wave and followed after. The way back was taken at a faster pace, so that by midday, they were clattering through the streets of Newton Abbot to where the town jail was situated.

Halting at the jail, they were greeted by a scruffy individual who poked his head around the studded door. "Whatcherwant?" he growled.

"What I want is for you to put this man in a cell whilst we go and find some dinner. We shall be back to start questioning him."

"Can't do that, whoever you be!" came the response. "Town constable doesn't allow anyone held here without his say-so."

Larkin dismounted and walked over to the man. "Let me introduce myself," he said, quite pleasantly. "I am Colonel Larkin sent here from Westminster to enquire into strange happenings and murder. Now – are you going to do as I ask, or do I take you by the scruff of your dirty neck and hang you up by your ankles from that post over yonder?"

Oh, the influence of senior rank and the trappings of power, Kent thought as he watched the man undergo a sudden and dramatic transformation.

"Murder, you say, sir? Then it will be my pleasure to do as you ask, sir. I shall keep him here safe and snug for when you return."

"Excellent!" Larkin beamed. "Keep him trussed and gagged – and disregard any protestation he may offer. A single cell, no communication whatsoever."

"It shall be exactly as you say, sir," the man almost touched the ground with his nose. Their prisoner was heaved down, taken inside the small jail, and placed inside a small cell. With the door locked securely, the four bade the jailer a good-day and went in search of some dinner. By the time they arrived at the nearest tavern, news had already spread. Larkin was regarded in some awe and that assured they were served quickly and with respect.

"And how do you intend to proceed?" Kent asked, his mouth stuffed with the crust of a succulent pie.

"With due formality," came the instant reply. "Bring down the weight of Parliament upon him – let him see that there is no appeal whatsoever – nobody higher to whom he might appeal! So, are you willing to act as my clerk in the matter? That would add somewhat to the formality of the occasion?"

"I would be delighted," Kent grinned. "I have writing materials with me as I assumed that sometime today someone would be required to make a proper note."

"Then I am grateful, Matthew. Today, I am Colonel. Tomorrow I shall return to being Paul!"

"Indeed, sir, colonel, not Paul!" Kent laughed.

Back once again at the jail, Larkin asked for the man to be brought out and to be sat on a hard stool. Kent sat at a small side table with paper and pen at the ready.

"Now," Larkin started immediately the man was sat facing him. "I am Colonel Larkin representing Parliament, at whose behest I am carrying out these enquiries. My clerk, Master Kent, will take down a complete account of the questions and answers. Trooper Hodge will stand behind you and hold you seated. Corporal Skinner will remove your gag so that you make response to the questions. You will speak only in response to those questions. Any infringement of those rules will result in damage to your knees. Nod if you have understood."

The man was glaring daggers at Larkin. That implacable face gave nothing away, so he nodded. Skinner removed the gag.

"Question one. What is your name?"

"Oliver Cromwell," the answer was almost spat back. It was followed by a howl of pain as the butt of Skinner's pistol butt cracked on his left kneecap. Larkin said nothing, merely cocked his head to one side.

"Bartholomew Preece," came the muttered answer.

"Bartholomew Preece. You were seen on at least two occasions conversing at The Three Tuns tavern with a young man by the name of Francis DeGruchy. That same Francis DeGruchy was found some days ago having been murdered and his body hidden behind the smithy in Bovey Tracey. So – question two. How did you know that young man?"

"I did not know him. I simply fell into conversation with him at the tavern."

"You and others sought him out. One other is now known to reside further along the coast at Maidencombe. We shall find him! DeGruchy is known to have been in the company of Abbe Justin, some short while before returning to England. That name certainly means something to you as I observed your reaction when it was uttered. He is a man very dangerous to England. You, Bartholomew Preece, are in deep waters. You are known to have been in long conversation with a young man, a young man murdered shortly afterwards, and also known to have been consorting with a dangerous enemy. By association, you are deeply implicated. Do not be in any doubt that you will be put to the most rigorous questioning. You can avoid that by answering every question that I shall put to you. I shall now leave you here until the morning. Use the time well and think very hard about your future – that is, if you have one. I shall be back again. In the meantime, you shall remain here in close confinement."

Preece was bundled back into his cell. The four were about to leave when the main door burst open and a very fat man waddled in, spitting venom.

"Who in blazes are you and what makes you so free with my jail?" he demanded, his jowls quivering with indignation.

"Are you able to read?" Larkin asked, removing his warrant from his pocket.

"Read? Of course, I can read, damn your insolence!"

"Then cast your eyes over that, especially the signature above the seal!"

The fat jaw dropped a good three inches. All bluster left as if wiped clear by a duster.

"I see you now appreciate why I am here. The prisoner I have left in your care is to be kept here overnight. He is to be fed. He is not to be spoken to. You are to disregard anything he might say – especially any important names he may utter. I shall return in the morning with my clerk and soldiers to question him properly."

"Indeed, colonel. It shall be as you order."

"I see you have manacles and chains. Make sure he is kept safe and sound with no chance for self-harm. I want him hale and fit when I return."

Back at Bovey Tracey, Kent and Larkin supped together at the tavern and mulled over what they had achieved.

"Well, we at least have one potential canary," Kent grinned. "I have little doubt that he shall sing very prettily on the morrow!"

"Hm – depends how deeply he is immersed in whatever this turns out to be," Larkin responded. "His fear of them – whoever 'they' are – may be greater than his fear of me and who I represent. We shall see!"

Mary received a very unwelcome visitor at the school the following morning, one she had to deal with in a far more peremptory manner than she usually adopted. She had been half-way through an explanation of the movement of the moon around the earth when there came a loud knock at the door and the jowly face of Hector Anstruther glared at her.

"I need immediate words with you," he demanded. Seventeen children sat back on their benches, all thrilled at such an intrusion. It bade well for an interesting interlude.

"And as you can see, I am otherwise engaged with the children," Mary retorted. "Whatever you need to say to me can be accomplished in the midday break which shall be in approximately forty minutes time.”

“My time is far more valuable than that! I demand that I speak to you now!”

“Master Anstruther – you may demand until you go blue in the face. My answer remains the same. Now, kindly go away until I have finished the lesson.”

“I shall appeal to have you removed from the will!”

“And you shall fail. Now, once again, go away!”

Even the irascible lawyer could see that he was not going to succeed. Slamming the door behind him, he could be heard marching off down the street.

“That told him, didn’t it Miss Mary!” one Charlie Plumb chuckled from the back row.

“Sent him off with a flea in his ear!” Peterkin grinned at his mother.

“Who is he?” his twin asked. Mary could see that she had to satisfy their curiosity, or she would get little peace.

“He is the lawyer retained by Lady Violette. He drew up her will. Now, back to the movement of the moon!”

When the bell sounded for the dinner break, Mary sent the twins home alone and walked up the street to the smithy. She had decided that a display of muscle would do no harm to the forthcoming conversation with Anstruther.

“Aha – we are visited by the town’s own genius!” her cousin Simon paused in his hammering of a piece of red-hot iron.

“Simon, may I borrow you for a while? There is a rather obnoxious man called Anstruther coming to see me at the school. He is the lawyer for Lady Violette, and he could just prove a hard man to shift.”

“I’m quite good at shifting obnoxious men,” Simon grinned. “Hold on for a moment whilst I cool this down and I shall be with you.”

Mary and Simon got back to the school cottage just before Anstruther. He neither knocked not asked permission to enter – just banged open the door and waddled in. He could hardly miss sight of Simon who was propping up the side wall and looking massive.

“And what is this *person* doing here?” he snorted at Mary.

"Oh, how remiss of me," Mary twittered. "Permit me to introduce Simon Smith, my cousin by marriage."

"There is no such relationship!" came the grunted reply. "Whoever he may be, he has no place in the conversation we are to have. Kindly ask him to leave."

"I shall do no such thing. Simon stays. So, unless you accept that stipulation, *you* have my permission to leave the school premises!"

"Insult Mary, and I shall toss you in the river, then summon twenty witnesses to state that you tumbled in all by yourself," Simon gave him his broadest smile.

Anstruther, both Mary and Simon could see, realised that his fate would be exactly as stated. He somehow managed to rein in his temper.

"I have just been appraised of the arrangements that have been made behind my back – that your husband's parents are to take up residence upon the demise of Lady Violette. I shall successfully challenge these arrangements at the next petty sessions," he at long last got around to saying why he had come.

"Then let me appraise you of our response to that threat. First of all, you were hired to draw up a will. That and nothing more. Lady Violette, of her own volition, made Matthew Kent her sole executor. The new arrangements as you call them have been set down on paper, signed and witnessed, and form a part of that will and testament. Matthew will very faithfully see that each and every term of the will be executed exactly as she has demanded. Your part in the proceedings ended with the presentation of the will. There are no grounds whatsoever for any appeal against it."

"It has the reek of nepotism!" snarled Anstruther.

"Garbage!" Mary retorted. "Matthew is no kin to me – or to Harry's parents. He will be the one executing the will, not I!"

"I shall plead undue influence!"

"Master Anstruther, you may plead whatsoever you want. You may even call upon the Archangel Gabriel. It will avail you nothing – and I suspect that you know it. All you are attempting is to browbeat someone you see as a helpless woman – and, as you can see – I am not one! Now, unless you have any further threats, this conversation is at an end."

"And the river runs very fast after the recent heavy rains," Simon laughed.

Anstruther made no reply, turned on his heel and stormed out, slamming the door behind him.

"Did you really need me here? You coped with that oaf perfectly well on your own," Simon put a huge arm around Mary's shoulders and gave her what he fondly believed to be a gentle hug. Mary winced.

"That's as maybe," she replied. "It did no harm to let him see that his opposition is formidable. I must seek out Master Kent and let him know what has just occurred."

"You have missed dinner. Far more important, so have I," Simon chuckled. "Back to Imelda we go and plead starvation."

Larkin had thought it unnecessary that his two soldiers accompany him and Kent to Newton Abbot. He was firmly convinced that a night of incarceration, plus his threats, would loosen Preece's tongue sufficiently without the need for more violence. Consequently, the two rode to the little jail and stabled their horses at the nearest tavern.

The jailer, all obsequious grovelling, stated that their prisoner had been kept alive for them to interview. Preece was brought out in his chains and was once again seated on the stool.

"Yesterday," Larkin began, "we established that you are Bartholomew Preece and that you were in close company with Francis DeGruchy on more than one occasion before he was found murdered. Also, we stated that DeGruchy had been in close contact with Abbe Justin, a known enemy of England. So, I now ask you why you and others sought out DeGruchy. What was your interest in him?"

Preece looked up and stared at Larkin. "I have spent a long and painful night thinking of my position. I have come to the conclusion that I need to be utterly frank with you less you form the very worst opinion of me. Should you do so, I dread to contemplate my inevitable fate. Therefore, I need to make a full and honest statement that I trust will be taken down verbatim."

"And that is why I am here," Kent looked up from his writing.

"Then I shall commence. Some many months ago, I was approached by two gentlemen who reside in Maidencombe. One is named Bernard Duplessis, the other is Claude Bruce. Why they singled me out is still a mystery to me. They arrived one morning at my home and asked if they might have words of a private nature. I was intrigued enough to invite them into my parlour and offer them wine and cake. They started off by asking my opinion on certain matters – what did I think of the way our Commonwealth was being governed? Did I believe it had been better served by the old king? Did I have any thoughts about the possible reinstatement of the old king's son as monarch? I took all this as being in the nature of the sort of discussion that occurs in every tavern throughout the land. As it happens, I do have views on all those topics, as I am sure does every thinking individual in England. I make no apology for stating that my thoughts do run along the lines of a reinstatement. That may not please you, Colonel, but I have said that I shall be honest. Anyway, having stated those views, I was asked if there was any way I would sanction the overthrow of the present parliament so that it might be brought about. It was then that I started to harbour the strongest doubts about the two. Reinstatement of the monarch, yes – I am very much in favour of that by peaceful means and at the wish of the majority. But overthrow had the stink of revolution and violence. It occurred to me that I could well find out a lot more from them and somehow get word to the authorities as I abhor violence of any kind."

"So, what you are claiming is that you would act as a spy and learn what you could so as to warn Parliament of their obviously treasonable intentions."

"Exactly, Colonel. And that is what I did. I attended meetings, made the appropriate noises. I also attended those two meetings with DeGruchy as he was said to be a leading light in whatever movement was being hatched. I was astounded when I learned from you that DeGruchy had been murdered. I had no knowledge whatsoever of it. I now see that I should have acted earlier and appraised someone in authority of what I suspected was being planned. I was foolish enough to believe that I could delve further into it all so that I had a fuller picture."

"And then, along we came and arrested you. Why did you not immediately tell me all this? Why wait until almost a day passed?"

"Again, I must plead a measure of panic. Last night served to waken me up to my predicament."

Larkin sat quietly as Kent's pen scratched away, taking down each and every word. When the pen was laid aside, Larkin spoke again.

"You will be held here – without the manacles and chains. I shall send soldiers to escort you to Exeter where you shall be held by the sheriff. In the meantime, I shall apprehend these other two. Then we shall see where all this leads."

Leaving Preece to the mercies of the scruffy jailer, the two mounted their horses and rode slowly back to Bovey Tracey.

"That was a load of utter bollocks!" Kent laughed. "Please sir, I was led by the nose into very muddy waters. I am innocent of everything other than utter stupidity. I was led, coerced, and decided to screw up my courage and do the right thing. Sheer bollocks!"

"Serves me right for allowing him the time to dream it up," Larkin admitted. "I should have hammered the man straight away. I shall not make the same mistake with Messrs Duplessis and Bruce!"

"So, a larger contingent and a ride to Maidencombe?"

"Precisely!"

"Gloves off right from the start?"

"No – gloves on! They hurt more when used as a fist!"

Mary made a detour after leaving the school that afternoon. Having penned a letter for Matthew Kent, she walked up to the tavern and left it for him with Sal Allen, then enjoyed a slow stroll back down the town and into Parke. Upon entering the house, she was intrigued to hear three voices coming from the parlour, the twins and Harry. She tiptoed to the door to hear more.

"Dung beetle!" Will shouted at his twin.

"Festering toad!" Peterkin retorted.

"Bucket of donkey piss!" from Will.

"Badger's turd!" back from Peterkin.

"Enough!" Harry shouted. "Enough, or I shall wallop the pair of you. Now tell me what is causing this exchange of insults."

"Peterkin refuses to treat me with respect – and I am the oldest!"

"Your mama would be horrified at your lack of grammar," Harry flung back at his son. "Between only two, the word is older, not oldest. In any case, you are older by the merest fraction!"

"I am still older, and I demand respect from my junior!"

"Pig's arse!" Peterkin shouted.

"I warned you," Harry again had to raise his voice. "In what manner has Peterkin not shown respect?"

"He says he is entitled to a half share in the new sledge when the winter snows come."

"And why should he not have a half share? He is your twin brother, for heaven's sake!"

"I should have the larger share being the older!"

"I have just about had enough of this," Harry grated. "Will – fetch paper and pen. Then work out what proportion of the sledge should be yours, based upon the proportion of time you are older than he is."

"But that will take hours and hours, papa!"

"It's is either that or you accept half-shares."

Mary, barely able to keep a straight face, opened the door and walked in – to be besieged by an aggrieved Will.

"Mama, papa has given me an impossible sum to work out!"

"No sum is impossible of being worked out. I heard the gist of it. So, how many minutes are you senior to Peterkin?"

"Ten."

"Then all you have to work out is the number of ten minutes you have lived, then subtract one for Peterkin's. Then present one as a proportion of the other. Then that proportion shall be yours and the slightly less proportion shall be Peterkin's."

"It shall take me all night and most of tomorrow to work it out!" the nearly eight-year-old moaned.

"Then my decision stands. Either prove it or accept half shares!" Harry grinned.

"Oh, all right – half shares it shall be," Will groaned.

"And now be off the pair of you. Go and wash before supper," Harry ordered.

From the far scullery could be heard soft voices muttering, 'cow's buttocks' and 'frog's vomit'.

Harry gave Mary a welcome kiss and a big grin. "It is quite lovely being parents, is it not?" he laughed.

"I wonder what they will make of a little sister or brother?" Mary wondered.

"Of one thing you may be absolutely certain. The twins will fight for his or her affections!"

CHAPTER IX

Once again, the weather was kindness itself as a small band rode out of Bovey Tracey the next morning. Blue skies with only the faintest trace of skimpy, high clouds, the gentlest of breezes coming from the south-west, and fairly firm going underfoot. They could not have asked for better conditions.

Larkin was saying exactly that to Kent as they rode side by side at the head of two ranks of mounted soldiers. Larkin had decided to bring six with him as a show of force.

"And what are your plans if we are unable to find these two men?" Kent asked as they left Newton Abbot behind them. Their planned route was to head for Combe, then onwards to Stoke. Then, instead of keeping on that road to Shaldon, to head to the right and make directly for Maidencombe.

"That has not even entered my head," Larkin admitted. "If we are able to trace them in Maidencombe, all well and good. If not, then we locate the house where one of them lives and see what that – and other residents – tell us. My bet is that they will not be that far away."

Sergeant Tamplin, riding directly behind his colonel, drew a bit closer.

"What level of arrest do we aim for, sir?" he asked.

"That, my bloodthirsty sergeant, depends entirely upon their response. Whatever happens, they must be in a fit state to answer the many questions we have for them. Preece has implicated them in whatever their mission may be. It could well be that Preece is spinning us a story, but somehow, I sort of believe the man."

"Hear that, Corporal Skinner?" Tamplin turned to speak to the soldier riding at his side. "No undue violence!"

"Aye, sergeant – I heard that!" came a somewhat disgruntled reply.

They clattered through Stokeinteignhead as the village clock struck eleven. "Another three miles or less, or so I was told,"

Kent remarked as the inhabitants went back into their houses once the small column had passed through. "It is all uphill, so may take us another hour. But once past Gabwell, we are as good as there."

"Strange names these places have," Larkin thought aloud. "Do you suppose the inhabitants of this Gabwell are prone to speak for hours on end?"

"I shall consult the oracle when we return," Kent grinned. "Avril Ramsey will know whence the names come."

At ten minutes short of midday, the eight riders drew up in the small village of Maidencombe. Immediately, they were the centre of attention as inhabitants from the nearby houses emerged to gawp at the apparent show of force. One man, probably well into his fifties, approached and almost saluted Larkin.

"Good day to you, Colonel. What may we do for you?" he asked.

"First of all, how do you know my rank?" Larkin was intrigued.

"Why would I not! I were at Naseby some fifteen years past, fighting under General Fairfax. I were a sergeant, just like that warlike chap behind you."

"Then you are exactly the person who can assist us," Larkin felt that his luck must be in. First the good weather, and then this chap. "We are searching for two men who are said to reside here. Bernard Duplessis and Claude Bruce."

Whatever he was expecting, it certainly was not the reaction of the old soldier who turned aside and spat on the ground.

"They two buggers! Sometimes here, sometimes not. Expect us to doff hats and treat them as gentlemen when we all know they be nothing more than arseholes with a bit of money!"

"Then, I shall make your day, old soldier," Larkin grinned down at the man. "We are here to arrest them and take them in for questioning. So – where may we find them?"

"If they be at home! Ride a bit further to crossroads and turn to your left. Tis a mighty steep hill you will be going down. Then, just past the back entrance to Orestone, you will find a cottage. Tis the only one and there they reside."

"And where may we find our dinner?"

"Ah, that be easy to answer. Around the corner from the cottage be a goodly tavern."

"Then I thank you for your assistance. Perhaps, if you look out for us after dinner, you may see us taking them away with us."

"Colonel, we all wish you luck and thanks for ridding us of the buggers!"

They had gone no more than a hundred yards down the hill when Kent turned gingerly to Larkin.

"He certainly was not joking when he said this was steep! I suppose it goes all the way down to the sea like this."

"Let your horse do as he wishes. He is far better able to keep himself steady than you are."

Kent's mount, like all the others, seemed to want to go down the hill almost sideways, skittering now and again on the loose surface. Soon, they passed on their right a lane that led into Orestone and, just beyond that, a cottage behind a tall hedge. Larkin turned to his men.

"Seargeant, we all dismount here. Take two and hurry to the back. I shall give you five minutes to get into position before going to the front door."

Kent accompanied Larkin to the front door with the other soldiers ranged left and right. Then, as Larkin reckoned five minutes had passed, he hammered on the door. He turned to Larkin with a broad grin as footsteps and whisperings were heard from within the cottage. The door opened slowly and a tall man in very expensive clothes stood and tried to look important.

"Bernard Duplessis?" Larkin asked.

"And what is that to you?" came the reply in faultless English, despite the somewhat French appearance of the clothes.

"If you are Bernard Duplessis, and your partner who I see lurking behind you is Claude Bruce, then I am here to arrest you and take you into custody."

The man drew himself up even taller. "Have you no idea who I am?" he spoke down his long nose.

"I care not a bull's fart who you think you are. You are under arrest. So, unless you want these soldiers to manhandle you – which I am sure they are itching to do – you will come outside here where you will be bound and made ready for a long ride."

The man behind Duplessis turned about and fled through the cottage. Larkin merely smiled and waited. He had not long to wait as Sergent Tamplin and his two soldiers appeared around the side of the house grasping a struggling man – portly and red of face.

"Look what we have found, sir," Tamplin grinned. Larkin faced the smaller man.

"Are you Claude Bruce?"

"You will be sorry you have manhandled my colleague," Duplessis grated. "We have *very* important friends in Parliament!"

"More important that this?" Larkin dangled his warrant in front of the long nose. "No, I thought not! So, let us commence with a simple question. Which one of you murdered Francis DeGruchy?"

Kent could not help observing that, whilst Duplessis maintained his aloof pose, Bruce turned a sickly white. Larkin glanced at Kent and nodded; he had seen it as well.

"Sergeant, I want these two kept very separate from now on. There is to be no communication between them, not even a glance."

"If I may make a suggestion, sir – why do we not keep them here in the house and in separate rooms until you are ready to make the return journey? That way, we can ensure there is no chance of them concocting a load of bollocks."

"And that's why we are unbeatable as an army," Larkin grinned. "Brains from top to bottom! I agree, sergeant. Two guards per man and we will relieve them when we have eaten."

"I shall stay with the first group of guards," Kent volunteered. He turned to the two captives. "Make no mistake, either of you. One move out of place and you get shot through the foot – very painful!"

"By heavens, we shall make a soldier out of you yet!" Larkin gave a shout of laughter. "Sergeant, detail three please to remain with Master Kent. The rest of us shall be back well in time for you to have your dinner."

Larkin, Tamplin and two soldiers went off to seek dinner at the tavern. Kent took one soldier with him and escorted Duplessis into the far kitchen, shutting the door to the parlour behind him. The corporal and another soldier remained in the parlour with Bruce. Kent motioned to a chair at the far side of the table, away from the doors to the garden and the parlour.

Duplessis glowered at him as Kent sat himself down on a chair in the middle of the room, his pistol in one hand resting in his lap. The soldier took up station at the back door, also with his pistol in his hand.

"I suppose you think you can get away with this sort of behaviour," Duplessis snarled. "When my friends in Parliament get to hear of this, you will not be so pleased with yourselves."

"Oh, believe me, when your so-called friends get to hear of this, they will abandon you like the plague. Let us see how you react to another name – how about Abbe Justin?"

"Who is he supposed to be?" came the quick reply.

"And there are you claiming friends in high places, and you pretend you have never heard of Justin! No, you are going to have to do a lot better than that!"

Duplessis glared back at him and relapsed into a glowering silence.

When all of them had eaten dinner, Kent and Larkin stood together outside the house to make a plan for the return journey.

"It is vital that they remain unable to communicate," Larkin insisted. "That is easily managed for the journey itself – we gag them and keep them well apart. But that does not answer the question of how we keep them apart when we get back."

"We already have Preece in jail at Newton Abbot," Kent mused. "Where can we keep these two apart from one another and away from Preece as well?"

"There is a small jail in Ipplepen – used for the occasional drunk," Larkin thought aloud. "One of them could be housed there, with some of my soldiers keeping guard. That should do for Duplessis. Bruce seems the most vulnerable. Is there anywhere in Bovey Tracey where he can be kept overnight?"

Kent thought about that for a while until he had an idea. "The mill by the bridge over the river has been empty for some time now. I am sure that your soldiers can keep him secure there until morning."

"Then let us get these two bound, gagged and mounted. When we arrive at Newton Abbot, we shall split into two groups. I shall take Skinner and two soldiers with me to Ipplepen and arrange accommodation for Duplessis. Sergeant Tamplin and the other two can go with you to Bovey Tracey and get Bruce settled down."

Duplessis struggled and bellowed defiance; Bruce accepted meekly. It was a silent and purposeful group that rode back.

Herb Grindley, unlike his partner Matt, was a light sleeper. The large barn had been extended considerably since the two had taken possession of it. The largest part was just inside the door and was given over to the manufacture of barrels. There were piles of oak, a steaming cabinet where the oak was softened before being shaped, large benches, racks of tools, and a template made of wood where the barrels were constructed. Beyond that was a small office where the two did their calculations and conducted the business. At the very rear were two small rooms where the friends slept and kept their possessions. What had woken Herb he had no idea. It might have been a sound of movement. Whatever it was, he was wide awake moments later.

And then he knew what it had been – he smelled smoke. He bounded out of his bed and hammered on Matt's door.

"What?" came a sleepy voice.

"Smoke! Something's burning!" Herb yelled, going through the office space to the workshop. It was in total darkness except for a burst of flame just inside the big doors. Herb ran to the doors and opened them wide, and then realised that a sudden draught of air was the last thing he needed. However, it turned out to be the best thing he could have done. He grabbed a large rake and set to pulling the heap of discarded off-cuts of oak out into the field. There had been quite a heavy dew and that alone slowed the burning pile into a hissing mess.

By the time the last of the burning rubbish had been raked clear, Matt and Herb regarded one another with eyes sore from the smoke. Matt was the first to start the thought process.

"Did you have to unlock the doors?" he asked.

"No, I bloody well did not!" Herb retorted. "Why the hell were they not locked!"

"One of us must have forgotten," Matt replied. "That pile of wood did not set light to itself! The bits of wood are too large – there must be smaller kindling – and neither of us would have left *that* there!"

The two wandered back inside the workshop and started looking at the place where the pile had been. Unmistakably, the blackened remains of wood shavings were evidence of how the fire had taken hold."

"That bastard from Taunton!" hissed Matt. "He had the devil's own luck finding the doors unlocked. Nobody else would have done this!"

"We shall have to report it to the bailiff. But first, we need to make certain that there is no fear of anything else catching fire."

It was nearly dawn before the two, washed and clean, settled down again to catch what sleep they could – with the doors firmly locked.

If Mary had envisioned a peaceful and productive day at school, she was to be sorely disappointed – it proved to be anything but peaceful and productive. And it was due mainly to her own relatives that her morning was to prove something of a trial.

Rosie, now twelve years old, had ceased to come to the school as she helped out at the small holding where her parents, Gil and Ella, grew vegetables, kept chickens, and sold their produce. However, their son Jamie, a somewhat precocious ten-year-old, and his disciple Jack, son of Simon and Imelda, both still attended – as did Mary's own twin children Will and Peterkin. There were ten other children who regularly attended – four from other families in the small town and six from small farms dotted about the heath. One of the latter, a very pugnacious lad named Robbie Chalk, had made it his lifelong ambition to get under the skins of young Jamie and Jack. That day, Robbie arrived at school with mischief very much in mind.

Mary had just finished the roll call and had put her ledger back into the drawer of her desk when the whole tenor of the day was rent by a screech of indignation. Her young nephew Jamie was on his feet brandishing a very dead mouse.

"Robbie just tried to put this down my neck!" he shouted, turning to the row behind him where Robbie Chalk sat with a look of cherubic innocence on his face.

"Miss Mary, Jamie's right. I saw him do it," Jack added his own indignation. Jack sat next to Jamie.

Mary called for silence in a voice that all the children knew brooked no argument.

"Robbie – did you try to put the disgusting thing down Jamie's neck?" she asked.

"Who? Me, Miss Mary? No – I never did. He's making it up to get me into trouble!"

Peterkin raised a hand from the very back row. "I saw him as well," he volunteered.

"So did I!" his twin Will added his own contribution.

"Well, you would, wouldn't you!" Robbie yelled. "You're all family and you stick together!"

"That is more than enough!" Mary was fast losing her temper – and that was a very unusual occurrence. Normally, Mary maintained a placid calm.

"You're a liar!" Jamie flung the mouse onto Robbie's desk. "I've a good mind to make you eat that thing!"

"I'll get my da to beat you silly!" Robbie yelled back.

"My uncle could slaughter your da with one hand!" Jamie flung back at him, knowing full well that his uncle Simon could probably beat everyone for miles around.

Mary was now reduced to yelling for silence – utterly ignored for the first time ever. Robbie picked up the mouse and threw it into Jamie's face. Jamie then lost all control and landed a very commendable punch at Robbie's nose. Blood spurted over the desk and Robbie gave a howl, rushed out of the schoolroom and was soon running like the wind down to his parent's small farmstead.

"Jack – run at once to get your father here now. Then go to get your uncle Gil. I want them here as soon as possible," Mary instructed. Jack needed no second bidding. He shot off up the street.

"Cor, Jamie, that was a good punch," Will gave his cousin a grin.

"What have I always told you about fighting?" Mary silenced the class with a shout and a bang on her desk. "I have always told you that I will not tolerate fighting – no matter what the provocation. Jamie – you threw the punch and you may well have broken Robbie's nose. You have certainly drawn blood – lots of it. You know that I'm going to have to punish you."

Jamie looked at his aunt and shuffled his feet. He knew that he had done wrong but could not hide an inner delight at the way he had immediately – and spectacularly – retaliated.

Silence reigned for a few minutes until the door opened and admitted Gil, the first to arrive.

"I've received a very garbled message from Jack," he said to his sister. "Jamie has attempted to kill Robbie."

"Hardly!" Mary did her best to hide a grin at the embellished tale from a very impressionable Jack. "Jamie punched young Robbie Chalk and made his nose bleed."

Gil looked at his son and saw defiance and something akin to pride in that young face. But before anyone else could say anything, the door burst open, and a very irate Gregory Chalk started shouting.

"My boy has been assaulted and I want that wretched boy severely beaten!" he yelled, pointing at Jamie. "If necessary, I shall beat him myself!"

"That, you will not do," Gill said very firmly, standing between Chalk and his son. "If there is punishment due, I shall administer it myself."

"And I intend to beat him until he begs for mercy!" Chalk roared, "And you shall not stop me!"

"Oh, indeed I shall," Gil stood his ground.

Chalk drew back a meaty fist but found it in the grasp of a hand bigger than his. He spun around to find himself looking upwards into a gently smiling face.

"Do not be ridiculous," Simon said quietly. "Jack came running and said I was needed," he said to Mary over the top of Chalk's head.

"It really concerns Jamie," Mary started to explain. "Master Chalk's son Robbie threw a dead mouse at Jamie. Jamie retaliated by throwing a punch that certainly drew blood from

Robbie's nose. It would now appear that Robbie's nose is broken, or so Master Chalk claims."

"And I have said that I shall administer whatever punishment is due to my son myself. I shall not permit anyone else to do it – certainly not in the state of anger that Master Chalk now shows," Gil stood defiantly in front of Chalk.

"And quite right," Simon nodded. "If anyone took a stick to Jack, I would not be best pleased."

Chalk somehow managed to squirm downwards and evaded the vicelike grip, He swung a vicious punch at Gil that somehow, to his amazement, scythed through empty air. Gil had been expecting something of the kind. He simply swayed to one side, extended a leg and tripped Chalk who landed in a heap on the floor. Gil seized the initiative, pounced upon Chalk's back and twisted one arm high up between his shoulder blades.

"Didn't know you knew that move," Simon chuckled. "Want me to sit on him?"

"Nay. I believe Master Chalk will agree that things are best left in my hands, will you not, Master Chalk?"

"Sod off, you bastard," came from the floor. Many of the children had not seen such entertainment for a long while and were thoroughly enjoying the spectacle.

Mary, as was her wont, retook control of the situation. "Master Chalk – we need to determine the extent of Robbie's injury. So, the first thing to be done is for you to fetch him to the apothecary where he may be properly assessed. Are you willing to go quietly and fetch the lad?"

"Ay, I am! And when it is found that his nose *is* broken, then I shall call upon a lawyer to demand compensation, and proper punishment of the hooligan who broke it." He suddenly broke off. "Hold still! The apothecary is another bloody Ramsey! I shall not get truth from that quarter!"

"That is an absurd remark!" Mary retorted. "But as you believe it, we shall ask Nell Dawkins to examine Robbie. Surely, you would believe her?"

"Aye, I suppose that I would. All know that she is trustworthy!"

"Then Gil, let him go and fetch Robbie. Jack, another task for you – run to the apothecary and ask Nell to come here."

Jack sprinted off, doing a very fair imitation of Hob when Hob was much younger – never walking anywhere but running at breakneck speed. Chalk, released, stormed out to go and fetch his son. The children erupted into chatter.

"Quiet!" Mary uttered the one word. Simon looked at Gil and grinned as there came immediate silence.

"She who shall be obeyed," Gil whispered to Simon as he regarded his sister with a big smile. Mary chose to ignore it. Instead, she embarked upon a lecture about the evil of physical violence. The children sat and listened quietly whilst Simon and Gil walked out into the fresh air.

"Sometimes," Simon laughed quietly, "physical violence is the only resort."

"That is because you are a giant!" Gil grinned at him. "But I agree with you; sometimes, it simply cannot be avoided. I swear that if that oaf had made a move towards Jamie, I would have flattened him."

"And quite right!" Simon nodded. "So, what punishment will you mete out to the young rascal?"

"Oh, something the like of which he will not expect," Gil chuckled. "It will not feature the rod or the cane but will entail something that Jamie loves more than anything – his freedom. He shall be allowed to attend school, but at all other times, he shall be weeding, hoeing, forking, and carrying from end of school until bed. Believe me, that will be just about the worst punishment he could imagine."

"Jack will miss his company," Simon thought aloud. "Those two are usually inseparable. But if that is what you consider appropriate, it is what shall happen. And talk of the devil and he appears."

Jack came tearing back up the street and skidded to a halt by his father.

"Nell be coming, pa," he said, not in the slightest out of breath. Indeed, walking far more sedately up the slope, Nell had a small bag in her hand.

"Jack says I have a boy to examine for a broken nose," she said.

"Aye – Mary will tell you the story. The boy is Robbie Chalk, and his father shall be bringing him here soon."

"Robbie Chalk? I am surprised it is merely a suspected broken nose! I would have thought that by this time someone would have twisted his neck!"

"He is known to you?" Gil asked.

"We have had to chase him from the shop many a time. His fingers always seem to be on the point of grabbing something before running off!"

It was not long after that Chalk returned with his son. Mary shooed all the children home for an early dinner and bade Robbie come and sit on a table so that Nell could examine his nose. That did not start well. Robbie perched up on the desk and leered at Nell, taking in her figure from head to foot. Nell simply ignored him. She opened her small bag and took out a square of clean linen and a little vial of alcohol. She put a few drops on her left hand and rubbed both hands with the liquid.

"What is that?" Chalk was immediately suspicious.

"Simply plain alcohol. It will remove any infection from my hands so that I do not pass any to an open wound." Nell stoppered the vial and picked up the square of linen. First, she removed the flakes of dried blood from Robbie's nose and upper lip. Then, putting the square to one side, placed one finger of each hand to either side of Robbie's nose.

"You hurt me, you bitch, and I'll set my brother on you. He likes to hurt pretty girls!"

Nell immediately removed her hands and took a step back. "I have no intention of hurting you, little boy," she said quietly, knowing that 'little boy' was the worst insult she could have levelled at the lad. "All I intend to do is to feel gently up the bone to see if there is any possible break. So, are you going to sit still and let me do that?"

Robbie, smarting from the taunt, grunted and nodded. Mary resumed her examination, feeling very gently up each side of the bone to between his eyes.

"There is no break," she announced. "Simply the rupture of the small vessels at the tip of the nose. They bleed very easily but heal just as fast."

"You did not feel down the tip of his nose!" Chalk grumbled. "Only at the top."

"That, Master Chalk, is simply because there is no bone at the bottom part of the nose. Bone ends roughly about half-way down. If you find that hard to believe, look at a skull and you will see what I mean."

"It would appear that there is no lasting damage, and that Robbie is well on the road to a complete recovery," Mary gave Nell a nod of thanks. "But before anyone leaves, what is all this about an elder brother taking pleasure from hurting girls?"

"Take no notice of him," Chalk grunted. "There is no elder brother. There are merely two elder sisters! But he was still hit by another boy, and I demand that he be punished."

"Oh, believe me, Master Chalk, Jamie will most certainly be punished – in a way that he is not likely to forget!" Gil assured the man.

Jamie, later that morning, howled with frustration when appraised of the nature of his punishment.

"Tis not fair!" he yelled. "All I did was to retaliate when he threw that stinking dead mouse at me!"

"You struck out and you could have caused injury!" Ella came back at him. She had been appraised of the whole story. "So, accept your punishment. Any more from you - and you would do well to remember that you are still young enough for me to box your ears!"

Jamie, for the first time in his young life, refused dinner and went to his room to sulk.

Harry received a visitor, one who was irate and had to be stopped, told to take a deep breath, then start again.

"That bastard from Taunton tried to burn us down last night," Matt at last made a coherent start.

"And how do you know it was him?" Harry asked.

"Who else has threatened us? Who else sees us as direct competition – even though we sell far from his own area?"

"I can see that you have grounds for suspicion," Harry agreed. "But first, take me and show me the damage done, when it was done, and how badly you have been affected."

Harry rode up to the field, left his horse contentedly nibbling at the roadside, and went across to the barn. Herb Grindley was still tidying up.

"See that pile we dragged out? It were well alight and it did not start itself!" Matt growled, pointing at the blackened remains that had scorched a small area of grass about two yards from the large doorway. Harry bent down and examined it.

"Aye – I see it. But where was it and why was it there?"

Matt, now a lot calmer, related the story – smoke, waking up, dragging the pile of off-cuts out, dousing it.

"So, you put old offcuts of timber in a pile by the doorway, plus old shavings. How did anyone get at it?"

"Ah!" Matt was a trifle shamefaced. "One of us forgot to lock the doors when we retired to bed."

"Then the story is as follows," Harry summed up. "One disgruntled chap travels all the way from Taunton and hides, hoping that the doors will be left open. His luck is in, and he is able, in the dead of night, to get in, find a miraculous pile of burnable stuff just inside the doors, sets fire to it, then goes all the way back to Taunton, not bothering to barricade you inside, or to stay and witness the success of his work. Sorry – without any proof, there is absolutely nothing I can do."

"But nobody else would have any reason other than him!" Matt exploded.

"Maybe not," Harry agreed. "But there is no proof – and without it, all you have is a pile of sodden embers and a heap of suspicion."

"We will not allow it to rest there!" Herb backed up his partner.

"Then let me give you both a friendly warning," Harry looked very serious. "Matt, I have known you for many years, but I have to tell you this. If you take the law into your own hands and pursue this man, do him or his business harm, I shall not be able to help you. In fact, it will be my duty to assist the law officers and bring you to justice. Think long and hard before you do anything rash."

And with that valediction, he rode off back to his office, wondering about something Mary had been talking about some days previously. Spontaneous combustion. Was it even possible?

Early October that year was turning out to be very benign – at least to those parts of the county to the east and south of the moor. By mid-morning, Larkin, Kent and ten soldiers were gathered outside the jail in Newton Abbot. Preece was being held securely inside. One group of four soldiers had Duplessis firmly under control – at a safe distance from the jail. Another similar group had Bruce under firm control at yet a further distance. Larkin signalled for Preece to be brought out. He watched as Preece blinked in the sudden sunlight, saw the other two prisoners, then swallowed hard.

"Take those two and keep them secure until I call for them," Larkin ordered, following the jailer, Preece and Kent back into the small jail. Preece was again sat on his stool.

"Well – as you observed, we have the two you accused under arrest. I wonder what their stories will be? Will they admit to the murder? Or will they accuse you in their turn?"

"What I told you is God's honest truth," Preece blurted out. "I was an unwilling participant and did no harm to DeGruchy. Duplessis is the more likely to have done the murder."

"Then for the time being, back you go into your cell. Let us see what Duplessis has to say about this latest accusation."

"Say nothing about me accusing him!" Preece wailed as he was shoved back into his cell. "He is very dangerous and will see me dead!"

"If you had any part, even the smallest part, you will be dead anyway!" Larkin grunted.

Duplessis was brought to the outside of the jail. He was surrounded by the four soldiers, two more who had accompanied Larkin, Larkin himself, and Kent.

"It has been suggested that you murdered Francis DeGruchy," Larkin opened the session. "You were seen with him, he had dealings with this Justin character, as no doubt did you. You were also seen with Preece, Bruce and DeGruchy. How do you respond to those facts?"

"I respond with silence. You have no proof whatsoever of these accusations. So, until you have something tangible, I shall not grace you with any response whatsoever."

Larkin thought about that for a while before announcing his decision. "Put this man in a cell next to Preece. I want two of you inside that jail at all times. Keep your eyes and ears keen. Anything at all that passes between them, I want to know."

Duplessis was marched into the jail and locked in his cell. Larkin then called for Bruce to be brought forward. Larkin gave Kent a wink before starting.

"It has been suggested to me that you were the one who murdered DeGruchy. You are in some sort of conspiracy with Duplessis and Preece. Somewhere in the background is this man Justin. How do you respond to that?"

Bruce proved to be made of far less stern stuff that Duplessis – in fact, he looked terrified. He gulped a few times before speaking in a tremulous voice that betrayed his Scottish ancestry.

"If I make a full and honest statement, will that be taken into consideration?" he quavered.

"Perhaps," Larkin gave him that much. "It all depends upon the nature of your statement – what it tells us, about whom, when, and where."

"I shall want it recorded in full," Bruce stuttered.

"Then we shall have to repair somewhere that can furnish us with the means of achieving that. Sergeant, have a horse brought for the man. Detail four to stay here for the purpose of supervising the jail. The rest of us will ride back to Bovey Tracey where we can use the back parlour of the tavern. We can also get a good dinner there."

Larkin used what he hoped was a psychological approach – he made sure Bruce ate as good a dinner as the rest of them. Then, with Kent armed with paper, pen and ink, Larkin told Bruce to start his statement. Mouths dropped open as the meat of that statement was uttered.

"You are correct in stating that there is a conspiracy," he had to clear his throat a few times before continuing. "The Abbe Justin is deeply involved, but there must be far more important people above him. It is well known throughout France, Scotland, Spain and The Netherlands that this parliament of yours is in deep trouble and cannot last much longer. The inevitable result of its collapse is a return of Charles as your king. But Charles is already beholden to Covenanters, Anglicans and others that France in particular find unacceptable. What they seek is certainly a return of a monarch to rule England, but not Charles Stuart. In many places are those who France would find far more acceptable – ones that would return your country to the rule of Rome. One of the real Scottish Stuarts is the preferred choice. That is the conspiracy – a plan to return England to the Catholic Church. The young man DeGruchy appeared some months past at the offices of Justin, saying that he had the means to infiltrate some elements in parliament that could well be of benefit to the plan. Another man, a very trusted man, was sent immediately to England to search for any verification of this claim. He was gone for four weeks, then returned and reported back to Justin. Preece, Duplessis and I were summoned to a secret meeting. It appeared that, far from being sympathetic to our cause, DeGruchy was acting as an agent for your parliament. But to end his life in France would immediately set bells ringing. He was told to return to England and continue 'the good work'. The three of us were ordered to return a week later and to devise the means of his death – in a manner that did not implicate France or anyone else for that matter. It took Duplessis only three days to devise the plan. He summoned DeGruchy to a couple of meetings and, after the last one was completed, for Preece to follow him in the dead of night, kill him and secrete the body far from the scene of the murder. Duplessis was the ringleader, Preece the murderer, and I the third party who took no part in the plan or the slaying."

Bruce stopped abruptly to take a long draught of ale. Kent scratched on with his pen for some moments, then laid down pen and gazed at Bruce.

Larkin was the first to break the silence.

"You say you took no part in the plan. But as a sane and sensible man, you know that to be a ridiculous claim. You heard it, you witnessed it, you acquiesced by your mere silence."

"But I have made a full and honest statement," Bruce wailed.

"Full and honest it may well be. But it in no way exonerates you from blame. You are guilty by mere association. Sergeant, get this man also taken back to Newton Abbot. There is a vacant cell. Also, ensure that every word uttered is taken down."

A shivering and still protesting Bruce was removed. Larkin looked at Kent and raised an eyebrow.

"Bloody hell" Kent muttered.

CHAPTER X

The next day proved that South Devon weather was as unpredictable as the mood of parliament – one day calm and serene, the next tempestuous. It rained – not the misty drizzle of the moor, but persistent and dreary. Kent woke to the sound of it falling outside his bedroom window; it depressed him as it did almost everyone else. The only people to view it with any welcome were Dick and Sal Allen. They knew that a day such as that would make their regulars tarry over their ale and food, making excuses to stay in the dry and buy another mugful.

Into that gloom came a message for Matthew Kent. Would he please make his way that afternoon to Brimley where he would meet Avril and Mary. It was some days since he had been to visit and hoped that this was not the precursor to the old lady's demise. Making his apologies to Larkin, he went up again after his breakfast to read again the draft of the will. He wanted to be word perfect so that he would be able to execute each and every provision as and when required.

Larkin had again changed his mind about the furtherance of his investigation. He had decided that the proper course of action would be to remove all three prisoners to Exeter, there to appraise the sheriff of his discoveries and to set the wheels of the law into motion. That decision would not sit very happily with his soldiers – who would have not only to ride for some hours in the rain but ensure the security of the three prisoners along the way.

"I shall take with me all the written reports you have made," Larkin told Kent as they both viewed the sullen downpour through a tavern window.

"In which case, I shall have to wrap them carefully first in blank paper and then in an oiled silk package. The last thing you will need is to present the sheriff with pages of meaningless inky splodges!"

"I can well imagine his face were such to happen," Larkin grinned. "He is not best known for a sunny disposition at the best of times!" He turned to Tamplin. "Sergeant, rouse the troops if you please. We ride to Newton Abbot in an hour, collect those three and then get to Exeter as soon as we can."

Sergeant Tamplin was *not* all that sorry to receive these instructions. He and his men would have dry and comfortable billets when they reached Exeter.

Meanwhile, Kent repaired to his room and started reading.

Mary sat in her classroom awaiting the arrival of her pupils, also considerably apprehensive at the summons to Brimley. Avril and Nell discussed it with James over breakfast.

"It simply cannot be much longer," James said, speaking aloud the thoughts in all their minds. "She has reached a very good age and has filled her life as she would have wished. In fact, as all three of us knows, she has lived considerably longer than most may expect!"

"You said that the message came from Meg, the steward's wife," Nell sat with her breakfast almost untouched.

"Aye – via young Jack Smith. He seems to have taken Jamie's place as Harry's chosen messenger."

"I think you will find that it is because Jamie has been forbidden to do anything other than school and work at home," Nell laughed. "Ella told me that Jamie is being punished for hitting that other boy at school. That aside, I cannot help feeling that this afternoon is not going to be a very happy time."

"That wonderful old lady is going to be sorely missed," Avril agreed.

Larkin. Tamplin and the troop left Bovey Tracey just past eleven o'clock. By midday, they had collected the three prisoners who were sat on horses and roped securely. Tamplin led the way with the three prisoners in the middle of a group of soldiers. Larkin came behind, talking to the soldiers who had been guarding them overnight.

"Anything interesting to report?" he queried.

"Not so as you'd notice, sir. There was just a lot of shouting and blame-shifting. That Duplessis character was the most vocal, blaming the other two for not keeping their mouths shut. He swore vengeance on Preece for not keeping *his* mouth shut.”

“Oh! Did he not level the same at Bruce?”

“No, sir. Seemed to believe that Bruce would back up whatever he said.”

“Hm! So, he is unaware that Bruce has put the blame on the other two. This could get very interesting indeed!”

The journey to Exeter, although normally taking a mere four or five hours, was made wretched by the persistent rain. The only relief came from the fact that it was borne on a wind from the south-west, behind them. Nevertheless, it was a wet and bedraggled troop that eventually stopped at Rougemont so as to get the three prisoners into separate cells. And then Larkin was able to send his soldiers to get dry and to partake of a hearty supper. He went in search of the sheriff.

He eventually ran the deputy sheriff to ground in the nearby tavern where the man was enjoying a dish of pork and vegetables.

“Aha! Colonel Larkin,” the bluff old man hailed him with a raised spoon. “You look passably like a drowned rat! Shed that cloak and get warm here by the fire, then eat some of this commendable fare. What brings you here?”

“Brought three prisoners in connection with my investigation. I’ve lodged them in your cells.”

“Investigation? Oh, yes – the murdered lad in Bovey Tracey. Guilty, are they?”

“That is surely for determination by a jury,” Larkin smiled, knowing what the rejoinder would be.

“But you have a good idea, what?”

“Oh, indeed. My belief is that they are as guilty as hell.”

“Then we’ll hang the bastards. But I suppose you’ve got to go through the motions and render pages of interminable scribble to those arse-bound buggers in Parliament.”

“That is my solemn duty,” Larkin sighed. “May I impose upon your hospitality so that I may interrogate them on the morrow?”

“Certainly, my dear fellow. Manacles and chains?”

“That would do no harm,” Larkin nodded.

Earlier that afternoon, Mary, Nell, Avril and Matthew Kent arrived together at Brimley where they were met by Luke Farmer and his wife Meg. Meg could hardly contain her grief.

"She's fading away and there is nothing that anyone may do to stop it," she managed between gulps. "Every now and again she is quite lucid, then lapses back into deep sleep."

The group ascended the wide staircase and paused before entering the large bedroom. From within came the sound of muttered prayers. Luke Farmer opened the door quietly for the group to file in silently. Lady Violette rested as always on her pillows. One hand was being held between the two hands of Reverend James Forbes who was muttering the appropriate prayers. Violette looked as if she was in a deep coma.

Forbes looked up at the group and gave a slight shake of his head. Nell was just about able to stop herself bursting into tears. Even Avril, accustomed by many years attending the dying, was looking grief-stricken. Mary, like Kent, just looked lost.

Something obviously stirred in the old lady's conscious, as she opened her eyes and surveyed the gathering.

"Ah," she managed. "All my dear, dear friends." And then closed her eyes again, her breath hardly moving her chest. Nobody said anything, just watched until the eyes opened once more.

"Bloody rain," she muttered, closed her eyes, and simply stopped breathing.

Avril went to the bedside and put her fingers to the old lady's throat, stayed still for a full minute, then knelt down beside the bed.

"Sleep well, My Lady," she whispered.

Nell and Kent joined her on their knees to offer prayers to speed the old soul to whatever rest she was destined. Only Mary stayed upright, knowing that to offer a prayer to something she did not believe really existed, would be the height of hypocrisy. Instead, she muttered to herself.

"One life lived to the full doing what was right and just. You, Lady Violette Charlton, will be sorely missed. I for one thank you for your friendship and constant support."

Eventually, Kent knew that what was to follow was his duty to organise. He stood up and cleared his throat.

"I would suggest, whatever arrangements are necessary under the terms of the will, be left until after the funeral."

"And that you may safely leave to me to organise," Reverend Forbes stated firmly. "I know full well what funeral she wanted. I shall make sure that she gets it in full measure. Who, may I ask, is to see to her now – lay her out in the proper manner?"

"That will be Mary, Nell, Meg and me," Avril spoke up. "We shall attend to that as soon as we may. And rest assured it shall be done with love and care."

"Dear Lord," Farmer stuttered. "It is my duty to inform all the staff. How the hell I do that I have no idea. Perhaps, Reverend, you would say some word of comfort to them when I get them all assembled?"

"Certainly. If I have any words that can do even the slightest justice to that dear lady!"

Within an hour, the whole town knew of the passing. There were many tears shed that night. Lady Violette Charlton had left a massive legacy - and a huge hole.

Larkin was up early the next morning, ready to do verbal battle with the one prisoner who had so far defied him. He was determined that would not be the case when he had the man brought in. Having broken his fast on sweetened porridge and newly baked bread, he felt ready for anything as he walked around to the castle entrance. The rain had expended its spite the previous day but had remained in a lowering sky as if to say, 'I can return at any moment'.

Having arranged for a small room to be made available, he supervised its preparation. One stool for the prisoner in the centre of the room. One chair for himself facing the stool. Absolutely nothing else in the room – bare walls, stone floor, small, barred window, thick iron-bound door. He nodded in satisfaction.

"Then let us commence. Sergeant – bring Duplessis and one extra soldier to stand with his back to the door."

Tamplin strode off to get Duplessis from his underground cell. The clanking of chains announced his imminent arrival. Duplessis was marched in, was sat down upon the stool. Tamplin stood just behind him, one huge soldier stood at the closed door,

Larkin sat and faced the prisoner. All this had been achieved in silence.

"And I suppose that this treatment is designed to intimidate me into betraying confidences," Duplessis snarled at Larkin.

"No, not at all Monsieur," Larkin gave him the vestige of a smile.

"And I am not French, so do not waste your time attempting to cast me in the mould of an enemy!"

"My dear Duplessis – you fashioned that mould all by yourself by consorting with sworn enemies of England. Now, to make a beginning. Your erstwhile colleague Bruce tells us that it was established young DeGruchy was not a collaborator but was in fact an agent of Parliament. Bruce further states on oath that you were given the task of eliminating the young man and set Preece upon the task. How say you to that?"

"I say nothing to that!"

Larkin thought, or pretended to, for a short moment.

"Sergeant Tamplin – do you have that thin knife with you?"

"Never go a step without it, sir," Tamplin brought out a knife with a blade about nine inches long and less than half an inch wide. It was wickedly sharp.

"Kindly insert the tip of that knife into his left ear, push it in a bit and then wiggle it about."

"Thus loosening the tongue, sir?"

"It is something I heard once. Of course, it may just be a tale told by an idiot. Still, it can do no harm to try."

Tamplin summoned his trooper to hold Duplessis head still, then laid the tip of the knife just inside the ear cavity. Duplessis let out a moan of terror.

"Seems like you were told a good tale, sir," Tamplin grinned from behind the stool.

"So, what say you now?" Larkin asked the shaken Duplessis.

"Bruce lied to save his own skin," the man faltered.

"His skin is past saving – as I told him yesterday. Simply by being there, knowing what was afoot, and doing nothing, makes him complicit. His life, like yours hangs by the merest thread. But to take things a step further. The three of you, plus the accursed Justin, did not dream up this by yourselves. There is a plot afoot to place a Scottish Stuart on the throne, one far more amenable to Rome. That plot simply must have originated from someone – or some people – a lot further up the ladder than you. So, next question. Who originated the plot, and to whom are you accountable?"

A look of cunning crossed Duplessis face. "Kill me and you shall never discover the identity!" he almost laughed.

"Did you hear that, Sergeant? If ever I heard an admission of guilt, that was it. I do believe that sterner measures are called for."

"Shall I ask the Deputy Sheriff to join us, sir?"

"If you would, Sergeant."

It took just a few moments for the crusty official to appear in the doorway.

"How do matters proceed?" he barked.

"They proceed apace," Larkin replied. "This wretch states that, should we kill him, we shall never know the identity of the people behind this plot."

"Then the bugger's as guilty as hell – by his own admission. I have just the fellow down below to drag the information from him."

"That may not be necessary," an emboldened Duplessis spoke up. "Give me a written and sealed guarantee of my freedom and I shall tell you everything you need to know. Believe me, I have no wish to go to the scaffold with limbs torn from their sockets!"

"First, tell me whether Bruce's statement be true or not," Larkin demanded.

"It is true in every respect, damn you!"

"Then Preece and Bruce stand trial on charges of treason and murder," Larkin nodded. "You shall be the guest of my lord sheriff until I have obtained the guidance of those in Parliament – those I know to be as yet oblivious to the plot and who would be appalled when told of it."

"Which damnable Stuart had you in mind to sit upon the throne?" the deputy sheriff asked.

"That, I was never told. All I *was* told was that it was anyone other than Charles himself with his hands tied to the cursed Covenant!"

"Keep this miserable thing here whilst I summon my jailers. He shall be afforded our best attention whilst you undertake your travels."

"With tongue loosened, sir?" Larkin prompted.

"Oh, have no fear on that score. He shall be brought forth undamaged in every respect. I have now to organise the trial of the other two. May God speed you on your travels, Colonel."

"Well," Larkin grinned at Tamplin. "That went as well as we could have wished."

Tamplin's brow was furrowed. "Surely, that sod cannot walk away from this a free man, sir?"

"Oh, believe me, sergeant, he will not be able to walk anywhere!"

"Oh, good!"

Larkin made sure that he had every piece of paper before he started on yet another trip to Westminster. To be on the safe side, he detailed four soldiers to accompany him on his journey. He left Tamplin in charge of the others, ate a very hasty dinner and was on his way just after two in the afternoon.

Preece and Bruce, told of their impending trial, sat in their respective cells and knew that their days were numbered. That deputy sheriff made sure that they knew exactly what to expect.

Duplessis, kept well apart from the others, sat alone in his cell and wondered if there was any real chance of his freedom in exchange for the information locked away in his brain. Being a supreme optimist, he began planning his future once he was released.

CHAPTER XI

It was as if Lady Violette Charlton had uttered a decree – the next day was cold but free from rain; even the breeze was gentle. Many people had been busy since daybreak readying the church with flowers and foliage, ensuring that every pew was dusted and polished, every window cleaned. Matthew Kent had also been busy making sure that the flat wagon that would bear the coffin was decorated and spotless, the single horse from the Brimley stable groomed and its tack gleaming.

By ten o'clock, both sides of the main street were lined with people – from the oldest inhabitant to the very youngest, a babe in arms. A few from outlying villages also thronged the sides of the street, all eager to watch the passing of the old lady.

Kent and Mary stood side by side at the entrance to the church along with James Forbes who had defied anyone to deny him the right to officiate at the service. The fact that nobody raised the slightest objection was testimony to the respect in which he was held.

Everyone from the Parke estate stood at the entrance gates to see the cortege pass, then to follow on up the town to the church. At half past ten, Luke Farmer, the Brimley steward, led the horse by its reins. On the bed of the flat cart the coffin sat with a single bunch of lavender atop its lid. Behind came every member of the Brimley staff. It passed Parke, the staff there following in its wake. Then up the main street past the throng of people, many openly weeping. It arrived at the church some thirty minutes later where the bearer party was waiting. Abel and Simon, much to their chagrin, had been precluded from the party – they were at least six inches taller than anyone else.

The coffin was borne into the church and placed before the altar steps on two trestles. By then, the church was filled to bursting, those unable to squeeze in had to be content to listen outside as the doors were thrown wide. Forbes led the service in his usual competent manner, then invited Mary to deliver the eulogy. Mary rose from her place in the front pew and instead of mounting the steps to the pulpit, stood by the coffin with one hand resting on it. She knew exactly what she was going to say.

"I have lived in this small town all of my life," she spoke loudly and clearly, her time as a schoolteacher standing her in very good stead. "Most of you gathered here today have also lived all of your lives here – some for far longer than I have. The very dear lady we celebrate today came here only comparatively recently. But her relatively short time here has left an indelible impression on our town, and that is something that is quite remarkable. I once had the temerity to call her – to her face – indomitable. She seemed to relish that, even laughed at it. Who amongst us here would deny her that description – she *was* indomitable. She arrived here to take possession of an estate that was in near ruins. She literally took it by the throat and shook it back into life until it is now the lovely place that she made it. Indomitable? Indefatigable? She was without any shadow of doubt both of those. But there was another side to her character, a caring and generous side. It was mainly through her efforts and generosity that we have the school – and she has made provision for it to remain not only just in existence but free from all debt. It would be fitting indeed were it now to be called the Lady Violette School. Brimley Estate will continue to be the wonderful place she has left us."

Mary paused a moment to collect her thoughts, and perhaps summon up her courage.

"What I am now about to do may be regarded by some as a sacrilege. I make absolutely no apology for it. You, dear lady, lived a life that very few of us would be able to emulate. I thank you from the bottom of my heart for a life well lived and applaud you for it."

So saying, she put her hands together and started clapping. Much to her great joy, she was immediately joined by Matthew Kent, her husband Harry, and all of her family and relatives. Soon, the whole church thundered with the noise of clapping, accompanied by many a tear. Mary blew a kiss at the coffin and resumed her place.

As the tumult died away, Reverend Forbes came forward to conclude the ceremony.

"Far from an act of sacrilege, that is praise indeed. Mary, thank you so much for that very fitting tribute to a lady of inestimable character. See – I can use long words as well!"

That brought again a bout of clapping and some laughter. The service ended and the coffin carried out shoulder-high to the waiting wagon. Back went the procession to Brimley where Lady Violette Charlton was interred in a place she had chosen for herself, a place previously blessed by Forbes himself.

Mary fled upstairs to the large bedroom and closed the door. She needed time and solitude to cry and to remember. A short time later, the door opened, and Nell came to join her. They sat together on the bed and silently remembered.

Luke Farmer, Meg and a host of helpers made sure everyone was fed and offered ale or wine. All of the Brimley staff wore sombre black. All were deeply saddened by the loss. All were profoundly grateful to their departed mistress.

Colonel Fisher made one of his usual visits to his friend James Forbes that same evening. He was entertained as usual with a very superior wine and some wafers that Forbes had at long last prevailed upon John and Evelyn Ramsey to produce at their bakery.

"What news brings you hot foot to me today?" Forbes asked.

"Believe it or not, Lambert has dismissed Parliament and has replaced it with the army."

"But that is a monstrous thing to do!" Forbes was aghast.

"Monstrous or not, it is what he has done. Many members of the Rump are now kicking their heels and threatening a new revolution."

"Lambert has the forces to quell any such uprising, does he not?"

"Indeed, he does, damn him!" Fisher grunted. "Those restless members will shout and scream until their throats be sore. But they know, probably better than most, that they are powerless to intervene."

Forbes retreated into his thoughts; silence reigned for a while as the logs crackled in the grate, the level in the wine decanter slowly lowered, and the evening thickened.

"Monck!" Forbes at last ejaculated.

"Monck, indeed," Fisher nodded. "There will be one very unhappy man. But what I know of him will cause him to think long and hard before he makes any move – even if he makes a move at all."

"Surely, he cannot accept this state of affairs," Forbes insisted.

"Let us play our usual game – hypothesis," Fisher raised a slight grin. "Let me make the first attempt. Monck does nothing and Lambert rules with his army."

"Monck does nothing and Lambert rules with his army until the population as a whole rise up against a state ruled by the military," Forbes countered.

"Monck comes south and raises objection, but Lambert outfaces him," Fisher passed the baton back again.

"Monck comes south with his army and threatens Lambert with conflict," Forbes batted back.

"Monck comes south with his own army and ousts Lambert, recalls the Rump parliament," Fisher managed a fierce grin at that suggestion.

"At this point, I mean to interject a question," Forbes even raised a hand. "You are the military man. If it came to blows, who would you see as victor? Monck or Lambert?"

"Monck, without the slightest hesitation. He is by far the superior tactician and the better general."

"Then here is my next hypothesis," Forbes relaxed again. "Monck recalls Parliament and sets someone in the top seat to run things."

"Cannot see that remaining the case for too long," Fisher grumbled. "Far too many would want the top spot – or seats near to it."

"There is, of course, one obvious solution," Forbes mused. "A renewed Parliament brings back Charles as king."

"That certainly would be one solution," Fisher nodded. "However, he would have to agree to a new set of rules – no 'divine right' nonsense, and rule *with* Parliament!"

"Could he bring himself to agree to that?"

"If he has an ounce of sense in his head, yes. Perhaps he would then bring himself to concentrate on his position as monarch instead of siring bastards around the continent! But there is yet another twist to the case – or so my contacts tell me. I hear there just may be a plot by certain people here and abroad to put a different Stuart on the throne – one far more acceptable to that fellow in Rome."

"Dear Heavens – another plot? Will we ever be free of them?"

"What would Westminster be without plots!" Fisher laughed at the thought. "Such a case would make it a very dull place indeed!"

"Do you know what, old friend – I *like* dull!"

"Even living a quiet life down here in the wilds of Devon, I still hanker for the machinations of Westminster, the comings and goings, the plots and counterplots that abound. Perhaps one of our hypotheses will come to pass and my bucolic monotony will be enlivened!" Fisher had the last word.

It was another four days before Peter and Laura Cove moved from their cottage on the Parke estate into the large Brimley mansion. As luck would have it, the weather again smiled on South Devon so that the move of both them and their belongings was accomplished with everything dry and in order. The two of them stood amidst a large throng in the large hall, a fire blazing away in the massive grate. Mary, Matthew Kent, and Hector Anstruther were also present. Kent, as the duly appointed executor, started off proceedings.

"Thank you everybody for meeting here today. As you all must know, Lady Violette appointed me the executor of her will. This is a duty that I neither sought nor wanted. However, the dear lady for reasons known only to her, appointed me and I shall carry out those duties as faithfully as I am able. Her friend of some years, Mary Ramsey, she appointed the custodian of the estate. All of you have known Mary for years and know that she will also carry out her duties fully and completely. Mary runs the school, now to be named the Lady Violette Charlton School. Therefore, she has a complex role, teacher, wife, mother, as well as custodian. You have all known Peter and Laura Cove for many years. Now that he has relinquished his role as Bailiff, he and Laura have agreed to come to live here. Someone has to, I'm sure you would agree – and who better than someone you have known and trusted for many years.”

He paused and had a quick glance at the many faces gathered there – and saw not one face registering disapproval. He then asked Mary to take over.

“My job is very simple,” she said. “All I have to do is to ensure that the estate carries on being run properly. From everything I have witnessed, the entire estate is in the best possible hands, from steward down to the most junior member of staff. Your positions here are guaranteed for as long as you wish to remain.”

That went down extremely well, even though everyone present had believed it to have been the case. It was just very comforting to hear the words said aloud.

Luke Farmer then raised a very valid point.

“What will be the case if some extremely rich person makes a bid for the estate?”

“In that case, he or she will be bitterly disappointed,” Kent replied firmly. “The final clause in the will states, and I can quote the exact words, ‘Brimley Estate shall continue in the manner and condition that I have left it’. Both Mary and I are the appointed trustees, and we shall ensure that *every* clause of the will be enacted and adhered to.

The final act was for everyone to raise a glass and toast the memory of the departed lady. Every member of the staff then went about their duties – most of them sad on the one hand and happy that things were not going to change.

Kent spent the rest of that day distributing purses of coins according to the bequests in the will – with the exception of young Felix who was not in attendance.

The only unhappy person was Hector Anstruther. He approached both Kent and Mary before leaving.

“The matter of the bequests were mine to administer,” he growled.

“Not so!” Kent had little time for the posturing lawyer. “I was appointed executor of the will. You were *employed* as its scribe. Your part ended with the signing and witnessing.”

"I shall scrutinise every word, comma and full stop. Believe me, I *shall* find some matter upon which I can enter an objection."

"Oh, for heaven's sake," Mary exploded. "Just go away. Scrutinise all you wish – you will not find any court to uphold your supposed complaint!"

Muttering dire imprecations, the lawyer made his exit. Kent and Mary exchanged a look and burst out laughing.

"Well, a good laugh is probably the best way to end a sad day," Kent grinned.

The next day was again raining, not blowing a gale, but a gentle, persistent rain that soaked you through before you had managed a hundred yards. Nell was, unusually for her, disgruntled with life as she vainly tried to adjust the collar of her cloak to stop dribbles going down her back. She was on her way to see Lou Crowley who had developed a nasty rash on her arms. It was not one that Lou could explain, so Nell had agreed to walk up to the school with an assortment of unguents to see for herself. She arrived at the large cottage and proceeded around the back. Lou and her adopted lad Felix lived on the upper story of the cottage.

Bemoaning the lack of strong sunlight, Nell examined both arms. Each was mottled with red patches about the size of a farthing. The rashes spread no further up than the elbows.

"It is obviously caused by something that you have immersed your arms in," Nell decided. "It is nothing like nettle rash, and certainly not akin to other rashes such as measles – they would not have confined themselves to your lower arms. Can you think of anything that you might have used on your hands or skin?"

"Nothing that I have not done for many a year. Only the other day I was washing out that new woollen blanket, and that is something I have done many times – washing woollen garments, I mean."

That caused something to fire in Nell's brain. She and Avril had been discussing that very subject some months before.

"May I see the blanket?" she asked. Lou went to Felix's bedroom and came back with the blanket – one that was obviously quite new. It was undyed, thick and very warm. Nell held it to her nose and inhaled the rich and somewhat fatty smell.

"I do believe I have the answer right here in my hands," she said slowly. "It is something Avril and I were discussing some time past. There seems to be something in sheep wool that can cause a reaction in a few people. We do not yet know what it is, but I am willing to wager that this is the cause of your rash. Over time, whatever the substance is, will probably wash out. But in the meantime, I have an ointment that will help reduce the soreness."

As she gently rubbed the ointment on Lou's arms, the older woman started talking about something that had also been worrying her.

"That money that was bequeathed to little Felix," she began. "It was typical of that dear lady to remember a child with such a past. I have lodged the money safely until he becomes of an age mature enough to appreciate it, what it may do for him and who left it to him."

"I have a very similar worry," Nell admitted. "The money has been given to me and I have done the same as you – lodged it safely and securely. I know I am now seventeen and am regarded as a grown woman. But I have absolutely no idea what I may do with it. My first thought was to distribute it to those unfortunate people down on the Heath – those thrown out of work when that wretched farmer threw them out of work. But I realised that Lady Violette gave it to me for a reason."

"Perhaps she had in mind that you keep it until you marry. It would buy you a very nice home of your own," Lou suggested.

"Oh, that shall never happen," Nell stated. "Marriage is not ever in my thoughts!"

"Goodness – why ever not? You are a very pretty young maid. Please do not tell me that you have no young men making bids for your affection!"

Nell blushed. "There may be such, but I do not encourage any of them. As I said, marriage is not for me."

"Nell, dear – will you listen to the advice of someone who has seen more of life than you – someone who has had a husband, then lost him, has had a son and has had him returned, and who now cares for a little lad as if her were mine own?"

Nell said nothing in response, wondering what the advice would be.

"It is common knowledge that your own mother died in the act of birthing you, that you were cared for most lovingly by your young father, who was also taken when you were but four years. Is what befell your mother causing you to shun marriage so that the same fate may not befall you?"

Nell was nothing if not honest. She sat glumly and nodded.

"Then, have you not applied the logic that you have gained from those years studying with James and Avril? Have you not seen how very rare it is for a mother to die in childbirth?"

"But it was at one time, very common!" Nell argued.

"Aye, it certainly was. But not now. Go through the records that Avril will have undoubtedly kept and do your sums. You are young, fit, healthy, and strong. Why should it apply to you any more than it does to others?"

"But we inherit traits from our parents," Nell was stubbornly fixated. "My dada always told me that my hair – blonde and curly – was exactly like my mother's. I have a snub nose and a wide mouth – exactly like my dada had. If I can inherit those outward signs, how more likely is it that I also inherit some internal ones?"

"My advice – go and speak with Mary. Avril is probably too close to you. Mary has two children – twin boys, and twins are notoriously difficult to birth. I believe you will find she is again with child. Mary will advise you better than anyone."

"I shall certainly do so," Nell agreed. "And I shall *still* keep that money safe until I find a good home for it."

CHAPTER XII

Things had changed dramatically, or so it appeared to Larkin as he rode into Westminster. Clouds threatened rain, the stink of humanity and its ordure was just as horrible as ever. Larkin, who had recently been used to the far fresher environment of the countryside, found himself aching to return there.

The three prisoners had been lodged very securely in underground cells, guarded by soldiers, not by civilian jailers. Larkin made straight for the office of the chief clerk to the justices. He needed advice more than anything.

The chief clerk, a strange man with a wig far too small for his bulging cranium, read the statements in silence. He then surprised Larkin.

"Satan's bunions! This is as fine a pickle as I have seen for many a day! I would advise seeking the brain of Justice Hackney – if anyone can sort out the best course of action it is he. Pay little regard to his appearance for it hides a very large intellect."

He summoned a very junior clerk to show Larkin the way but had a parting word of advice.

"Be brief, succinct, and do not embellish. Justice Hackney is himself a man of few words and hates nothing more than blather."

Larkin was led down corridors, up and down stairs, until he was utterly disoriented. Eventually, the young man knocked on an imposing door, opened it and announced, "Colonel Larkin to see you sir", then promptly disappeared.

Larkin approached a large desk behind which sat a diminutive figure. Justice Hackney was dressed in black, had long hair hanging lankly to his collar, which sported the puritan double white hangings called a rabat. He was obviously perched atop a few cushions. Two piercing blue eyes regarded Larkin as the Colonel stopped and saluted politely.

"Sir, I come in need of legal advice," he said quietly.

"Sit, be brief, explain!"

With as few words as possible, Larkin related the tale – the finding of the body, the discovery of the three prisoners, the connection to Abbe Justin, the conflicting statements. The judge said nothing, merely extended his hand for the written statements. He read them through once, then again more slowly.

"DeGruchy *was* acting for Parliament. That is for your ears and those of his family. This Duplessis demands written indemnity. He shall not get it. Tomorrow, go to his cell at nine of the clock, and you will be met by someone who will have the truth out of him. Take a clerk to record what is said. Return to me when it is over."

Sensing that he was being dismissed, Larkin rose, offered a word of thanks and then got hopelessly lost trying to find his way back to the main doors. He was convinced that the 'someone' in question would be far harsher with Duplessis than he had been.

Nell had made her excuses to James, saying she needed to talk to Mary on a personal matter. She then waited patiently for Mary to finish school that afternoon and walked with Mary and the twins back to Parke. Mary sent the two boys out to help in the stables where they were always at their happiest. Both seemed to have developed an affinity with the horses.

"Please may I speak to you on a confidential matter?" Nell asked politely.

Mary, who was nothing if not perceptive, had a fair idea what the subject matter would be, but did not interrupt whilst Nell spoke of her own mother and her fears for her future.

Mary, now some months pregnant, sat Nell down and regarded the young maid with a smile.

"These fears have been with you ever since you learned of your own mother's death when delivering you, have they not?"

"My dada told me the week before we first came here, the week before he also died. When I was old enough to understand, the fears multiplied and have stayed with me ever since."

"Aunt Avril and I have attended most births for the last ten years. In all that time, we have lost not one mother. Admittedly, one did die a few weeks afterwards, but that was because her miserable husband failed to care properly for her – and she had no relatives or friends on whom she could call for help. Believe me, Nell – it used to be the case that mothers died in childbirth, almost as many as the babies who died at birth or soon afterwards. But even then, it was never more than one or two in a hundred."

"I have helped Avril with childbirth recently and I know that what you say is true. But I simply cannot rid myself of the terror."

"Have you a prospective father in mind?" Mary asked, thereby hoping to bring a lighter note into the conversation.

"Indeed, I have not!" Nell replied with a deal of vehemence.

"Please do not tell me that you of all girls have not received advances from the young men hereabouts!"

"Oh – well, yes, I have. But I do not encourage any of them."

"Now, be honest with me Nell – does not any one of them spark the slightest interest?"

"Not one!" Nell was adamant.

"But what if another young man arrived here one day and sparked that interest? Would your fears make you spurn him – just in case you were tempted to marry him and possibly become with child?"

"I honestly believe they would," Nell admitted. "I know that it may appear irrational, especially when I see you and Meg and Ella and Imelda – and all the others with children and witness the joy that they bring. But that fear simply overrides everything."

"Aunt Avril's greatest sorrow is that she and Uncle James have not been able to have children of their own. That is why they lavish such love and care on you. Can you see yourself in another fifteen or twenty years from now, alone and childless?"

"That is the whole point – I *can!* And I do not relish the prospect. But how can I ever get past these fears, stupid though they may appear to others?"

"Believe me, Nell – there is only one way that you will *ever* overcome the fears – when the right young man comes along. The desire to be with him and to have children with him will be the only way those fears will fade. Do you think I did not have such hesitation? Or Ella? Or any other of us women? Of course, we did. But the desire to be with Harry and to raise our own family simply overrode those hesitations."

Nell went quiet as she digested this. Mary wanted to have the last word.

"Do *not* shun the company of these young men. If you continue to do so, then a lonely future is all you have. Give yourself the chance to find happiness and fulfilment. You at least owe that to yourself – and that would be something indeed for you to relate to your dada when you visit his grave!"

Larkin spent his afternoon visiting the DeGruchy family at the warehouse.

"Do you mean to tell me that my son was acting in the best interests of his country, despite all the rumours to the contrary?"

"I have it on the highest authority that such was the case. You must surely now be very proud of your son."

"Proud, certainly. Sad, overwhelmingly so. That pain will be with me to the grave, as it will be with the rest of his family. I have to assume that, as he was working clandestinely, we should keep this intelligence within our own family group?"

"Indeed, that is what I have been instructed to relay to you. I know that this will be hard for you, but I would implore you to do so."

"Please stay whilst I gather my family to tell them the news."

A while later, the rest of the family had been told that Francis, far from being an enemy agent, had been working for his own country. Larkin watched closely as this information sank in. There was much relief when it had been told, especially on the face of one very young lady. Larkin made his farewells, but followed young Letty as she made her way back to the warehouse where she had been making a tally of some imported goods.

"You knew, did you not?" Larkin spoke softly.

Letty looked downcast but nodded. "Francis told me his mission before he went abroad. Why he did so, I know not. But he swore me to silence. I have now to spend my life pretending that your news came as great a shock to me as to the others."

"Oh, I'm sure that a young lady of your capabilities will be able to dissimulate," Larkin gave her a friendly grin.

"Oh, I do hope so!" Letty waved him goodbye and went about her tallying.

That afternoon, two weary travellers stopped for the night in the cover of a small wood on the southern fringes of the town of Taunton. They unhitched the horse from the wagon and tethered it on a long rein so that it could feed on the long grasses. On the wagon were two large barrels – their excuse for being away from Bovey Tracey. They would eventually deliver the barrels to a customer in far off Bideford, explaining that they had to take a long break to repair a wheel that had been badly damaged. They needed but a few more hours to complete the task that they had set their hearts upon.

The fire was discovered just after midnight, but nor before the entire cooperage yard had been abandoned to the flames. Neighbours rallied frantically to stop the fire spreading to their properties. In that, they were to prove successful. In the darkness, the Taunton Barrel maker surveyed the ruins of his business. He raged and swore that he knew how the fire had started. However, there was little or no proof that the fire was either accidental or deliberate arson.

By five the next morning, two very tired young men from Bovey Tracey rumbled onwards towards the town of Bideford, past Barnstaple and along the river. Barrels delivered, they made off due south again to go home, stopping only at a village blacksmith, a distant relative of one of the men. This relative agreed to state, if questioned, that he had repaired the wheel the previous day.

CHAPTER XIII

Larkin was met at the entrance to the dungeons by a man somewhere in his forties. He was neatly dressed in black, was quietly spoken, and had the air and grace of a gentleman.

"Colonel, my name is Jack Peters. Judge Hackney tells me that there is a person residing here who is reluctant to divulge information that you need most urgently."

"Ah, you must be the person he spoke of. The man is Bernard Duplessis and says that he will tell me all if he is granted immunity from prosecution."

"Does he indeed! I would ask that you relate to me all that you know so that I may conduct the interview with full knowledge."

It took Larkin a good half-hour to bring Peters up to date. Peters said nothing for a few moments, then gave a smile.

"Then, Colonel, let us go and confront this chappie, shall we?"

The jailer led them down some slimy stone stairs to an underground corridor that had iron-bound doors on either side. He unlocked one in the middle on the left and ushered Larkin and Peters into the evil-smelling cell. It contained two things, one prisoner and a bucket that was half-filled with human waste. The smell was diabolical. There was a small grille in the roof that allowed some light to illuminate this hellhole.

Duplessis rose from his position squatting at the far wall. He was dishevelled and obviously in some trepidation until his eyes lighted upon Larkin.

"Ah, the good Colonel brings me written absolution," he said with as false a smile that Larkin had ever seen. Duplessis extended a dirty hand for Larkin to shake.

There came a sickening crack as a short, iron rod descended on his outstretched fingers. Peters put the rod back into his pocket.

"No, Monsieur Duplessis – we do *not* come with anything at all except questions. You now have one broken hand. I shall now ask you one simple question. Say a fond farewell to the other hand if you fail to answer to my satisfaction." Peter's voice remained calm and perfectly modulated.

"You have done me false," Duplessis wept as he nursed the fingers of his right hand. Two were at very strange angles.

"Indeed, I have done nothing of the kind," Larkin said, secretly quite sickened at this turn of events. "I gave you no indication that your demand would be met."

"So, my first question," Peters went on in his urbane manner. "Are you the mastermind behind the plot to put a Catholic favourable to Rome upon the throne of England."

"No, I am not," Duplessis sobbed in pain.

"That I believe. So, on to question two. Do you know who is? And bear in mind that you agreed to divulge this information in exchange for a pardon!"

"Yes, I know."

"Again, I believe you. And now we come to the next, and very vital, question. Who is this mastermind?"

"I dare not tell you," came a quiet whimper.

"Oh dear! Contemplate this if you will, Monsieur. A hurdle bearing your broken body is hauled to the scaffold. The crowd is jeering and hurling filthy things at you as you pass. You are hauled up by your neck until you are choking in your death throes. Then you are cut down and a wicked long knife rips open your belly so that your innards may be torn out to be burnt before your eyes. And then, almost as an act of mercy, your head is severed from your body, that body is chopped into small pieces to be displayed for public viewing. I take it that the picture I have painted is firmly in your mind? So, again, I ask, who is this mastermind?"

Duplessis gave a groan of defeat. "Lord Percival," he whispered.

Larkin gave a start of utter surprise. That was not a name he would have ever considered. Peters did not even raise an eyebrow.

"There," he said. "That was not so hard, was it. I shall have a physician come to set your hand and allow food and drink to be brought. You will remain here as the good Colonel continues with his investigation. I bid you a good morning."

Back in the daylight, and removed from the stink of the dungeons, Larkin turned to Peters.

"And what happens to Duplessis now?" he asked.

"Oh, that is simple. You use whatever powers you are able to summon and make whatever enquiries you need. That man has more information to divulge – of that, I am sure. At the appropriate time, we shall interrogate him further until we have drained every last drop. Then, he will be quietly executed."

Peters gave Larkin a cheery goodbye and went on his way whistling softly to himself. Larkin went straight back to Judge Hackney.

Nell was sitting in her usual place – on a high stool behind the counter of the apothecary shop. She was busy counting small tablets into little glass vials. She had spent some time earlier that morning pressing the paste into little moulds, the paste being a mixture of ground willow bark and a harmless filler that James had devised years before. She became aware of a dark shadow over her work and looked up into a pair of large brown eyes.

"I apologise if my sudden appearance startled you," came a pleasant voice from a mouth hidden between moustache and beard.

"I also apologise for my mind being miles away," Nell replied with a smile. "What may I do for you?"

"My father and I are travelling through here on our way to Saltash. He suffers regularly from pains in his belly and awoke this morning at that rather splendid tavern with the pain more severe than usual. The landlord recommended that I come here to consult you as his usual tonics seem to have little effect on his suffering."

Nell's interest was immediately aroused – any pain or irregularity interested her, no matter whom or when.

"It would be most unwise to recommend any medicine without first seeing the patient and coming to a proper diagnosis," she remarked. "I shall ask either James or Avril to visit your father as soon as possible so that it may be properly determined the cause of the trouble. For whom should they ask?"

The young man seemed somewhat taken aback by two things; first, the young age of the girl who was speaking to him, and second, the precise and almost pedantic delivery of the speech. However, he rallied and gave her a polite smile.

"My father is named Josiah Clements," he announced. "He will be found still in our room at the tavern as he is unwilling to leave his bed at the moment."

"Either the apothecary or his wife will be in attendance before dinner," Nell went on. "Please tell your father that, if anyone can ease his suffering, they can."

"Then I am very grateful for your help. My name, by the way, is Adam." And with that, he turned on his heel and left the shop. Nell finished her batch of tablets and went in search of Avril. She found her immediately in the room behind the shop.

"Worry not – I heard the conversation," Avril grinned. "Did you not think him a most charming and handsome young man?"

"I cannot say that I noticed," Nell protested. But being a very honest young lady, admitted to herself that she had noticed – sort of.

Avril was determined that the matter would not be allowed to rest there. "Both James and I are far too busy at present to attend the father. There is no reason why you cannot go and examine him. You have all the knowledge you need to come to a correct diagnosis. So, take with you what you need and go and examine the poor man."

Nell put a few items into a bag and made her way up the street to the tavern. She was in a bit of a quandary; first, she was fascinated to carry out a full diagnosis of an ailing patient – she always was! Another part of her said that she looked forward to seeing the young man again. Her fear of the consequences of any sort of relationship had faded into the background.

Dick Allen showed her up to the bedroom where a man in his early forties lay atop the covers, both hands clutched around his abdomen. Adam Clements sat by the side of the bed but rose to his feet as Nell entered.

"You are neither the apothecary nor the apothecary's wife," he stuttered.

"Indeed, as you say, I am neither of those. But I am a certified apothecary – despite my age and gender," Nell went on the immediate defensive. "The first thing I need to ascertain in that your father grants permission for me to examine him. Without a thorough examination, nobody can reach even the beginnings of a proper diagnosis."

"My physician in Tiverton has cost me a fortune already with his so-called examinations – and not to mention his arsenal of medicines!" the father grunted from the pillows.

"Then let me rest your mind on that score," Mary gave him a smile. "If I can reach no proper diagnosis, I shall charge you nothing whatsoever."

"Then, examine as you will."

Nell first went to the wash bowl and cleansed her hands, wiping them on a piece of clean linen from her bag. Then, approaching the man, bent forward and drew up the shirt, thereby exposing the chest and upper abdomen. Nell rubbed her hands together to ensure that they were warm, then gently started to probe, following the route taken by food – out of the stomach, across to the start of the small intestine, then across it. She stopped at a wince of pain from her patient.

"Please bear with me – I believe I have located the cause." She gently massaged across the line of that small intestine, hearing gurgling and rumbles. The man winced at every movement. Nell stood up and again washed and dried her hands.

"Those movements within cause emissions of wind, do they not?" she asked.

The man blushed and admitted that it was so. Nell gave him an encouraging grin.

"Believe me, there is nothing seriously amiss. What you have wrong is an excess of flatulence. This can be caused in many ways. Eating too much fresh bread – its yeast can start to bubble up again within you. Again, the same may be said for overindulgence in ale. Excess flatulence in itself sounds innocuous but as you have experienced, it can be most painful and incapacitating."

"But what may be done about it?" the man asked wincing as a ripple of pain lanced across his exposed belly.

"Milk," Nell almost laughed as the man looked at her with an incredulous expression. "Yes, I know that seems almost too simple. But you will find it very beneficial. My advice to you is to replace ale with milk, eat eggs and beef – but in moderation. Avoid an excess of anything."

"And I do not need expensive medicines?"

"Certainly not! They will reduce nothing but the contents of your purse."

"I shall slaughter that physician," the man growled. "He has never even laid a hand upon me – simply stands and looks clever and pronounces yet another expensive so-called remedy."

"Why are you not a physician?" Adam asked. "Your knowledge would appear to be far greater than his!"

"And who ever heard of a female physician?" Nell retorted in exasperation. "We are allowed the title of 'wise woman' but are never allowed anything more professional. One day, perhaps, we shall be allowed into the realms of professional medicine. But those days seem a long way off."

"But why milk?" the father wanted more information.

"Two reasons," Nell assured him. "One of your symptoms – which you never mentioned, and I have guessed – is a rising of acid. This can be particularly unpleasant. Milk will act as a soothing agent and reduce the acidity. The second reason is that milk eases the passage of matter through the intestines – besides being an excellent food in itself. After all, babies thrive on it!"

"And that is your advice?"

"Not only that. Keep to a more bland diet. Avoid rich sauces. Eat vegetables that are never overcooked. Above all, replace ale with milk at least twice every day."

"That sounds to me to be a very boring existence!"

"Aye – boring and less painful!"

"And what do we owe you for this examination and advice?"

"Nothing at all at this moment. I would advise that you stay here for some days and keep to the new regime. Then, when you have come to enjoy its benefits, visit us and pay what you deem us worthy to receive."

"Dear Lord above. Do you hear this, Adam? An honest practitioner" Whoever would have thought it? It shall be as you say, young lady. And I thank you for everything. I shall certainly honour your establishment with a visit to report progress."

"Then may I escort you back to your premises?" Adam rose and went to open the door.

"That would be most kind," Nell answered, careful to avoid looking at him so that her blushes were hidden.

"And what brings you from Tiverton to Saltash?" she asked as the two walked slowly back down the street.

"Ah! Sordid business, I am afraid. My father owns three cargo vessels that ply regularly between Saltash and Portugal. We take wool there and bring wines back."

"And have you ever been on that journey?"

"Many times since I was sixteen and deemed old enough to start learning the business. I am my father's only son. I have two sisters younger than I am, but he intends to make me so conversant with the business that he can safely leave it to me when he grows too old."

"So, you shall be a rich merchant in the fulness of time?"

"Only if I do not make a complete hash of it all!" Adam laughed.

Back at the shop. Adam gave Nell a polite and very gentlemanly shake of the hand and said he would return daily with news of his father's progress.

That evening, Nell having gone to bed early, Avril grinned at her husband.

"Have you noticed that all afternoon and evening, it has been Adam this and Adam that. I do believe our Nell is quite smitten with the man."

"He certainly appears to be a young man of excellent character. Is our Nell emerging from her shell, do you think?"

"If so, it is a happening long overdue!" Avril nodded.

That same afternoon, Larkin was again in with Judge Hackney. He related in detail what had occurred in the underground cell – and the part that Jack Peters had played.

A faint smile appeared on the judge's normally stern features. "Aye – persuasive bugger, is he not!"

"Indeed so, sir. But I now need urgent advice on how to proceed. After all, the name of Lord Percival is not one that I can bandy about without permission."

"Stalks about the corridors of power, giving off an air of sanctimonious piety. You shall now accompany me to meet someone who has all the necessary power to direct your efforts."

Larkin followed Hackney along corridors that grew steadily more impressive as they went. Finally, they came to a pair of large doors guarded by a couple of soldiers.

"Judge Hackney and Colonel Larkin. It is imperative that we see the General immediately."

One of the guards opened the door and relayed that to someone inside. Then the doors were both opened wide and the pair were ushered in. A bevy of clerks were busy at desks. One of them went to a further set of doors and announced them.

General John Lambert, effective leader of Parliament that consisted of members of the army, beckoned them towards his surprisingly small desk. He waved them to chairs.

"General, Colonel Larkin has come across serious evidence in the case of DeGruchy. You need to be made aware of it."

Lambert bent his head towards Larkin and simply motioned him to speak.

Larkin gave a precis of the events that had led up to the questioning of Duplessis, omitting the means by which the name of Percival had emerged. Lambert grunted, then rang a small handbell. The door opened and the same clerk entered.

"Arrange for the immediate arrest of Lord Percival. It is to be done quietly and, if possible, secretly. He is to be taken to the Tower and housed there in moderate comfort. Also, prepare a document for Colonel Larkin that authorises him in the name of Parliament to conduct whatever enquiries he may deem necessary. Bring that document to me for signature as soon as it is ready."

The clerk hurried out to get matters under way. Lambert faced Larkin.

"I take it, Colonel, that you wish to be associated with this enquiry?"

"Indeed, sir. I have been with it ever since it came to light. I would certainly wish to bring it to a successful conclusion."

"Please see that you do so. You will report directly to me at the close of each day."

Larkin swallowed, realising that a lot depended upon this investigation.

The shop had hardly been open for ten minutes the next morning when Adam Clements came to report progress.

"He is significantly improved since your visit yesterday." Nell was pleased but hardly surprised at this news. "I do believe he is contemplating a claim of false practice against his physician."

"Then give him a word of advice," James had been in the shop working with Nell. "All the physician has to do is to say that he prescribed the medicines in good faith from the symptoms that were reported to him and no court in the land will penalise him. You and we know this to be wrong and utterly unjust, but that is what will inevitably happen."

"Also, tell him to beware spreading complaints throughout his friends and neighbours. That physician would then have a case against your father for spreading malicious gossip, if not downright slander," Avril joined in.

"The law seems to be slanted in the wrong direction!" Adam snorted. "However, as well as giving a report, I have another reason to call upon you. I would dearly like to invite Nell to take dinner with us at the tavern − if that would meet with your approval."

"Nell?" James raised a quizzical eyebrow.

"Oh, ah, um, I believe I would like that very much," Nell managed, knowing that she was blushing a deep red.

Adam went off seemingly a happy young man. Nell faced James and Avril.

"I agreed only because I need to see progress in my patient," she said on the defensive.

"Oh, of course you did!" Avril grinned. "The mere fact that he is a very presentable young man with seemingly impeccable manners, not to say a handsome face, never entered the equation!"

"Oh, piffle and nonsense!" Nell stormed out of the shop and into the back parlour.

Colonel Larkin rode through the city of London from west to east, marvelling at the way in which the crowded inhabitants seemed to be blissfully unaware of the foul stink of the place. Not that he was unused to the foul odours - far from it. But his time spent in the Devon countryside had made him realise that massed humanity was something he could well do without. He was even more dismayed when he entered the Tower. The stink of animal dung and human ordure was even worse, being contained within mountainous walls.

Having handed his horse to a stable groom, he was met in the inner courtyard by a smiling Jack Peters.

"Good morning, Colonel. I take it you are here to see Lord Percival. Maybe I can be of further service?"

Larkin was a bit startled to know that the interview was to be conducted in a manner similar to the previous day. He followed Peters across the courtyard and into a door at the base of the Bell Tower, climbed a staircase and was halted at a door that was being guarded by two soldiers of impressive stature. Apparently, Peters was well known as the door was opened for them.

The room was tastefully furnished with bed, chairs, table, garderobe, rugs and a fire held within a brazier. The window was barred. A gaunt and very resentful man was standing at the window gazing outwards.

"I sincerely hope that you come with abject apology for this insult!" he barked, noting that one of his visitors was a Colonel.

"No, Lord Percival. I come with a list of questions that you are required to answer – and before you start objecting, please read this warrant."

He displayed the warrant and the seal and signature. Percival gave a gulp, but then returned to his indignant pose.

"And what possible information do you suppose I may have for you?" he barked.

"Abbe Justin, Bernard Duplessis, Claude Bruce, Bartholomew Preece – not to mention a certain Francis DeGruchy," Larkin sat down uninvited in a chair.

It took just a few seconds for Percival to form a reply.

"And those names are supposed to mean something to me?" he sneered. "I have never heard of any of them!"

"Monsieur Duplessis has certainly heard of the illustrious Lord Percival. It was he who gave me to understand that you are the instigator of a plot to place a Catholic pleasing to Rome upon the throne of England. Your French counterpart is this Abbe Justin. It has already been firmly established that Francis DeGruchy was acting for Parliament, seeking out the details of this plot. He was murdered by Preece at the direct command of Duplessis. Preece will be executed in due course. Duplessis came up with the plan to give us your name in return for a pardon. He did indeed give us your name but received certain injuries instead of the pardon. He will face execution in due course. So – now we come to you, my lord. How may you help me in the furtherance of my investigation?"

"It would seem that my name was extracted after torture," Percival went on the attack. "What possible credence can you place upon that? A person under torture will blurt out anything to stop the pain!"

"That is indeed so. But let me further inform you that your home is being searched from roof to cellar. I am certain that some small thing will have been overlooked by you. They *will* find it. And, when they do, this comfortable room will be but a fond and distant memory."

"And what is to stop them *finding* what has already been forged and placed there?"

"And what of your staff?" Larkin countered. "Are you so sure of them that one at least will seek to save his or her skin by adding to my store of evidence?"

That caused Percival to stop for a moment before replying.

"Not one member of my household could tell you anything. Because there is nothing to tell!"

Larkin decided on the spur of the moment to try an idea.

"The Fitzalans and the Howards might yield useful information," he mused aloud.

Both of those families had been known for many years to be Catholic. It had got them into some trouble in the past. Percival sat for some moments, before Larkin stood up.

"I shall leave you to contemplate," he announced. "Be under no illusion that this is the end of the matter!"

"I look forward to another meeting," Peters added, giving the seated peer a wicked grin.

Harry was busy in his small office bringing the list of the estate's tenants up to date; this was an exercise that was becoming all too regular. Tenants seemed to come and go with far more frequency than they ever used to. He sat back and wondered why this should be. After all, he reasoned, other large estates in the vicinity did not suffer such regular upheaval. He was interrupted by the arrival of Hob.

"Do you recall that irate barrel maker from Taunton?" he asked. "Well, the blighter is here again at the door swearing that our barrel makers set fire to his cooperage yard and have destroyed his business. Oh, and he is spitting anger and venom!"

With a sigh, Harry set down his papers and followed Hob to the door. There stood the enraged man from Taunton, hopping from foot to foot in frustrated temper.

"I demand the immediate arrest of those two villains!" he shouted. "They have destroyed my business!"

"And what evidence have you to support that demand?" Harry asked.

"Who else could be responsible? They swore vengeance and they have accomplished what they swore!"

"That hardy constitutes evidence," Harry pointed out. "I grant that you have reasonable grounds to *suspect* that they have done so. But suspicion alone is nowhere near enough. Did anyone actually see them? Can anyone identify them?"

"Nay – bastards were canny enough to set the fire in the early, dark hours when all would have been asleep."

"Then all I can do is to question them," Harry replied. "I shall do so now – and you will remain quiet as I do so!"

"Then you will have wasted your journey for they are not there! I checked as I rode past."

"I sincerely hope that you did nothing amiss, or I shall have to hold you as well."

"Nay – I want this done properly this time. Arson is a serious crime, and I shall laugh aloud as they swing from a gibbet!"

"I shall still have to go there and see for myself," Harry stated. "Hob – fetch our mounts and we shall ride up there now."

Harry and Hob rode up the street to the top by the church, then tethered their horses to the gatepost that led into the field. They walked across to the barn and found as they had been told – nobody home.

"Told you so!" The Taunton man grunted as he drew up in his horse and small wagon. "Scared to show their faces!"

Simon Smith with his wife and children went past as the three arrived back at the gate.

"They've gone to Bideford delivering barrels," Simon offered. "Left three days past. Probably be back any time this afternoon."

Jack and his sister Rachael went to the horse and started to stroke nose and neck.

"If these be your brats, tell them to keep their dirty hands off my horse," the man spat.

"Oh dear," Simon grinned as Imelda walked up to the irate man.

"Those are indeed our children," she said, almost too sweetly. "Their hands are not dirty, and they always pat horses. So, unless you want to feel my hand across your face, keep a civil tongue in your ugly head."

Simon, Harry and Hob looked on with broad grins. Imelda in a temper was a sight to behold. But any further action was postponed as another horse and wagon trundled around the corner.

"There they be!" roared the man. "Arrest them!"

"I told you before we left to leave this to me," Harry reminded him, holding up a hand to arrest progress of the wagon.

"Afternoon, Bailiff. What seems to be the trouble?" Matt Crowley asked, knowing full well what the trouble was – it was staring at him on two stumpy legs with a face infused with anger.

"Perhaps no trouble at all," Harry replied. "But first, tell me where you have been."

"Where have we been?" Matt hoped he looked mystified. "We've been delivering barrels to Bideford. Why?"

"Have you been anywhere near Taunton?"

Matt managed to look even more perplexed. "Taunton? No, that would have been miles out of our way. We went across the moor to Okehampton and had to stop in Hatherleigh to have a wheel mended."

"Lies!" the man almost screamed. "You two burned down my yard!"

"Did we, bollocks!" Herb Grindley retorted. "Look at the wheel and see the repair that was necessary. And if someone burned down your bloody yard, tis no more that you tried to do to ours!"

"So, you went across the moor, through Hatherleigh and onwards to Bideford, where you delivered barrels, then came straight back here?" Harry wanted a complete statement.

"Aye – we did exactly that. And you may enquire at Hatherleigh and at Bideford if you need. We have been gone nearly four days, just enough time to do as we say. And not a moment to spare to go all the way to Taunton to burn down this idiot's yard!"

"Then they commissioned others to do it for them!" the man would not give up.

"Fancy a ride over the moor?" Harry grinned at Hob. Hob never turned down any opportunity to ride long distances.

"Aye, I shall leave at first light tomorrow," Hob grinned back. "I trust that I shall find proof of what you say?" he looked up at Matt and Herb.

"It will be exactly as we say – despite what this oaf alleges!" Matt answered.

"Then you had better be on your way back home," Harry said to the irate cooper. "If I have need to contact you further, I will send Hob. In the meantime, stay away from here – and do not even think about taking any unlawful action!"

Later that evening, Hob relayed all this to May. May, who had known Matt for years before he had disappeared to serve his king, gave a hoot of laughter.

"Of course, they did it!" she chortled. "And you will not be able to prove it!"

"Aye – what I thought," Hob grinned back.

CHAPTER XIV

The twenty-first of October was a date that would for ever be etched in Colonel Larkin's memory. It was the date that he confronted a peer of the realm and unravelled a plot – that had it succeeded – would have altered the religious face of England for perhaps a century or more. It was also the date when he came into contact with some of the leading legal people in Westminster.

It all started innocuously enough. The previous evening, Larkin had reported to Lambert that his 'search squad' would be back early the following day, and that he would again be confronting Lord Percival. Lambert then told Larkin that he would be sending two senior judges to witness the interrogation.

Just after he had finished breakfast, Larkin was visited by his faithful Corporal Skinner. Skinner had been in charge of the 'search squad' that had been ransacking Percival's domain. Skinner was bursting with information, plus a package of papers.

"That was a job extremely well done," Larkin grinned. "Consider yourself promoted to sergeant with immediate effect. You may now accompany me to the Tower and bear witness to the dismantling of a peer of the realm."

Later that morning, Larkin and Skinner met up with Jack Peters and two very austere men in legal robes. They introduced themselves as Judge Cartwright and Judge Wheeler.

"We are here simply to hear and see what transpires," Wheeler said. "Our presence will add to the gravity of Percival's position. I assume that you have further grounds for suspicion?"

"Indeed, sir. Proof instead of mere suspicion!"

Percival's relatively comfortable room was only just large enough to accommodate the six people gathered within. Percival was again peering down his nose in disdain.

"I take it from the presence of learned judges that I am to be exonerated and released," he grated.

"On the contrary, you are going to listen to what I have to say – and then required to answer questions."

"I shall do no such thing – whatever you have to say!"

"Very well – let me see if I can change your mind. First – let me recapitulate the happenings of May this year. The French king – Louis, entered into an agreement with our own Commonwealth and the Dutch Republic that became known as the Concert of the Hague. In it, England agreed with both other parties to cease any hostilities whilst cooperating to ensure free trade passage in the Baltic Sea. It seems strange, does it not, that a fierce radical such as the Abbe Justin would seek to interfere in the affairs of England when his own king is making friendly gestures. But this is what is happening – and you are a prime mover in that unrest. Please do not start remonstrating and uttering stupid attempts at refutation. My sergeant here has just returned from a very fruitful search of your house. Can you guess what he has found?"

"Whatever the wretched man claims he found will have been placed there simply to incriminate me!"

"Damien and Gertrude Bolsover," Larkin could hardly contain a smile.

"My steward and housekeeper. What of them?"

"They seem to bear you little good will. The first thing they did was to introduce the good sergeant and his men to an underground room that is very cleverly hidden from view. Inside that small room were an altar and the accoutrements necessary for the conduct of a Catholic Mass. Now, these in themselves are no crime, nor is it a crime to attend such a service. But it points to the religious leanings of the person who owns that house. However – it does not end there. Sergeant Skinner has earned himself the nickname of The Ferret – and for one very good reason – he ferrets out every nook and cranny. And here are the fruits of his labours."

Larkin fished about in his satchel and brought out the sheaf of papers. Percival's facial expression did not alter, bit turned slowly white as the blood seemed to drain out.

"Two of these papers were found in a secret hole beneath the altar. Five more were discovered behind a loose brick in the end wall. Six more were discovered in a panel behind the desk in your study. Shall we see what these papers tell us?"

"I deny any knowledge of those papers. They are clearly either forgeries or are put there to bear false witness against me!"

"Hmmm." Larkin had picked that up from somewhere. "Paper one is an instruction from three leading French bishops. They instruct their principal agent – the Abbe Justin – to start the movement in England that is led by one Lord Percival. The movement's purpose is to seed the thought of a Catholic king being installed in England. The second paper instructs the said Lord Percival to use whatever means he thinks appropriate to gather a small band of followers who are committed to the cause. And now we come to the other papers – and one in particular. Lord Percival is instructed to use his band of followers to eliminate one Francis DeGruchy who has been discovered to be an agent of Parliament – instead of his professed adherence to the cause. So, what have you to say in answer to all that?"

"Forgeries, the lot of them!"

"Hmmmm. Then, what about this final one – a letter from a certain Bernard Duplessis saying that DeGruchy has indeed been eliminated as instructed. It is addressed to you - and bears out exactly what Duplessis has already admitted."

Percival said nothing, simply slumped in his chair. Judge Cartwright then spoke for the first time.

"Colonel, your job is done – and very well done, I might add. This case will now be taken over by the judiciary, including your other three prisoners and the paper evidence you have gathered. Lord Percival, you will immediately be transferred to a different part of this building. Prepare yourself for charges of treason. Colonel, you may now leave matters entirely in our hands. You have the thanks of a very grateful Parliament."

"What's going to happen to the bugger now?" Skinner asked as he and Larkin strode from the Tower precincts.

"Oh, I would imagine a trial in secret, a sentence of death on all four of them – and a somewhat fiercely worded communique to Paris. Anyway, our job is done."

"So, back to barracks then, sir?"

"For you, yes. For me – well, at the present moment, I have no idea. I have a hankering to return to Devon and seek a far quieter life."

For the third day running, Nell took her dinner up at the tavern, followed by a walk arm in arm with Adam Clements. She was honest enough to admit to herself that her feelings towards this young man were deeper than mere friendship. And that frightened her when she contemplated where such a relationship might end.

She was also honest enough to admit to herself that she was very much smitten with this personable man. She made herself think about never seeing Adam again – and that thought was unacceptable. She knew that Adam was as smitten with her as she was with him – probably more so. She knew that the next step he would take would be to declare his intentions in an honest and open manner. Could she cope with the undoubted consequences?

Instead of merely walking her back to the apothecary shop, he led her onwards to the crossroads and on towards the entrance to Parke. A wooden seat stood at the side of the road beneath the shade of an old elm tree. He invited Nell to sit and then took his seat beside her. Nell just knew that she was going to be faced with the most important decision of her young life.

"I have already pleaded with James and Avril to allow you a further half-hour before you go back to resume your duties," Adam took Nells hand in his and faced her.

"Nell, it will, I am sure, come as no surprise when I say that I have enjoyed your company the last few days. So much in fact that I am loth to end our meetings before I state my honest intentions. Not only do I admire your knowledge and skill, I have developed a love for you that I never dreamed possible. I love the way you walk, the manner in which you speak, the loveliness of your face, in fact – I love every facet of your being."

Nobody had ever said anything like that to her. She had been the recipient of lascivious glances, even somewhat crude comments. She knew that she was attractive but had never thought that anyone would feel so deeply moved by her that words like that would come her way. She was almost overcome with the depth of feeling in which they were delivered. She was deeply moved by them.

"Adam – are you proposing marriage?" she asked, going straight to the point as was her wont.

"No – not until I hear from you that my feelings for you are reciprocated. Such would not be correct!"

"Then it is up to me to be as honest with you as you have been with me. I like you very much, Adam. Whether or not that would blossom into love, only time will tell. I know that you and your father have to travel back to Saltash soon, so my counter proposal is this. Let us spend as much time together as we may. I promise you that, should I feel love for you, I will tell you – and then will be ready for your proposal."

"I accept that counter proposal with gratitude. Let me further state that I shall always honour you, seek your advice, and treat you with respect. We shall be as equals in our partnership. And now, I seek just one small kiss."

That kiss went a long way to dispel any reluctance of Nell's part. But being the sensible young lady that she was, rose and asked to be escorted back to the shop.

"And will you accept his proposal?" Avril asked that evening when Nell had reiterated word for word the conversation with Adam.

"I really want to," Nell admitted. "But it will mean the end of a life here that has been my joy and my refuge for so many years."

"And so it is for any young girl when she enters marriage. I relinquished a life of love and security when I agreed to James' proposal. I have never regretted that decision for a single moment."

"I should damned well hope not," James grinned. "You have been the daughter we never had. You have brought us nothing but joy and happiness. That also means that we want nothing for you but that same joy and happiness that Avril and I have found in each other. My advice is this – go up to your own dada and tell him all your hopes and fears. Open your heart to him – and then follow your own instincts."

"I tell him everything," Nell nodded. "I always have."

Larkin had been as good as his word in that he had sought leave of absence and had ridden slowly back to the place he was coming to think of as his home. He was received with laughter and handshakes at the tavern, Dick and Sal regarding him as a friend from his regular visits.

"May I have my usual room for a month as I have a lot of thinking to do," he admitted.

"Would those thoughts concern our little town?" Sal asked.

"Above all else, yes, they would."

"Then you will be most welcome!"

Larkin had just finished a late dinner when he was joined by Reverend Forbes.

"Aha! I see that our little town proves irresistible, does it not?"

"Indeed, Reverend. It most certainly does – and I cannot fathom the reason for it."

"Then perhaps a dose of enlightened company is what you need. This evening an old colleague of yours, Colonel Lionel Fisher, will be calling on me for our usual chat – plus sampling a rather precious Bordeaux. You will be most welcome to join us as you are most recently back from the seat of power and can regale us with the latest news."

Larkin accepted eagerly, finished his dinner and went for a long walk. Past the gates of Parke, over a small stream and past the gates into Brimley estate. He then turned northwards along a track that led him steadily up and up towards the south-east corner of Dartmoor. He stopped in a small clearing, sat down on a fallen ash trunk and breathed in the clear air, listened to the birdsong, and gave a very contented sigh. He grinned to himself as he compared this to the stink and noise of London.

"No – this is where I wish to be," he decided. That thought, once settled deeply into his brain, would never be dislodged, even though it meant resigning his commission. He had more than enough funds to settle down comfortably. Mind made up, he went back to the tavern and made himself ready for an evening of company.

Nell took a single, very late blooming rose, and made her way for her weekly visit to her father's grave. She had been doing this every week of every one of the thirteen years since his death when she was a mere four years of age.

"Hello, dada," she said quietly as she knelt by the small headstone. She pressed the stem of the rose into the soil. "I have a lot to tell you this time. Last time I was here, I told you about a young man named Adam Clements. Well, he has declared his love for me and has said that, should I return his love, he intends to propose marriage. I have to admit that I like him very much for his courtesy, the respect he shows me, and his very good manners. I am sure that, should I accept him, he will treat me with that same respect when we are married. But you know my innermost thoughts as I always tell you of them. I am still scared of the consequences of such a liaison. Should I do as Avril and Mary say and ignore those fears – trust to God to look after me?"

Nell was a very sane and sensible young lady and knew that there was no chance of a reply. Some people, she knew, swore that dead relatives spoke to them. Nell had no such beliefs. When a person died, all their faculties died with them and only their essence – perhaps, their spirit – remained. Nevertheless, she still used those visits to clarify her own thoughts, knowing that somewhere her long-dead father would be aware of her.

She knelt for quite long enough for the early evening dew to soak through her dress and slowly made her aware of very wet knees. She stood up and blew the usual kiss.

"Next time I come to talk to you, I may well have a fiancé – or perhaps not!"

Larkin was ushered into the large parlour where he was greeted by Forbes. He was introduced to a stern and bluff character – Colonel Fisher. To his surprise, Matthew Kent was also there.

"Well, we are now a quartet!" Forbes grinned as his servant handed glasses of the promised Bordeaux around.

"So – yet another Colonel!" Fisher boomed. "Retired years ago myself and never regretted one second of it."

"I have now resigned from my role as a roving Parliamentary agent," Kent informed the group. "Have a lot to do winding up the estate of dear old Violette – may she rest in peace."

"Amen to that," Forbes nodded. "A great lady and a great benefactor to this town of ours."

"So – what news from the seat of power?" Forbes steered Larkin back on course.

Larkin gave the chapter and verse of the case he had been working on. It took some time as he went into minute detail.

"Percival, you say?" Fisher grunted. "He was at that fiasco in Worcester back in '51 – when young Charles fled for his very life. He fled northwards and sought shelter in a place called Boscobel House. I've seen the priest hole where it is alleged that the blighter hid. Percival is, I believe, a very distant relative of the Giffard family who owned the house and assisted Charles in his onward flight out of England."

"Ah, there I have to correct you, Colonel," Larkin said. "I was interested enough to look into Percival's antecedents. There is no direct connection to the Giffard family, although he most certainly was well acquainted with them."

"Then I take your word for that. And none of this 'Colonel' nonsense. We are of equal rank. You are Paul and I am Lionel. Kent over there is Matthew, and our esteemed ecclesiastical host is James."

"Then, like you, Lionel, I shall soon be resigning my commission. I have a yearning for the quiet and gentle pace of life hereabouts."

"Can get a bit rowdy of a Saturday evening in the tavern," Kent grinned. "But Dick and Sal always have it strictly under control. Apart from that, young Harry Cove is proving to be as good a Bailiff as was his father before him."

"Is that right – Peter and Laura Cove are now at Brimley as sort of guardians?" Forbes enquired.

"Aye, they are – and proving to be excellent and well-received guardians."

"So, Paul – where do you propose to live? Lionel here found an excellent cottage towards Teigngrace."

"Perfect for my simple needs!" Fisher nodded.

"As yet, I have not decided whether to be here in Bovey – as I know the residents call it – or somewhere not that far distant."

"Only people who do not live here call it Bovey Tracey," Forbes laughed as he topped up four glasses.

"As the people of Newton Abbot call it simply Newton – or 'Noot'n' as they pronounce it," Fisher added.

"I rode down through Dorchester," Larkin remembered. "Although the people there looked at me as if I was from Jupiter. Apparently, they call it 'Dorch'."

"Strange lot, us English!" Forbes chuckled. "But back to Percival. What is happening now, do you know?"

"As I understand it, various learned judges made the connection straight to this Abbe Justin, and thence into Paris and the court of Louis. I doubt that they will get much further. However, the plot has failed. Percival and his conspirators will be heard of no more. Quietly executed and the whole matter rolled up as if it had never been."

"More than can be said of Lambert and Monck!" Fisher growled. "If what I hear has even a grain of truth, Monck will move against Lambert in the not too distant future."

"And where is your wager?" Kent asked.

"Oh – Monck, without a moment's hesitation. Both are excellent generals, but Monck beats him hands down on strategy and long-term planning. No – Monck will prevail. What happens after that is mere speculation. He may well call back the remains of the Rump Parliament. He may even go so far as to invite Charles back – with his wings severely clipped."

Forbes, who had at one time been Prince Charles' chaplain, held his peace. Secretly, he hoped that would indeed be the outcome. But there were hurdles strewn in vast numbers to be surmounted before that could even be thought of. But he had his hopes.

CHAPTER XV

The month of October had but three days left. Even the weather seemed reluctant to see it end as the sun shone, the clouds were mere wisps, and the breeze was kindness itself. School had ended early, so Mary was on time for the meeting at Brimley. Her mother and father-in-law, Peter and Laura Cove, were already sitting at the large dining table. Matthew Kent was sitting at the other end in front of a pile of papers. Mary sat down about half-way between and gratefully accepted a glass of watered wine and a slice of very delicious fruit cake.

"I have asked all of you to attend so that I may keep you up to date on the execution of Lady Violette's will," Kent announced. "There is very little left for me to attend to now, so I shall resign my position of executor knowing that I have faithfully discharged all of her wishes."

"Can one merely resign such a position?" Peter Cove asked. "What if, subsequent to all this, there arises a complication or – heaven forbid – a challenge from that weasel Anstruther?"

"Mary?" Kent turned to her. "You are co-trustee. What are your thoughts?"

"I think the same as Peter," Mary nodded. "It would be far more prudent for you to retain the office just in case there is a need to defend the merest clause in the will."

"Then I shall certainly stay on as executor – until such time as we all agree there is no further need for one. Now – progress. Peter and Laura are in situ and have rendered account. Mary – have you seen and agreed it?"

"Despite there being no need, I most certainly have. There was never the slightest doubt that they would be in good order – and the estate is showing a nice profit for the quarter ended last month."

"And on that subject," Laura broke in, "we would like to place on record the excellent work done by Luke Farmer. A better steward it would be hard to find!"

"Every monetary bequest has been fulfilled," Kent went on. "Mary – the bequest to the school – what has happened to it?"

"It is very safely and securely invested so that the school may draw down the interest every month to defray the running costs. I cannot see the need to touch the capital sum until and unless something unforeseen happens. I have also kept back a portion of the interest so as to set up bursaries for any child who requires to attend but whose parents have not the means to pay."

"That is entirely what the dear lady would have wished," Peter Cove added. "She was ever concerned with the proper welfare of children."

"And how is Kit Warden coping with the duties of head gardener – now that he is in sole command?"

"In all matters excellently," Peter replied. "He is also, or so we are told, seeking the hand of Meg's senior cook-helper. And Meg is an absolute gem, despite being in constant warfare with her Hal, her son. The boy is close to eleven years of age and seems to believe that every creature from the largest cow to the smallest chick is fair game for his catapult."

"I well remember being of a somewhat similar bent," Kent laughed. "Is Farmer not disciplining their son properly?"

"Sticks and beatings seem to mean nothing to him. He absorbs them and carries on as if nothing has happened."

"Why do they not apprentice him to Abel and Simon Smith?" Mary thought aloud. "If there are two people on this earth capable of instilling discipline, it is those two!"

"That is a brilliant thought. I shall speak to Luke Farmer this very evening," Peter grinned at her daughter-in-law.

"Hal will not like it!" Mary chuckled.

"Hal will do as he is told just this once!"

"On a more personal note," Mary was always inquisitive. "Where do you intend to live, Paul – or have you decided to remain permanently resident at the tavern?"

"Far from it," Larkin grinned. "Or to be more precise, not that far from it. I have taken a lease on that large cottage between the now vacant mill and the apothecary where you used to reside yourself."

"Then you have indeed become one of us at long last. That is good, but that place is large and will need either a good servant or perhaps a wife?"

"She is relentless!" Larkin grinned back. "To set your minds at rest, I have nobody in my sights at present."

"Then that shall be my very next project – finding some gorgeous lady suitable to a man of distinction!"

"Dear Lord, cannot anyone rein her in?" Larkin pleaded.

"Many have tried – none has succeeded, not even our own son." Laura snorted.

The four sat down to an excellent early supper supplied by the magic of Meg's kitchen.

Adam and his father called in at the apothecary shop on the first leg of their onward journey to Saltash. The nearest practical crossing point of the river Tamar was to the north-west of Tavistock at a village called Gunnislake. Then they would have to ride due south through St. Mellion and Carkeel to get to their final destination.

Nell went out to have a private word with Adam. She knew that what she now said to him would determine the course of her life – either she agreed to his proposal, or she declined it. However, being still very undecided, she attempted procrastination.

"Adam – I have thought long and hard about you. I know that you want an answer, whether or not you actually make the proposal. You will readily understand that I am still not decided either way. But to make your life a little easier, I am about seventy to eighty percent clear in my mind. May I beg you to ask me again when you return from Saltash – or is that too much to ask?"

Adam's face fell, but he rallied. "I take it that the eighty percent is in favour and not against?"

"Yes – it is. I will probably never get to one hundred percent – I doubt that any woman ever does. But the weeks we are apart will help me to think even harder."

"My father and I have also been discussing possibilities," Adam thought it only right that he gave Nell all the information she would need to come to a firm decision. "At present, we have our offices in Exeter – down by the harbour nearer to Topsham. But we have decided that an extra office in Newton Abbot would be advantageous. We are presently negotiating the purchase of two more ships, both to be docked at Teignmouth. There is a fairly new business starting up on the moor, extracting granite. The granite will be brought down from the moor via this town of Bovey, then onwards to Newton Abbot, where it can be transferred to barges towards the port. That granite will be in great demand as building material. My father has suggested that I manage that operation from Newton Abbot – so your move would not be that far distant."

Nell, like most people in the town, was aware of the new, burgeoning enterprise up near Hay Tor, but had never thought that her home town would be a part of the business. It made a lot of sense to have an office somewhere along the route – and Newton Abbot was indeed a sensible choice.

"That does make a difference," she admitted. "One small part of me has always been reluctant to move from this little town. It is all I have ever really known – apart from being constantly on the move as a little child."

"Then, father and I will be back in the early spring to set up the office. May I expect a firm answer from you by then?"

"Yes, Adam. I shall be ready to give you my firm answer – I promise."

She stood in the street as the two men rode down to the crossroads. Their journey to the south of the moor, then north to the crossing point, then south again, would take them about another week. But at least, Josiah Clements would not be suffering as he had been on his arrival.

The next morning saw a somewhat apprehensive Hal and his father at the town's smithy. Luke and Meg had jumped at the idea of apprenticing their wayward son to Abel Smith. If there were any two people in the town capable of instilling discipline into an unruly boy, Abel and Simon fitted the bill perfectly.

Hal gazed at the array of implements, the air of purposeful industry as Abel and Simon – two huge figures – went about heating, hammering and shaping bits of iron into complicated shapes. He looked closely at the massive biceps as they worked, then glanced down at his own, spindly arms and wondered whether he would ever be able to emulate even the simplest operation.

Luke, on the other hand, looked at the work being done so expertly and easily – and came to the conclusion that this was indeed the place for Hal – if the two men agreed to accept his son. Abel glanced at Luke standing with his boy, put down a large hammer and strolled across.

"And what may we do for you today?" he asked. "Brimley in need of a new pair of gates?"

"Actually, no," Luke was a bit unsure how to approach the matter. "Meg and I have been advised that young Hal here needs to be kept out of mischief. It is no good whatsoever sending him to Mary at the school. We tried that and Mary begged us to take him away as he spent all his time looking out of the window. It was Mary herself who came up with the idea of apprenticing him into a worthwhile occupation – and yours seemed the very best available."

Abel scratched his head and called his son across.

"You are asking us to take the lad on as an apprentice?"

"Aye – if that is at all possible. If anyone can keep him in order, teach him something really useful, it is you and Simon."

Abel looked closely at the young lad and again scratched his head. Simon gave a loud grunt.

"He's very young to be apprenticed anywhere," Abel noted. "Probably not too young to be taken on at somewhere a lot less strenuous, but this work requires strength and stamina."

"Believe me, he's a lot stronger than he looks," Luke argued. "I've seen him pick up a milk churn and try to hide it – and that earned him a clout from Meg."

"So – reasonably strong for his age and one for making mischief. Try that here, Hal and you will get more than a clout!"

"Does that mean you will consider it?" Luke could hardly believe his luck.

"Aye, we shall consider it," Abel nodded. "He will have to do a lot of fetching and carrying for some time – learning the types of tools we use, cleaning them so that they are ready for us when we need them. He will also have to spend a deal of time working the bellows – and that is hard and very hot work by the side of the furnace. Let me and Simon discuss it together and we shall let you know by the end of today. If we agree, Hal will have to be here every morning except Sunday at eight of the clock."

"Then, I would thank you for your time and look forward to hearing good news," Luke took Hal's elbow and pulled him back to the street to walk back to Brimley.

Meg, her red hair liberally speckled with flour, regarded her husband and son as they entered her kitchen.

"Let us hope that they agree," she said, and then fixed her son with a gimlet eye. "If they do take you on, you will have to put aside all your fun and mischief. Those two are not to be trifled with."

"Aye, mother. They have lots of wonderful tools there. But I shall get very tired!"

"Excellent!" Luke grunted. "Perhaps you shall be so tired that you will cease being a plague to everyone else. But I warn you – this is a chance for you to make something of yourself. Play us false and we will send you to the pig farm down on the heath where you will be one of many mucking out and living with the other lads, sleeping on straw and with little future."

Hal mumbled a reply that sounded like acceptance, wandered off to play what he promised himself would be his last prank. He eyed one of the young gardeners who was using a pitchfork to load piles of cut long grass onto a barrow. He had an idea.

CHAPTER XVI

Colonel Larkin, wrapped up in many layers of clothing and covered by a huge cloak against the bitter cold, rode from his house to join the other three for Christmas dinner at Forbes' house. Despite the horrible weather – snow flurries, driving wind, freezing temperatures – he looked forward eagerly to the dinner with his established cronies. He had been without any real news for a month, getting his large house in order with cook and two young servants. He had made ample provision for them to enjoy their Christmas dinner in his absence.

Arrived at last, he shed the outer layers and joined the others in the parlour, warmed by a large fire and an equally large bumper of mulled wine. He slowly thawed out and was soon sprawled in a deep armchair with his toes slowly being toasted before the grate. He gave a contented sigh.

James Forbes bustled in with the news that dinner would be served in an hour from then. He also joined the others, making a very contented quartet. He turned to Colonel Fisher – always a fount of information. Fisher acknowledged the prompting with a loud 'harrumph'.

"Country's in bloody chaos!" he began, making no allowance for the presence of a clergyman. Forbes, well used to the bluff Colonel's method of speech, merely grinned.

"Most want the monarchy restored. Been several uprisings already. Lambert seems out of his depth. Rumours are that Monck and Fairfax are getting together to do something about it. Whether or not that will result in Charles being welcomed back is anyone's guess. London is in a state of near anarchy, screaming for new elections and a recall of the Rump parliament. God alone knows what is going to happen once the Christmas festivities are over!"

Having been without news of any description for weeks, Larkin was anxious to learn more about the investigation he had been involved with.

"And is there any news about the outcome of the Percival affair?" he asked.

"Oh, indeed!" Fisher boomed. "My sources have informed me of the entire outcome of that disgraceful affair. It seems that Percival went to his death as silent as the grave into which he was dumped. Those other three – Preece, Duplessis, and Bruce. Well, Preece was executed for the murder, as was right and fitting. That damned Frenchie Duplessis was also executed for instigating and arranging the murder. Again, right and fitting. However, the Scotsman Bruce – well, he was another matter entirely. He made a very subtle bargain with his inquisitors. In exchange for his information, he was sentenced to indefinite imprisonment. And now, I suppose you want to hear what he had to divulge?"

"Not only our esteemed colleague, but Kent and I are also itching with impatience," Forbes chuckled. "Although I fear what he divulged will not be to my liking!"

"It appeared from his testimony that there was a small gathering in Scotland that was involved to a major degree. They had in mind some distant Spanish relative of the Stuarts who they wanted seated upon our throne. A devout Catholic no less. As for that Abbe Justin – seemingly secure in his bolthole in Rouen, he had a direct line of access to Louis – whom they are now referring to as The Sun King. Bloody impertinence! Anyway, to cut this story short, groups of agents were sent clandestinely to both Scotland and to Rouen. The five major players in Scotland suddenly perished in a mysterious house fire. Justin and two of his cohorts were shot as they processed together from a meeting towards the large house where they were living. So, my friends, the plot failed and is no more. Even Louis, parading in his finery, will have got that message loud and clear."

"Then I feel entirely justified in my part of the exercise," Larkin breathed a sigh of relief.

"And I am relieved also that there is no other contender for the throne," Forbes gave a quiet smile. "I suppose that, as a man of the cloth, I should deplore the taking of so many lives. But the plot involved a degree of wickedness that I cannot forgive."

"And now, onwards to more harmonious topics," Kent was determined to lighten the mood. "My home in the town is now running smoothly. May I suggest that we four convene a monthly meeting, taking it in turns to be the host?"

"I heartily second that proposal," Larkin nodded. "My house is near as dammit to being ready for entertaining. I would be very glad to be a host."

"As would I," Fisher nodded.

"Excellent!" Forbes beamed around the room at his three guests. "Our dinner is almost ready. May I further suggest that, not only do we meet on a regular basis, but that we name ourselves The Sane And Sensible."

"The Sane And Sensible!" Four glasses were raised in a toast.

A similar gathering was being held at Brimley – on a far more populous basis. Gathered in the large main hall were Peter and Laura Cove, the current principal occupants. They were acting as hosts. Their son Harry, along with his wife Mary and their two children, Will and Peterkin, were joined by the steward Luke Farmer, his wife Meg and their son Hal. Down in the large kitchen, the staff were gathered around a large table partaking of their own Christmas dinner. In the main hall, punch was being drunk, along with mulled wine. The noise of chatter was deafening.

Peter Cove, now fifty-one years of age, took a large knife and hammered the hilt of it on the table to still the noise.

"My dear family and friends," he spoke when silence had descended. "This is the first Christmas we have enjoyed in this wonderful house. But let us never forget the one person who made all of this possible. I ask you to raise your glasses to Lady Violette Charlton – may she enjoy eternal peace and rest."

The toast was drunk in respectful silence, followed by a longer silence as each remembered the old lady, some offering a silent prayer for her eternal repose.

"And now, let us sit down for dinner," Laura added. "That is, of course, if Hal has not engineered some diabolical mischief!"

"I would not do such a thing!" young Hal stated. "I am an apprentice blacksmith and am beyond such antics!"

"That I shall believe when the entire world freezes over!" Meg his mother declared.

In the main house at Parke, another gathering was taking place. This one, hosted by Luke Barton, the longtime steward. He and his wife Grace had lived there ever since they had been appointed some thirty years previously. Hob, his wife May and their two little daughters Kitty and Poppy, were sitting around in a group, listening to Grace Barton telling them a story of a Christmas many years before.

Maud Fletcher, May's unmarried sister, sat quietly on the outskirts of the group, bound up as usual in quiet contemplation. May often expressed her deep concern for her sister. Maud had rebuffed every young man who had ever come near her, not that she was happy in her isolation. She had never come to terms with the loss of her parents who had been taken from her during the previous winter sickness. Now nearly nineteen years of age, she took in darning and sewing, assisted daily at the bakery, and still managed to maintain the small family cottage. She seemed destined for a life of spinsterhood. She spoke rarely, and then almost in monosyllables. May was determined that, somehow or other, she would break through the defensive shell.

One other very large Christmas gathering was held at the large parlour behind the smithy. Abel and Faith, Simon, his wife Imelda, Jack and Rachael their children, were joined by Gil, Ella, Rosie and Jamie.

Jack, just over nine years old, was desperately trying to inveigle Jamie, one year older, to join him in a prank to be played upon the tavern the following day. Twelve-year-old Rosie and Rachael, a mere eight, were just as determined to deter their brothers from such a rash undertaking. Dick and Sal Allen at the tavern would seek drastic measures as the prank would inevitably be discovered and the miscreants easily identified.

Simon, well aware of his son's ability to endeavour to outdo the practices of Hal – who seemed to have turned over a new leaf – was well able to hear the muttered plans. He reached out a massive hand and grabbed his son by the collar.

"If I hear one more word about this proposed prank, I shall send you to your room and you shall not eat one mouthful of this wonderful dinner. Do you understand me?"

"Er, yes, father," Jack looked upwards to see the determined face glowering down at him.

"And Jamie – disregard whatever this young oaf has been telling you. Stay well clear of his pranks. Your own father will have something to say on the matter if you take even the smallest part!"

"Aye, that I will!" Gill gave his son a fierce glare.

The tavern was destined to pass the next day - Saint Stephen's Day - in relative peace, undisturbed by childish pranks.

James and Avril Ramsey had opted for a very quiet Christmas with only Nell for company. Nell read aloud the letter she had received only two days before. She had already read it many times to herself. It was the latest in a string of letters she had received from Adam since he had left for Saltash. Each time she had received one, she had read it to James and Avril, effectively her foster parents since she had been orphaned at the age of just over four.

"My dearest Nell," she started reading, leaving nothing out. "Things are not going to plan. No, that is not exactly true – things *are* going to plan – it is the timescale that is stretching out interminably. Father, who is probably the most astute man of business I have ever encountered, seems to understand the reason – so I shall try my best to explain it to you in his own words. The country is in a state of chaos; nobody seems to know from one moment to the next who is in charge of things so, nothing is done, no decisions are being made. Trade depends entirely on a state of certainty, and there is none of that commodity anywhere in either Westminster or in the large cities. Father says that in a state of chaos like the one we currently experience, a prudent man does little or nothing other than what he knows best. In other words, neither expand nor contract; take on no new ventures but concentrate solely on what you know has worked satisfactorily for years.

As I told you before we left, Father's intention is to open an office in Newton Abbot, take on two more cargo vessels, then join the venture that ships granite to wherever it is required. It is a solid venture. Now – progress so far. We have, via a land agent, taken the lease on the new office in Newton Abbot. This was accomplished in early November. Since then, things have sunk into the mire and all new ventures are being held in abeyance until there again is a proper parliament making proper decisions. We have since then taken options on two very good cargo vessels, but will certainly not finalise the purchase – or, indeed, proceed with the venture – until things again settle down.

Father is now convinced that the inevitable result of all the chaos is that Prince Charles will be invited back. Once again, a country with a king. Neither he nor I are enamoured with the prospect. We were staunch supporters of the Commonwealth as it existed under Cromwell. There was stability and certainty. However, since his death, things have slipped from muddle into utter chaos. Rumours persist that Generals Monck and Fairfax will soon become so exasperated that they will oust Lambert and his military and recall a proper parliament. That is our fondest hope. Should this happen, then rest assured that we will proceed apace with the whole plan.

Your letters to me are my greatest joy. They are the glimmer of light in an otherwise dark existence. I miss you more than I would ever have thought possible. No matter what occurs, it is my intention to come for a visit in the next two weeks. Ostensibly, of course, I shall be inspecting the new office and the manner in which the business may be conducted – once things return to normal. However, my main reason as you might imagine, is once again to see you and to forget for a short while the frustrations of this state of nothingness. Until then, I assure you of my love. Your devoted Adam."

"That young man could well be a writer of some distinction," James gave Nell a grin. "That letter, like all its predecessors, is an example of grammatical exactitude, as well as being highly informative."

Avril had another aspect of the letter on her mind.

"Leaving aside business ventures, parliament, and all this chaos – what are your feelings towards this erudite young man?"

"I miss him terribly," Nell admitted. "When I was with him, I felt truly alive. I cannot wait until he comes to visit."

"Is that an admission that you have love for him?" Avril asked quietly.

"It is so strange," Nell mused aloud. "How is it possible to grow to love someone when he is not even here?"

"And do you love him?"

"Yes – I honestly believe that I do. I shall know for certain the moment I set eyes on him again. I shall know whether I greet him as a wonderful friend – or as the man with whom I wish to spend the rest of my life."

"If it is to be that latter, then both Avril and I thank the Good Lord that you will be not too far distant. We shall come regularly to visit you and you shall always be welcomed here as our daughter."

It was two days after the Feast of Stephen that Cuthbert and Honor Hopkins came to take up residence in a cottage mid-way up the main street. Things were indeed set to change.

CHAPTER XVII

The New Year of 1660 was just four days old when the weather took a turn for the better and matters in the town took a turn for the worse. Very unseasonal sunshine bathed South Devon in warmth, rain and snow clouds disappeared, the breeze was gentle. People strode out with purpose, no longer huddled inside warm cloaks, bent against the biting wind. Gil and Ella were again able to turn the soil of their vegetable beds, much to the annoyance of Rosie and Jamie who were cajoled into helping catch up with the necessary manual work. School was to reopen the next week, so there was no excuse for non-compliance.

Young Hal had settled into *his* apprenticeship at the smithy. He had started to develop muscles from constant pumping the bellows, hefting very heavy lumps of iron, and fetching and carrying the myriad tools. He and young Jack got on very well together, albeit with some friendly rivalry.

John and Evelyn at the bakery sweated at their ovens, Dick and Sal sweated in the tavern's kitchens. Even James, Avril and Nell at the apothecary shop worked with shutters, doors and windows wide open.

"We shall suffer for this," James predicted. "Who ever heard of working in this way in January? It is not natural, and we shall pay dearly when the season returns with a vengeance!"

Bovey Tracey, Parke and Brimley went about life with a smile and a laugh – except in one small cottage half-way up the main street. That cottage had its shutters closed and its upstairs windows cloaked in dark curtains. The inhabitants, the newcomers Cuthbert and Honor Hopkins spent frugally on food, said little or nothing to anyone, spent most of their time indoors. Had they but known it, they were taking over where Hubert and Mercy Green had left off some years before. Hubert had been taken with a winter fever; Mercy had taken passage to the New World along with others of a serious Puritan bent. Their bookshop had been bought by the Huguenot family, the Bessants.

The son, Gaston now ran it with his wife Glory, the daughter of the Allens in the tavern. Bessant father and mother had also been victims of a severe winter fever.

Cuthbert and Honor were radicals – religious radicals. Every waking moment was spent in either work, contemplation, or prayer. They asked for nothing except forgiveness – forgiveness for their multitude of sins. These did not include murder, incest, arson, theft or anything serious enough to be punished by hanging. These sins were sins of omission – not praying hard enough, not working hard enough, eating one mouthful too many, sleeping beyond cockcrow. Most people did these things as a matter of course and it never occurred to them that they were doing anything incorrect. Not so the Hopkins! To them, these were absolutely unforgiveable. Not for them a laugh and a joke. Frivolity was a serious sin. Life was hard, full of drudgery – and rightly so.

For some days, they had endured the laughter and capering of the children playing in the street, the laughter and jokes of the parents (who should have known better!). As for the ribald behaviour when the tavern closed for the evening, well – by rights these people should have been struck down by bolts of heavenly wrath.

Cuthbert had not long since been the beneficiary under a will of a distant relative, leaving him with funds sufficient to buy a cottage and the means to live frugally. He spent his days writing religious tracts – mostly concerned with the wages of sin. He and Honor then copied them onto small sheets to be distributed throughout the neighbourhood. So far, there had been no response to the first of them.

The one nailed to the door of the church had been blown into the mud of a field, unread and hence ignored. Others, poked through doors, had been seized upon as excellent lighting material for fires. Not one had been read. Most had glanced at the heading and had screwed it up with a grunt or a 'pah' of annoyance.

That day, being a day blessed with sun and unseasonal warmth, prompted a larger gathering than normal of children playing with hoops and whipping tops. The noise eventually sent Cuthbert into a fit of rage. He hurled down his pen and strode out into the street. At least twenty children were having a great time, laughing and cavorting around. Cuthbert stood at his open door and felt the rage burning up inside him.

"Silence!" he bellowed. "Have you no respect? Have you no sense of decency? Children should be hard at work, either studying or helping their parents. They should *not* be making noise and disturbing God's peace. Go to your homes this instant and pray for forgiveness!"

"Sod off, you old misery!" came from somewhere to his right. He glared at the boy – a lad with bright red hair and a face covered in freckles.

"And get your father to wash out your foul mouth with soap! Begone, the lot of you!"

"Piss off!" came the response to that.

Cuthbert, enraged beyond breaking point, reached inside the front door and emerged with a blackthorn stick. He made straight for the lad, stick raised.

"Strike that child and I shall march you straight to the town lock-up!" came an authoritative voice from lower down the street. He glared at the newcomer with fury.

"And who are you to tell me not to discipline this hooligan?" he demanded.

"Hob Slater – Deputy Bailiff!" came the reply from the twenty-three-year-old. "I order you to drop that stick immediately!"

"I take no orders from such as you. I shall discipline this unruly child as I see fit!"

"Children – go to your homes and leave this to me," Hob ordered quietly. Within a minute, the street contained only one enraged Cuthbert and a quietly determined Hob. The Deputy Bailiff approached and stood within touching distance.

"I told you to drop that stick!" he said very quietly.

"I am about the Lord's work. There shall be silence as I do so!" came the shouted response.

"Dear Lord above – Hubert Green arisen from the dead!" Hob muttered to himself, having as a young boy been on the receiving end of that fanatic's wrath. "I give not one fig what you are about," he retorted. "Whether you are on the Lord's work or merely standing there picking your nose. You will *not* threaten little children. Now – do as I say, drop that stick and go indoors."

Goaded beyond reason, Cuthbert Hopkins raised the stick, ready to bring it down onto Hob's head. Had it made contact, it would have resulted in serious injury. But it did not land. Hob simply hopped sideways, stretched out a foot and tripped Cuthbert into a heap in the road. He placed the other foot firmly on the hand that held the stick.

"Well," he managed a grin." Now you really have annoyed me. Attacking an official with deadly intent – I shall have to see whether I shall have you locked up for a bit. I shall report to the Bailiff, and then see what happens."

"I saw it all and can be your witness," came a voice from across the street. Lou Crowley stood at the door to her cottage. "The children were doing no harm – simply playing and enjoying the sunshine. That man came bursting out with his stick and threatened to beat young Horace. He is exactly as Horace said – a miserable old sod!"

Lou, a widow and the mother of Matt Crowley, had adopted a little baby named Felix that Hob had himself found abandoned some years before. She was acknowledged as an honorary auntie to many of the children of the town.

"I seem to remember many similar happenings when the Greens were living here at the bookshop. Surely, we have not been saddled with another pair like them!" Hob grimaced.

"Aye, Hubert and Mercy Green. Mayhap this was just one incident and will not be repeated," Lou said, fingers crossed.

"Somehow, I doubt that," Hob grunted. "I also remember when I was a wild, young lad, putting slugs on their doorstep and a dead frog through their window,"

"There was also a rumour that a dead frog magically appeared in Gil's and Ella's wedding bed," Lou laughed.

"Now, who would sink so low as to carry out such a disgraceful prank? Hob, grinning at his younger self, strode off down the street to report what he had witnessed to Harry. Cuthbert Hopkins slammed his front door and stormed into the parlour to report all that had happened to his wife. Honor, in sombre black from head to foot, was equally appalled.

"We shall have to redouble our efforts," she stated in her usual gravelly voice. "The people of this wretched place have urgent need of our messages."

Cuthbert, only slightly less belligerent, had the beginnings of doubt creeping into his mind. He sensed that they would be met with fierce opposition, especially from those who exercised a dubious control. However, undaunted, he sat down at his desk and started to pen a vitriolic message of hellfire and damnation.

The following day the weather was slightly even more benign in that the breeze dropped to a mere whisper and the temperature rose another notch. Once again, school having not yet recommenced, the town was entertained to choruses of childish laughter and games. But these were kept away from the vicinity of the Hopkins cottage. Even the ebullient Horace deemed it wise to keep a distance.

Nevertheless, the noise of laughter penetrated into the cottage, causing both Cuthbert and Honor to growl at what they deemed an unholy disturbance. But the happenings of the previous day gave them pause to sally forth and do something about it.

A slightly different disturbance happened down at the apothecary shop. James and Avril were busy in the shop preparing pastilles and serving a customer when a horse clopped up the street from the crossroads, stopped and was tethered to a post outside the shop. Avril glanced up expecting to see just another customer.

"Nell," she called over her shoulder into the parlour where Nell was poring over a pile of unpaid accounts. "You have a visitor."

Hoping against hope that it was Adam, Nell hurried past the customer in the shop and stopped in the threshold. It was indeed Adam, and his appearance brought on a feeling of joy mixed with a sudden dose of acute shyness.

"Hello, Adam," she managed.

"Do I not merit some warmer welcome?" Adam said, suddenly apprehensive.

With a shake of her shoulders, Nell broke into a broad smile, went down the two steps and into his waiting arms. "Is this a warm enough greeting?" she asked.

The few people about, including the customer in the shop – not to mention James and Avril, were entranced by the sight of two young people so obviously happy to see one another.

"Nell," James called out. "Fetch your shawl and go for a walk. Those accounts can wait until after dinner."

Adam, Nell's hand in his, walked with her back to the crossroads and then up the lane that led to Lustleigh. When they were out of sight, he sat Nell down on a fallen tree trunk, they sat beside her.

"This is far better than a letter," he grinned. "I arrived yesterday at the new office in Newton – see, I even call it by its local name! Everything is in perfect order. All that now remains is for matters to settle down and we shall start the new venture in earnest. I rode over here at the first opportunity as I could not wait to see you."

"And now that you see me, what do you think?" Nell had regained her composure and was determined to find out face to face what his feelings were.

"What do I think? I think that we have been apart for far too long. I think that I have missed you terribly. I think that I love you more than ever. That's what I think."

"Ah – but thoughts are less than firm intentions," Nell was determined to keep matters light. "And what do you believe are my thoughts?"

"As to that, I have desperate hopes that you think as I do. Am I right or am I wrong?"

"You are right on two points at least. One – I have missed you. I feel truly alive when I am with you. Two – I agree that we have been apart for much too long."

"Then that at least is a good start. But we come to point three, do we not? Have you developed a love for me?"

Nell looked down at the ground at her feet, scared at what she might next say, worried in case she made a wrong decision. She looked up into Adam's open and honest face. She made her decision.

"Yes, Adam – I have indeed developed a love for you," she said, almost trembling at her words.

Adam said nothing for a while, simply looked at Nell at his side. Then, very gently, he planted a kiss on her lips. "I could have hoped for nothing better," he said quietly. He was well aware of Nell's history and had a sudden idea. He stood up, held out his hand for her to stand beside her.

"We have a visit to make," he said, leading her back to the shop. Instead of going inside, he hoisted Nell onto his horse and led it quietly up the street to the church where he lifted her down and made for the churchyard.

"Show me where lies your father," he said.

Nell led him to the corner where a single bunch of early snowdrops adorned a grave. Adam looked at the stone and read the words. He reached for Nell's hand.

"Master Hal Dawkins. I stand here with your beautiful daughter and ask your blessing on what I am about to say to her. I give you and Nell my solemn promise to honour her, to respect her and to care for her as you would wish. I will never do or say anything that will harm her. Nell – I love you with my whole being. Will you consent to be my wife?"

Nell was so moved at this unforeseen gesture that she was struck dumb for a few moments. Then, raising her face to Adam's, she knew that what she was about to say was absolutely right.

"Yes, Adam – I consent to be your wife."

"Then, even in this hallowed place, I shall seal that with a kiss – the first of many thousands."

They stood side by side, looking down at the grave. Then Nell blew her usual kiss to her dada and led Adam back to the street. In silence, they walked together back to the shop to break the news over dinner.

In the field opposite the church, Matt Crowley and Herb Grindley put the finishing touches to a couple of very large barrels that had been ordered by a brewer in Ashburton. Having satisfied themselves that the barrels were watertight, they stopped for their own dinner.

"Well," Herb grunted as he spooned soup into his mouth. "We have heard nothing from Taunton. Perhaps that wretched man has indeed given up."

Matt swallowed a mouthful of fresh bread and ruminated. "Do you know, I have sincere doubts on that score," he muttered. "Did he strike you as one who would simply fade away and do nothing?"

"But he no proof at all that we were responsible," Herb argued. "If he did anything, he would be deemed to be in the wrong. Harry said as much to him. No, we are safe from any reprisal."

"But what is to stop him from doing what we did to him?" Matt argued. "If we can destroy his business and leave no trace of proof against us, what is to stop him doing the same? After all, he never struck me as an idiot!"

"What we did was in response to what he attempted to do to us," Herb retorted. "He struck the first blow – we did not!"

"Aye – that is true enough. But he was unsuccessful. We were totally successful in destroying his entire business. There is no way that we would allow such an action to go unpunished! So, why should he?"

"Then, if that be so, how may we defend ourselves?" Herb was getting slightly apprehensive at the force of Matt's argument.

"A dog!" Matt had a sudden idea. "If we had a dog here, the mutt would hear and sense someone prowling about. Now – where might we obtain one that is amenable to training?"

"None better than a sheep dog," Herb grinned at the idea. "Let us seek down on the Heath. There are many flocks thereabout."

"Better still, what about young Bernie Wheatcroft, the shepherd at Parke. He will certainly know where one may be obtained. And he will know whether or not the dog is suitable."

"You seem to know him better than I," Herb stated. "Why do you not seek him out this very afternoon?"

"But he may be miles distant," Matt observed. "Parke has extensive fields where his flock may be grazing. I may be away for many hours."

"It was your idea," Herb grimaced. "So, go and fulfil it!"

James and Avril watched as the two young people came back to the shop, hitched the horse again, then walked hand in hand into the shop.

"Do not tell us, let us guess," Avril gave a peal of laughter as the two stood looking a bit sheepish.

"Er, Nell has agreed to become my wife," Adam stuttered.

"Then James and I wish you nothing but a life of happiness," Avril hugged them both. "It has taken someone very special to break through that shell that Nell has grown about her. Welcome, Adam."

"Aye, indeed, welcome," James gave Nell a kiss on her cheek and exchanged a firm handshake with Adam. "Let us close up a bit early and eat our dinner – when you can tell us all about your plans."

"Plans? We have none at present," Nell admitted.

"Then it is just as well that James and I are probably the best planners in Bovey – perhaps the best in the whole of Devon."

"I have a feeling, Adam, that our future is about to be drawn up on paper in diagrams, down to the smallest detail," Nell laughed.

"Aye, that is precisely what my own father would do," Adam nodded.

"Oh – your father. Has he any knowledge of what you intended?" Nell gasped.

"To settle your mind on that score, he not only knows, but is delighted that I have chosen a wife who he regards as a jewel, a prize beyond price."

"That is simply because I diagnosed his problem and sorted it out for him!" Nell argued.

"You really have no idea the impression you give, do you?" Adam. "You did far more than just diagnose; you gave peace of mind – and that is worth far more!"

"Before this young lady expires from embarrassment – or indeed gets a swollen head – come in and join us at dinner. And then I have to insist that Nell returns to those accounts, many of which are becoming overdue!"

By mid-afternoon, the news had inevitably spread throughout the town, encouraging many residents to call into the shop on the pretence of needing some medicament for unspoken minor ailments. Nell had waved Adam off after dinner for his ride back to Newton Abbot. He promised he would visit regularly – if only to keep an eye on the plan that Avril was determined should be all-encompassing.

By nightfall, three things had happened. Matt and Herb were the proud owners of a young sheepdog. They had made a small wooden bed for the creature, upholstered with old blankets. The dog, which they named Spotty as he had white spots about his muzzle, seemed quite content to prowl about the barn, lap from his bowl of water, and gnaw at some large bones obtained from the butcher. The two conducted an experiment. They stayed quietly in the barn with the doors firmly closed whilst young Jack – whom they had briefed – crept silently up to the barn. Spotty raised his head from his paws and growled. Success!

Cuthbert and Honor Hopkins went to bed quietly satisfied with their afternoon and evening work. A pile of handwritten papers stood ready on the parlour table to be delivered to as many doors as possible the following morning. They planned to be up well before sunrise so that they could deliver them well before most people were up and about. The message that they had laboriously copied was, in their opinion, written is such a manner as to awaken all who read it to the perils of this life and its temptations.

'Beware the temptations of the flesh; beware the temptations of the table; beware the temptations of strong drink. Above all, beware the temptation to allow your children to do other than learn to serve the Lord in everything they do. Gone must be the noise and disturbance. God's holy silence is a blessing to be revered, not abused with wild noises! Pray quietly in your homes. Idolatrous churches are not for you. Stay pure and you will reap the reward of eternal salvation. Follow any other path and you are damned for all eternity!"

Nell paid another visit to her father's grave before going back home for supper and bed. "Dada, have I done the right thing? I just about remember you telling me about my mother – how you and she were so happy together. Shall I be as happy? Adam gives every indication of being a good man, honest and true. But I am still a little apprehensive of what is to come. Perhaps most maids think as I do, although I know of some who are happy enough to be maids no longer! Pray for me, dada, as I pray for you and the mother I never knew, every day of my life."

Nell awoke the next morning, very surprised to find that she had slept extremely well. She had fully expected to lie awake for most of the night, thoughts a-jumble in her head. Maybe, she wondered, my ability to sleep like that is a good omen, that I am content with my future.

The next day saw a return to typical winter weather. Rain sheeted down from the west; strong winds whistled down from the moor. Outside work of every description was impossible – and would have been time wasted should anyone have attempted it. Fires were heaped with precious fuel, children arrived for the first day of school thoroughly wet and miserable. Sheep down on the Heath and in surrounding fields, huddled together against hedgerows and Devon stone walls.

CHAPTER XVIII

The month of January had just four days remaining; the people of the South-West could not wait to see the back of it. January had been, after the first few balmy days, wet, cold and decidedly miserable. The previous autumn's harvest had been good, so there had been enough to see most people through. But a wet February would start to put a severe strain on supplies. Even Gil and Ella, secure on their smallholding, were hard put to it to get out for brief periods for hoeing, planting and general husbandry.

Mary had struggled with school as most of the children were inevitably late arriving and necessarily early in leaving. She had been hard put to keep their attention, despite the warmth of the classroom where a large fire burned constantly.

Colonel Fisher, warm and bored to distraction in his cottage, was very surprised to receive a flying visit from a messenger on his way from Exeter to Bodmin. The news that he brought was enough for the old Colonel to defy the weather, don his finest weatherproof cloak, and ride through mud and flowing water to his friend in the Bovey Rectory.

"Somehow or other, a message must be sent to gather the entire group as soon as maybe," he announced as he dripped puddles upon the rectory hallway.

"Kent is easiest as he is at the tavern," James Forbes muttered. "However, getting a message to Larkin will need a short journey. Is the meeting so urgent?"

"Indeed, it most certainly is. Pray forgive me not telling of it straightaway as it is complex and needs telling just the once."

It was not until late that afternoon that the whole Sane and Sensible group was gathered around a blazing fire, sipping this time a fine Rhenish wine and nibbling on seed cake.

"Well, here goes!" Fisher looked around to see three eager faces looking back at him. "This very morning I received word about the happenings in Westminster. It would appear that Monck and Fairfax marched on London just two days past.

Lambert rode out to face him with his army at his back. Unfortunately for him, Lambert then reaped the harvest of his failure to pay his troops properly for many months past – they simply melted away and left him virtually defenceless. He is now languishing in the Tower. Monck is at this moment recalling the Rump Parliament. It would appear that soon we shall have representatives again sitting in the chamber. The common feeling is that Charles will be invited back very soon. Well, those are the bare bones of the information I received. James will no doubt be cock-a-hoop. For my part, I am relieved that Monck is again in virtual control, although he will no doubt transfer that control to Mister Speaker – whoever that may turn out to be. Although I have been a soldier all of my adult life, I have no liking for a military dictatorship – as that was what Lambert effectively achieved.”

“I second that sentiment,” Larkin nodded thoughtfully. “This country has never been content without the stability of an elected parliament – or has not been since one was properly established. However, that may mean, as you say, the return of a king sitting on a throne. How can we be sure that curbs on that regal power are effective? We all saw the utter chaos when Charles’ father insisted on his right to divine rule. That can never be repeated!”

“Constitutional Monarchy!” Matthew Kent spoke for the first time, raising eyebrows at his sudden utterance. He grinned at them. “That is what must surely come about,” he went on. “A king as the head of state, with a parliament making and passing the laws.”

“That would make any king into a mere puppet!” Larkin argued.

“No, not at all,” Kent was seeing far into the future if he had but known it. “The king would retain the right to call parliament, to examine its proposed legislation, to question, but never to refuse assent.”

“Next, you will be calling for a drastic enlargement of the franchise!” Fisher grunted.

“And why ever not?” Kent countered. “At present, the only ones with a vote are those with holdings in land. How about the yeoman farmers who hold smaller parcels under their landlords?

Do they not have a right to make their view known? After all, without them, this country would starve!"

"But they already have access to those same landlords, who may well use their votes to represent their own tenants," Fisher argued.

"Oh, come on, Colonel! You know as well as I that any vote cast by a landlord will represent his own interests! Those of his tenants will come a very poor second."

"And how about the women and children? Are we to have every single person in the land casting votes? Such a system would be unworkable at best and utterly disruptive at worst!"

Kent was not going to have his idea ploughed under a mountain of argument. "Let us take one simple example. Master Abel Smith is a mature and extremely sane individual. He makes the best ironwork for miles around. He pays his tithes faithfully and serves the town and the estate properly. Why therefore, is he not capable of thought beyond the confines of this small town? Why is he not thought competent to think larger matters through? And if he be so, why is he not to have any say in who represents him?"

"But he is already represented by his own landlord!" Fisher shot back. "What more safeguard does he need?"

"Colonel, you know as well as I. His own landlord rarely makes an appearance here. He is certainly not cognisant of the problems of the estate as he is almost never here to be told of them. And, even if he were, would he feel even the slightest need to make those problems known in Parliament? Bailiff Cove and Steward Barton know a hundred times more than he does. And have they a vote? No, of course they have not!"

"But they are servants of their master!" Fisher was not going to lose the argument without a fight. "On that basis, my own cook and houseboy would have a vote!"

"And why should they not? Are they not also people with rights?"

"We seem to have nurtured a radical in our midst," Forbes laughed. "But Matthew does have a very good point. There are many in this country who do the work, see the problems, work out for themselves the right answers – and they are seldom those who lord it over their estates. Their knowledge and acumen should be acknowledged, not kept in silence!"

"Even though I was a soldier and a servant of parliament, I have to admit that I see some distinct merit in Matthew's view of things," Larkin was forced to admit.

"Before we delve even further into the semantics of power, let us have a vote on the statement – that the Sane and Sensible welcome the return of Parliament," Forbes assumed the chair.

That vote was passed four to nil.

"And now upon the statement that the Sane and Sensible welcome the idea of a return of Charles as King."

"Can't support that without a rider that it is welcomed under proper and restrictive terms!" Fisher growled.

"And who is to state the nature of those terms?" Forbes passed the ball back.

"I shall!" Fisher insisted. "None of this divine right nonsense; no return to Rome under any circumstances; no veto of legislation already agreed by parliament."

"That I can agree," Larkin spoke quietly. "My vote is 'aye'.

"And mine," Kent nodded.

"Well, I suppose that accords with my own thoughts," Forbes admitted. "So, the Sane and Sensible agree with a return to proper parliament and a return of a king with those restrictions placed upon his power. And now, let us turn our thoughts to lamb chops and minted vegetables. A supper will soon await us."

It took Avril a mere two days to present Nell with a very detailed plan for the wedding and the wedding feast. Much to James' amusement – and Nell's frustration – Avril spent those two days almost secreted in the parlour with paper, inks of various colours, and a screen around her to keep prying eyes away. James and Nell were perforce kept unusually busy with preparation of medicines and pills, seeing customers, advising on treatments, and generally keeping the business running.

On the evening of the twenty-ninth of January 1660, Avril spread four sheets of paper across the table and deigned to allow Nell and James to survey the results of her labours. James was secretly amused and proud of his wife's ability to concentrate upon the minutest detail. Nell was overwhelmed.

"I am sure that Adam never in his wildest dreams considered such an elaboration!" she exclaimed as the enormity of the event proposed was outlined in four different coloured inks. "I certainly did not! I truly believed that I would meet Adam at the porch, make our vows to one another, then proceed into the church for the service – and then retire to the tavern for a simple meal of celebration."

Avril threw up her hands in horror. "There is nothing *simple* about two young people becoming wed," she gasped. "It is the greatest moment in your life – and one that must proceed without even the slightest hitch. To achieve that, every smallest detail needs to be anticipated and planned so that one event proceeds smoothly to the next."

"But that simply makes it sound like an order of battle!" Nell argued. "I can well appreciate a general needing to plan in such a manner, but this is just another marriage."

"Oh, for the love of all the angels and saints!" Avril was getting exasperated. "It is not just another marriage. It is *your* marriage!"

"Aye – I am well aware that it is unique in that respect. But surely it cannot need such minute detail. For an example, why does it matter when the groom arrives at the church to await my coming? As long as he is there some time *before* I arrive, that is enough!"

"And that is why you need such as I to plan the whole thing! It matters because his groomsman needs the requisite time to ensure that the groom is correctly attired, for the rector to brief him on the correct procedure of greeting his bride. These things cannot be properly accomplished in a few minutes!"

"Cromwell could have done with you when planning his battles," James grinned at his wife. "Bullets to be in sufficient number at the correct places at the correct time; Halberds and swords sharpened to the correct degree at least a day before the battle! Muskets cleaned and oiled by nine in the morning!"

"You may both scoff as much as you like!" Avril retorted. "But on the day, you will be grateful that someone has planned it in proper detail. After all, you cannot want something serious to go awry and thus spoil the occasion!"

"Please do not misunderstand me," Nell was quick to reassure Avril that she was indeed grateful. She had always regarded Avril as the mother she had never known – and James as her foster-father. "I am indeed truly grateful for your concern. I am sure that, on the day itself, we shall both be eternally grateful for your planning. But may we first of all decide *when* this is all to take place?"

"Did not Adam say that he needs to have the new venture established first so that he may then concentrate entirely upon the marriage and not be concerned that the business itself is running smoothly?" James reminded them.

"Aye, that he most certainly did," Nell spotted a way of diverting Avril from the minutiae of the plan. "And I agree with that concern. After all, that venture will form the basis of our security and wellbeing."

"And from what I gathered from his thoughts, that will be May at the very earliest," James added.

"May we await Adam's next visit?" Nell prompted. "He will be here on this coming Sunday. He may well be able to set a proper timetable by then."

"I shall *not* relinquish these plans," Avril gathered her papers into a tidy pile. "I shall keep them in readiness so that I may brief everyone on what he or she is to do, how it is to be done, and importantly when it is to be done. I shall never tolerate mistakes be laid at my door!"

"And that is that!" James grinned. Nell gave in with good grace. Avril gave a snort, then realised that she was being just a touch overbearing – and gave a soft laugh at herself.

School during the winter months ended at half past three in the afternoon. Some of the children had long walks home down onto the Heath. It was considered dangerous for them to make that walk in the dusk – or even the dark.

Mary, having deposited her children back at Parke, saddled her pony and rode out to Brimley for a meeting with Kent. He had pointed out that, as trustees, he and Mary had a duty to, at the very least, discuss the eventual disposal of the estate.

Harry's parents, Peter and Laura Cove, were spending that particular week on a much-delayed visit to Laura's married sister in Okehampton, so Kent and Mary used that opportunity to sit before the fire in the hall, eat cake and sup weak ale provided by Meg, shoo various children out of the hall, then sit down to the very necessary discussion.

"Remind me of the clause in the will," Mary prompted. Matthew pulled out the folded document and found the requisite paragraph.

"My appointed trustees shall at their discretion dispose of the entire estate of Brimley to whomsoever they shall regard as a trustworthy and deserving purchaser and shall divide the monetary proceeds from the sale according to the following stipulations. Three tenths shall be invested in the town school; two tenths shall be allocated to the provision of a library for the town; two tenths shall be held by the trustees for the maintenance of the poor and needy of the town; the remaining three tenths shall be given without restrictions as to use to my dearest friend Mary Cove. I place only one stipulation that the trustees shall be of one mind in selecting the eventual purchaser."

"My heart does a somersault every time that clause is read," Mary admitted. "I have already allocated the initial bequest to the maintenance of the school. With the three tenths of the sale proceeds, the school is provided for adequately – indeed, generously. What I may decide to do with all this money, I have no idea! There is more than enough to provide bursaries for every child for miles around!"

"But that aside, have you any thoughts concerning a prospective purchaser?" Kent asked. "After all, you are far more conversant with the people hereabouts that I am."

"Do we not have a duty to advertise?" Mary asked. "I have one person who just might be interested, but we cannot afford the charge of favouritism should we not seek a wider audience."

"Aye, I suppose you have the right of it," Kent nodded. "But on one thing I am determined – we shall *not* involve that damned Anstruther in any further discussions. His job ended with the grant of probate."

"You shall get no objection from me on that score. He is quite the most obnoxious man I have come across since Hubert Green departed this world."

"Aye – I have heard of him. But are you not aware that there is mooted to be a replacement for him in Cuthbert Hopkins? Apparently, according to the gossip I hear in the tavern, this Cuthbert is just as mean-spirited as Hubert ever was."

"I have indeed heard mutterings from some of the children. I just put it down to childish resentment at something that he had done or said that curtailed their high spirits."

"I fear, although I have no personal experience of the man, that he will prove just as troublesome a thorn in the side as his predecessor! However, we wander from the point. May I suggest that we seek out an honest lawyer in Newton or Ashburton – perhaps even Totnes. We shall certainly need one to write the contract for sale and to see it through."

"An honest lawyer? Does such a creature roam this earth?" Mary could not help a smile at her own words.

"Such cynicism from one so young!" Kent laughed. "I do take your point – but surely, there must be one somewhere!"

"Let me enquire at Parke," Mary suggested. "Luke Barton the steward has to my certain knowledge negotiated some legal business for the estate during his many years there."

"Then, may we reconvene this meeting when you have more information? And who, may I ask, is the person who you think may be interested?"

"Well, how about that young, retired Colonel – Paul Larkin? He has settled here and seems to have funds saved from his years of service."

"Saved funds, maybe," Kent argued. "But a sufficiency for the purchase of an estate the size of Brimley? He must have been thrifty indeed if that is the case!"

"You are better acquainted with him than I," Mary pointed out. "Is there any way you might probe the matter with him?"

"Oh, hello, Paul – have you enough money to buy Brimley? I hardly think that even I have the bare-faced effrontery for such an approach!"

"Matthew – you have more than sufficient delicacy to put the matter to him in a much more guarded manner. I would be surprised if he were not in a position to think seriously about it."

"And what, pray, draws you to that belief?"

Mary wriggled and had to admit that it was 'just a feeling' that she had. Kent, who had come to know and admire Mary for her wisdom and thought, certainly did not dismiss that 'feeling' out of hand. There could well, he knew, be some real substance in it.

"Then, in a very roundabout way, I shall endeavour to probe his thoughts. But I shall have to be extremely oblique – simply mention the need for a buyer in the general conversation."

"So – you approach the Colonel, and I shall probe Steward Barton. Shall we say the same time next week?"

CHAPTER XIX

Just to confound all predictions to the contrary, the month of February started with snow – not the deep, drifting snow of the moors but persistent small flurries that did nothing but annoy anyone planning any outdoor activity. Gil and Ella were particularly affected as they knew not from one minute to the next if they would be able to get one whole hour of weeding, turning soil, or digging in manure before having to flee indoors. Jamie, an observant and inquisitive ten years old, had his vocabulary enhanced as his father came and went.

That did not stop Adam doing as he had promised. He arrived in the late morning of the third day of the month resembling one of the snowmen that the children had erected on the Heath. People who relied on horses – and it was most folk who ventured further than five miles – made the horse their first consideration. Adam was no exception, stabling his horse at the remains of the old mill by the bridge. Some enterprising soul had erected a long shelter where horses could be left with hay to eat and water to drink. Having given his faithful mount a good rubbing down, Adam made his way up the street to the apothecary shop.

"Good grief! A snowy apparition to see you, Nell," James called.

Nell burst into a fit of giggles as she looked at Adam. "Come away in, but first shake all that snow off your cloak or you will never hear the end of it!" she greeted her betrothed.

Some minutes later, Adam was standing before the fire in the parlour emitting clouds of steam as the remainder of the snow slowly thawed. He was sufficiently warmed and dry a little later to accept very gratefully a mug of warmed ale.

"That was not the best journey I have ever undertaken," he gave a wry grin. "However, you may now believe that nothing would have stopped me from visiting my lovely wife to be."

Nell could not help blushing at this fulsome compliment but was quietly very happy to hear it. "May we talk things through over dinner?" she asked.

By the time the distant church clock chimed twelve, James had shut the shop and the four sat down to a warm and very welcome stew. Nell, eager to hear the latest news, prompted Adam who swallowed his mouthful before replying.

"It is better news than I had feared I might be bringing," he began. "Father joined me the other day to see progress for himself. The office is completely finished, as are the four rooms above it. We have a parlour, two bedrooms, and a kitchen. Neither of us would dare to decorate the rooms – that is for the new lady of the house to determine. As for the business, we have already purchased one of the ships and have entered into an agreement with the major dealer in the granite. Our ship – hopefully, two ships – will moor at the jetty and be loaded by the crane with granite blocks that arrive from the moor. We will have mooring charges to pay, also fees to pay for use of the crane, but there are so many customers for the stone that we will be hard pressed to choose between them. So, things have moved on very satisfactorily. Father and I anticipate that we shall take our first cargo at the end of this month, probably for an eager customer in London. Now – as to the finances of the business. At present, we have an agreement with the owner of the business that quarries the stone. He sells the stone to the end customer. He pays us for transporting the stone from Newton to London. Although we pay port charges at Newton, the customer has agreed to defray the port charges in London. We anticipate a high profit from each shipload – greater than we receive from shipping cargoes of wool. When we have both ships plying between Newton and London, we shall show a very tidy profit indeed!"

"So, Nell shall not be obliged to take in washing to provide bread for your table," Avril remarked.

"Indeed, she shall not!" Adam laughed. "However, I am fully aware that Nell will hardly be content with a life of leisure. I have not been idle on your behalf," he assured Nell. "There is more than ample room behind the office for Nell to open her own business. There are two physicians in the town, plus two apothecaries – and all of them need pills and potions prepared for their use. The fame of this apothecary is well respected, so Nell will be able to use her knowledge and skill to great advantage. All four people I have mentioned are keen – indeed, eager – to shed a part of their work to one whose skill is fully appreciated."

That was the one thing that had been preying on Nell's mind – what would she do with her time. There was no way she would have ever settled for the existence of a lady of leisure. It was not in her nature. The prospect of having her own small business was a huge load off her mind.

"I do believe that such an arrangement would suit our Nell very well," James acknowledged.

"Indeed, it most certainly would," Nell nodded. "And I am truly grateful for your kind thought and consideration."

"I cannot have my wife unhappy, can I?" Adam said in all seriousness. "Now – as to timing. I have already said that we plan to start shipping at the end of February – weather permitting, of course. We are both confident that the business will be running smoothly after another two months. Then, after that, I shall be able to devote my time to Nell. May I propose a date somewhere towards the end of May for our marriage?"

"That is nearly four months distant!" Nell objected.

"But I want to devote myself entirely to our wedding," Adam replied. "And I cannot in all honesty promise to do that any earlier. Besides, Nell has to come and see to the finishing of our home to her satisfaction – and that cannot be done quickly, knowing her insistence upon proper standards!"

"Aye, that is indeed true," Avril grinned at Nell. "I cannot envisage her being satisfied with anything less than utter perfection."

James had been doing some calculations. "It certainly cannot be early May – the May Day celebrations will occupy everyone's minds. Then there is the Spring Fair; everyone will be very busy at that – and we all know that a whole host of people will want to come to celebrate your wedding, Nell. May I suggest the twenty-fifth of May? All other celebrations will be over and done with by then, leaving every opportunity for as many as wish to, to attend the wedding of the year!"

Adam and Nell exchanged a look. Nell gave a slight nod.

"Then the twenty-fifth of May will be the date," Adam agreed. "I shall have to notify the church here to call the banns well in advance. It will give time for the business to start to flourish, Nell to finalise our home and to organise her attendants. Have you any idea who they may be?"

"Oh yes," Nell laughed. "And there shall be plenty of them, you may rest assured!"

"And I have to organise my groomsman. My cousin Alfred lives not too far distant in Totnes – and he has already agreed to carry out the duties. By heavens, it is all proceeding better than I had ever hoped!"

Adam rode his snowy way back to Newton Abbot when dinner had been concluded. Nell spent the afternoon making mistakes, her mind far away from pills and ointments.

By the fifth of the month the weather had done yet another of its unfathomable turnabouts – it was quite warm, the snow had turned to slush, and the roads and lanes were yet again in a filthy mess. However, as the sun shone fitfully, no one was grumbling too much – with the exception of those whose livelihoods depended upon constant travel.

The Sane and Sensible met again in mid-afternoon, this time in Kent's cottage where a fire was burning merrily, ale was warmed, and a massive fruit cake waited to be cut into slices. Matthew had ordered it the day before from the bakery, knowing that Evelyn Ramsey's cakes were known and relished for miles around.

"By heavens, young man – you have certainly made yourself comfortable here," Fisher looked around him and nodded in appreciation of the furniture, the wall hangings and the general air of homeliness.

"It suits my very modest needs," Kent replied, making sure his three colleagues were sitting comfortably and nursing large beakers of the warmed ale. "And now, has anyone news to impart?"

"This time, it is I who have the news," James Forbes acknowledged. "Only yesterday, news reached me from a travelling cleric on his way to Buckfastleigh where it is mooted that changes are to be made to the church there. What those changes are I have no idea as the news he started with eclipsed any inquisitiveness I may have had in ecclesiastical matters. It seems that, only three days ago, General Monck entered London and immediately set about the reinstatement of Parliament – the very same one that Lambert dismissed."

"So, the old Rump Parliament will again rule our lives," Larkin mused. "At this present moment, I have no idea whether this is a good or a bad thing!"

"Surely, it can be nothing but good," Forbes insisted. "Also, may it not herald the reinstatement of a king upon the throne?"

"Ah! That poses the same dilemma as Paul just voiced – will that be a good or a bad thing?" Kent took the sting out of that question with a wry smile.

"If I did not know you better," Forbes smiled back at Kent. "I would take that as a personal affront. Instead, I take the point you make. Charles, when I was his Chaplain, never seemed to me to be wholly enamoured with the idea of the goodness of God. He seemed to be far more interested in the goodness of his female attendants!"

"On that score, he already has sired a small army of illegitimate children, notably James Scott – or James Crofts as he was first known – born of Lucy Walter some eleven years ago. I wonder if, should Charles be reinstated as king, that he will eventually become known as James Fitzroy – son of the king?" Fisher pondered. "It would pose a pretty question should Charles die without legitimate offspring!"

"Then, the very first thing that *must* happen, should Charles be reinstated, is that a suitable wife must be found for him. Parliament will know without any prompting from outside that this is a dire necessity!" Larkin offered his thoughts.

"We are all assuming that a reinstatement is a fait accompli!" Kent laughed. "What if our newly reinstated Parliament does no such thing?"

"I suppose that such an eventuality *is* possible," Forbes grunted. "After all, Monck and Fairfax together are a formidable duo. They may indeed shy away from what would be, with the best will in the world, an experiment. But, on the whole, I cannot see it. No – Parliament is not so stupid as to ignore the feeling throughout the country that a restoration is what is wished."

"Then you and I have to be on our very best behaviour!" Larkin grinned across at Fisher. "Also, Matthew here as he was an agent for Cromwell's Parliament."

"My profile shall be as low as necessary," Fisher laughed.

"Then, may I record that The Sane and Sensible regard a restoration as necessary, inevitable and desirable?" Forbes made ready to pen the words.

"Inevitable, I suppose," Fisher acknowledged.

"Both inevitable and necessary as far as I am concerned," Kent voiced his thoughts.

"And I echo the words of Matthew," Larkin nodded.

"And I remain the lone voice calling for desirable," Forbes made the final note. "Now, any other business before we ask Matthew to slice that magnificent cake?"

"One matter that may be of interest," Kent seized the opportunity. "As you all know, Mary Cove and I are trustees for the estate left by dear Lady Violette. We have determined that it is right that the estate be offered for sale – and are in the process of instructing a solicitor to draw up the necessary contract. The availability for sale is to be made widely known in the next day or two." He watched intently to see whether this excited any interest other than mere curiosity.

"It cannot be allowed to fall into the wrong hands," Forbes growled. "That wonderful lady would be outraged were it to be so!"

"Oh, believe me, Mary and I shall be scrupulous when enquiring into the motives and background of any prospective purchaser," Kent assured them. "Luckily, we have a fund of knowledge hereabouts – people of proven reliability and honesty who have a deep knowledge of most folks – and that includes you, Reverend."

"Indeed, I know of some whom I would be most reluctant to see owning and probably desecrating what Violette created."

"We may have need to call upon your thoughts," Kent nodded to Forbes.

"Well, I for one would not wish to be regarded as a prospect," Fisher admitted. "I am well catered for as I am and have no wish to add to my burden of responsibility – those days are well behind me."

Larkin had said nothing up to that point. And then raised eyebrows when he posed a question.

"Is the estate entirely unencumbered?"

"Yes – it is a totally unencumbered freehold," Kent replied, wondering where this was going -and hoping it was going where he hoped it might.

"Then you should have no difficulty in arousing widespread interest," Larkin dashed those hopes. Kent tried to ensure that his face did not register any trace of disappointment.

Mary had some days before prevailed upon Rosie to come to the school to draw portraits of each of the children. That afternoon, each child had left the school proudly carrying the portrait to show their parents. Rosie, a bit tongue in cheek, had done a combined portrait of Will and Peterkin and had added underneath, 'Will and Peterkin – or is it Peterkin and Will?'

Mary was delighted with it and planned to pin it to the wall in their parlour. She was walking down the street to go home with her twins, Rosie at her side to be returned to Gil and Ella. Rosie was now nearly thirteen and had serious admirers amongst the young lads of the town. These same lads had a grudging respect for Gil, and certainly for Ella, whose father was the fearsome blacksmith and whose brother was the equally fearsome Simon.

The foursome had almost reached the smallholding's cottage when they were accosted by Cuthbert and Honor Hopkins. The two were dressed all in black as usual and walked side by side but not touching.

"Shame upon you for consorting with such evil," Honor accosted Mary, causing the four to stop in their tracks.

"And to what manner of evil are you referring?" Mary asked, determined not to provoke.

"What this maid does is not natural – and therefore, ungodly," Honor pointed at Rosie, who retreated slightly behind Mary.

"Oh – would you be referring to these drawings?" Mary asked, displaying the portrait of her twins. "In what manner can this be called ungodly?"

"By being the work of an unnatural person. Anything unnatural is by its very nature ungodly. Girls and women were never intended to do such things!"

"Piffle!" Mary was slowly losing her good intentions. "You shall next be accusing me of the ungodly act of teaching children!"

"Aye, tis a most unnatural and ungodly thing!" Cuthbert broke silence and glowered at Mary. "A woman's place is in the home, caring for that home and devoting all her work to Almighty God."

"Then you are as twisted in your mind as you are sour in your face," Mary was becoming goaded. "Where in your Holy Bible does it say that a woman may not exercise the gifts bestowed upon her by that same God?"

"It says in the very first book – Genesis, to be precise – that God created man in his own image and likeness, and that he created woman to be his companion. That infers subordination."

"To be grammatically correct, it *implies* subordination. It does not order it!"

"I have not the time to bandy semantics with the likes of you, an unnatural woman!" Hubert was equally goaded.

"Thank the Good Lord for that. It would be a waste of precious time arguing with a bigot and his wife!"

"Did you just accuse me of being *wife*?" Honor screeched. "I will have you know that Hubert and I are brother and sister!"

"Hm – brother and sister living into middle age under one roof – and you say that I am unnatural?" Mary gave a hoot of laughter.

"How dare you impugn my sister of unnatural behaviour!" Cuthbert started to shout, thereby drawing a very interested audience of passing folk, plus some drawn from their homes with the promise of some entertainment.

Mary turned to her new audience knowing that she would have the backing of the vast majority. "I simply made the natural mistake of assuming that these two people were husband and wife."

"And they be not? Be they living in sin, then?" Came from the back of the crowd, and thereby causing a gale of laughter.

"Apparently, they are brother and sister – and sin does not enter into it!" Mary informed everyone.

"Well, that comes as a great surprise," came another voice. "We all assumed they were wed!"

"This is intolerable!" Honor screeched. "We live quiet and godly lives, unlike the majority of you – drinking strong liquors, causing ribald merriment, living sinful and wasteful existences!"

"But unlike you miserable sods, we enjoy our lives!" came a third voice. "Mayhap were you to run and dance upon the Heath, you would start to enjoy yours!"

"Amen to that!" came a chorus.

"May the Lord call down curses upon you! We shall *never* besmirch our godly lives with such behaviour – nor shall we ever do as you do, indulge in matters of the flesh!"

"You therefore desire that all men and women refrain from matters of the flesh?" Mary saw a path through this balderdash.

"Most certainly, we do!"

"Do you regard God's greatest achievement is the creation of men and women?"

"Of course, we do!" Honor said in her most pious manner.

"Then you also must believe that the best way to thank Almighty God for that superb achievement is to bring it to an end – no more children and thus no more men and women. That is indeed a strange way to thank Him for his great work!"

"Got you there!" One woman near the front sneered openly at the pair. "Cross swords with our Mary and you lose every time!"

"And now piss off and go and read your bible," came that original voice from the back.

"Better still, start reading the works of Thomas Aquinas. He has a fund of logic that you could only benefit from learning. And now, we must away home," Mary suited action to words and led her trio down the street.

"You were brilliant, mama," Will grinned as they passed out of earshot.

"Logic beats stupidity every time," Mary grinned to her son. "Always look for the logic and you will seldom go awry!"

CHAPTER XX

A small council of war was held in the diminutive church hall on the very last day of April. The next day would be the first day of May when, by a tradition dating back many centuries, the town of Bovey Tracey would hold its May Day celebrations – not that Bovey was unique in that respect – nearly every town and village throughout the country would do the same. One very important part of that celebration was the crowning of the May Queen – elected from the young girls of the neighbourhood. And that was what the council of war had been called upon to thrash out. Isobel Bessant, daughter of Gaston and Glory Bessant, elected by popular demand, resolutely refused to have anything to do with it!

Gaston and his parents had escaped some years before from France. They were Huguenots and had been appallingly persecuted by French Catholics, spurred on by the Pope. Thousands had been killed. The two older Bessants had died of the winter fever, leaving Gaston running the town bookshop with his wife Glory, daughter of the Allens at the tavern. Isobel, now nearly thirteen, was as a result of her parents' shop, a very well-read young lady. She was also a determined and resolute free-thinker – much to her parent's joy, and sometimes to their despair.

Evelyn Ramsey, baker of distinction, had been for many years the organiser of the May Day pageant; Evelyn was not happy.

"For the sake of heaven and all its angels," she was almost at the point of pleading with the recalcitrant young girl. "Why will you not do his one thing? You respect Mary, do you not? She was May Queen!"

"That is as maybe," Isobel stood defiantly in the centre of a circle of adults. Evelyn, Gaston, Glory, Reverend Forbes, Mary, Harry the Bailiff, Hob and his wife May – all had jobs to do with the pageant.

"And what is that remark supposed to mean?" Mary asked. Secretly, she was not in the least surprised at the intransigence of young Isobel. She knew how deeply Isobel thought about things.

"It is not a Christian thing to do," Isobel aimed her remarks directly at James Forbes. "It is a continuation of a pagan ritual – like the images of the Green Man, Pixies on the moor, Robin Goodfellow the Hobgoblin. Mistletoe and so on. As it is not a Christian thing to do, I shall not do it!"

Everyone looked at Forbes, who seemed at a loss how to respond. Mary, who had indeed been May Queen in her time, attempted to sooth Isobel's ruffled feathers.

"Actually, you are quite correct when you say that the celebration of May Day is not a Christian tradition. But it *is* a tradition, and one that does nothing but bring joy and happiness to people. It is, if you like, a harmless bit of fun. Why cannot you put your sincere beliefs to one side for one day? You would not be betraying them in the slightest bit. You would be doing one small thing for your community – and that is all it would be!"

"I am truly sorry, Miss Mary, but I cannot and will not do it," Isobel almost stamped her foot. Mary was addressed by every schoolboy and schoolgirl as Miss Mary, instead of the more correct Mistress Cove. Even those who had left the school did so – and Isobel had left a year before to help in the bookshop. Her compendious knowledge of books was her pride and joy.

"Then, what are we to do?" Evelyn had never come across this attitude in all the years she had been the organiser. "Who else is there who could step in at this late hour?"

"There is Simon and Imelda's daughter Rachael, but she is but nine," Mary thought aloud. "But there is also Bess from Harvey's farm. She is thirteen and as pretty as a picture."

Harry grunted. "She is also furious that she was not elected! May and I heard her crying and storming about the farm only the other day, yelling hellfire and damnation on everyone who elected Isobel in the first place. It would not surprise me if she were to refuse point blank, seeing that she was regarded as a poor second choice."

"Yes – I can readily see her doing that," Mary nodded. "The same would probably be the case with Milly Hooper and Kat Baldwin. We have a paucity of young girls who are about the right age. Three who would have been, perished from winter fever. I know it flies in the face of tradition, but may not Rosie be prevailed upon to do as she did last year?"

"But that has never been done!" Evelyn objected. "The same girl two years in succession. Some would see it as blatant favouritism! She is my own granddaughter!"

"Then it shall have to be up to me to explain why Rosie is doing a double duty," Forbes shrugged. "I am sure you would all trust me to use words that are appropriate, saying why the choice became necessary – rather than disappoint the town with an absence of a May Queen at all! I shall announce that Rosie, despite her own reluctance, has been prevailed upon to stand in rather than disappoint the town."

Evelyn hurried down to the smallholding where she was relieved to find Gil, Ella, Rosie and young Jamie all hard at work in the field behind the cottage.

"Look – grandmama is here!" Jamie shouted, making a beeline for the visitor and giving her a massive hug, despite muddy hands.

"Then let us all stop for a while and go indoors for a drink," Ella ordered.

"And what brings my respected mother looking like her world has suddenly collapsed?" Gil grinned at her over the top of a mug of weak ale.

"Isobel has absolutely refused to be May Queen, that is what has happened!" Evelyn sat disconsolately on a stool. "We also fear that Bess, Milly and Kat will also refuse, having been passed over in favour of Isobel.

"But why would Isobel refuse?" Rosie asked. "It is an honour to be asked!"

"She maintains – and she is absolutely correct – that it is not a Christian celebration, and that it harks back to pagan times."

"But it's fun!" Rosie insisted. "Being dressed in all that finery, crowned with flowers and smiling at everyone!"

"But what brings you here?" Ella had the beginnings of a suspicion.

"Because there is nobody else, we all wondered if Rosie could be persuaded to do it for a second year."

"But everyone will hate me!" Rosie wailed.

"Reverend Forbes has said that he will tell everyone that Isobel has refused and that you have been brave enough to step in at the last moment so as not to spoil everyone's day," Evelyn explained. "Rather than hate you, they will be very thankful."

"Oh! Then I suppose I could do it," Rosie slowly came around to the idea of being the centre of attention again.

"You will have the two little girls from Brimley as your attendants," Evelyn added. "They at least, have not raised any objection!"

"Kitty and Poppy? They are very young!" Ella pointed out. "What are they – six and four?"

"But they are absolute poppets," Evelyn retorted. "They will look absolutely adorable – and will do exactly as they are bid."

And so, at the very last minute, Bovey Tracey would have its pageant complete. Everything would proceed as normal, and the town would not be denied its day of happiness.

Matt and Herb, pleasantly tired after a day of work, returned from their supper of pie and ale and decided on an early night, although it was only just past dusk. Everywhere they went, Spotty went with them. He was particularly attached to Matt Crowley. Spotty had also enjoyed a small pie and a dish of weak ale – something for which he was slowly developing a real liking. The barn was completely different to the original structure. Large, double doors opened onto the work area, with racks for tools and special places for oak planks and the steaming cabinet. At the rear were a set of wooden steps that led to two small, partitioned rooms – one for Matt and one for Herb. In each of these they had a bed, pegs for clothes, shelves, and small tables and stools. Spotty had a special bed with his own blanket just to the side of the double doors. Matt, being a tidy soul, had insisted upon a separate privy that was housed in a small shed at the rear of the barn. Another, much larger wooden construction housed the horse and the large cart. Both men were particularly careful with their horse – no horse, no deliveries. It enjoyed fresh hay daily, clear water from the pump, and a warm stable.

They had been asleep for about an hour, missing completely the church clock striking nine, when Matt became aware of a soft growling coming from the front of the building. He raised himself onto one elbow and realised that Spotty was making the growling. Very quietly, he rose, pulled on breeches and a shirt, thrust his feet into shoes and crept towards the doors.

"What is it, boy?" he whispered, fondling the dog's silky ears.

In answer, Spotty turned his muzzle to the side and gave a low growl. Matt went over to the tool rack and selected a short-handled splitting axe. It was one with a very long blade that they used for splitting planks down the grain of the wood. It was heavy and wickedly sharp. He crept to the doors and silently removed the bar that held them firmly closed. Motioning Spotty to follow him, he opened the left door a crack and peered around to the side that the dog had indicated. As his eyes became accustomed to the faint moonlight, he became aware of a shape slowly moving around to the back of the barn. He waited until the shape had disappeared around the corner, then crept along the wall and peered around. The shape was kneeling at the back wall and pouring some substance from a can up the wooden wall. Matt was then faced with a dilemma. Should he use the blade of the axe to safeguard him, Herb, and their business – or should he try to incapacitate the man in some other way? He decided on the latter course of action. He turned the long blade sideways, shot towards the figure and brought the flat of the blade smartly down on the back of the man's head.

There came a satisfactory 'clunk', followed immediately by a stifled groan – and then the man slumped sideways. Matt gave it a few moments just in case the man was feigning, then tentatively reached out to feel the pulse in the neck. It was there and regular. However, the figure did not even moan as Matt tested again with a kick to the ribs. The man was definitely unconscious.

"Spotty – fetch Herb," he ordered. The dog looked up at him with a puzzled frown as if to say, 'what?' Matt repeated the order with much signalling with his hands. Spotty gave him another look that Matt interpreted as, 'right, got that!' The dog raced off to do as bid. Matt stood over the slumped figure with the flat of the axe ready to administer another whack should it become necessary. Finally, he heard the unmistakable sounds of a man being woken from a deep sleep.

"Bugger off, Spotty. And stop making that bloody row!" Matt used the wooden end of the axe to beat on the back wall.

"Herb – get yourself out here and bring some rope. Spotty heard movement and we have someone here who was pouring oil on the back wall!"

"Shit and damnation!" came a shout. "Kill the sod!"

"Nay – bring rope and we'll hand the bastard over to the Bailiff."

Still muttering dire threats, Herb appeared partially dressed, but with a long coil of rope. The man's hands were roped together behind his back, his legs drawn up behind him and roped to the bound wrists.

"There – the harder he struggles, the tighter it will get," Matt grunted as he straightened up. "Now, one of us will have to stand guard whilst the other runs to get Harry Cove."

Herb regarded the axe in Matt's hand.

"If that had been me with that axe, I would have sliced the bugger's head off! What made you let him live?"

"Did we not both see enough mutilated bodies at Worcester?" Matt argued, remembering vividly the carnage wrought by Cromwell's army on the Scots supporting Charles at the very last battle – the one before Charles fled abroad.

"Aye, I suppose so," Herb grudgingly nodded his agreement. "Then it had better be me fetching Bailiff." He disappeared to get properly dressed, then started trotting down the street. Matt sat down well clear of the oily wood. Spotty curled himself up at Matt's feet and promptly went to sleep – as if he was satisfied that his part in proceedings was over.

Meanwhile, Nell was busy regaling Avril and James with an update on her soon to be new home. She had spent the day at Newton Abbot and had been brought back before dusk by Adam – riding pillion behind him. Adam had turned about and gone back.

"The rooms are a delight," she was bubbling over with excitement. "I have had the plaster on the walls painted in light green, with dark green borders at top and bottom. Each room looks like a forest glade. I shall have to ask Rosie to draw pictures so that I may hang them to make the place even more homely." She then blushed a deep red as she went on to talk about the bedroom and the large bed with its curtain hangings.

"So, looking forward to being a wife, are we?" James gave her a wry smile.

"Well, for the most part, yes I am," Nell acknowledged. "I am more certain than ever that Adam will be a very good husband. He spent most of the day with me and seemed just as delighted as I was. And the other blessed thing is that I shall be no more than an hour's ride away."

"And how is your own new venture coming along?" Avril wanted details of the small workroom that would be where Nell would do her preparations.

"Oh, that could not be better," she enthused. "The workmen have done exactly as I asked them, making sure that my worktable is lit properly under a large window. There are shelves aplenty for the jars and bottles, I have stills and pestles and mortars, spoons and weighing scales, plus moulds for pills and pastilles. I could not be more pleased!"

"The wedding is less than four weeks away – and you are still as happy with the prospect as you were?"

"Yes, I honestly am."

"Then James and I are as happy as you are," Avril drew a deep breath of relief.

Herb arrived back with both Harry and Hob. He led them around to the back of the barn where a very slowly recovering man was starting to struggle with his bonds.

Harry strode to the figure and pulled back the hood to reveal the features.

"Aye, the same man I warned before," he stated.

"Thought it could not be anyone else," Matt grunted as the craggy face looked up at him through bleary eyes.

Harry knelt down and started rummaging through the man's pockets. He drew out a small knife, a steel, flint, and a small wad of cotton waste.

"Came prepared with a pot of oil and the means to start the fire," he stated. He stared hard at the man. "I warned you before not to take matters into your own hands – yet here you are again disregarding that advice. It is plainly obvious that you intended to fire the barn. Two people sleep just the other side of this wall, so you shall be charged with attempted murder. I shall have you taken to the jail in Newton Abbot to await the next assize. I have little doubt that the evidence I have seen here will ensure that you are found guilty. The penalty – well, you know what that will be!"

"May you both rot in hell," the man spat in Matt's and Herb's direction. "You did exactly this to me and have escaped any punishment. I sought only to do the same to you."

"But we had no hand in the destruction of your business!" Herb was a far better liar than Matt. "We have never even been questioned, never mind charged. You have no evidence whatsoever!"

Harry and Hob between them heaved the bound man over one of the horses and went off with their burden – and the evidence of the large oil bottle, steel, flint and wadding. Herb gave Matt a broad grin and looked down at the recumbent dog.

"Tomorrow, I visit the butchers and obtain enough bones to keep you happy for weeks!" he grinned down at Spotty.

That same evening, Colonel Fisher received news that he instantly knew he had to divulge to his friends. The best way he could do that was simply to ride the short distance to James Forbes and then to rely upon the Reverend's tried and tested network to see that it reached as wide an audience as possible. It was news that he knew would be of great interest to most people. Consequently, just after the sun had set, he mounted his favourite horse and gave him his head to gallop as fast as he liked. He drew up at the church, dismounted like a twenty-year-old and ran up to the Rector's house.

"Reverend baint there, midear," an old woman called out to him. "He be in tavern with everyone about tomorrow's May Day."

With a word of thanks, Fisher went back to his horse and led it on the rein to the tavern, where he left it with the ostler. He hurried into the main taproom where a sizeable crowd were discussing the nest day's pageant. Rosie was in the centre of the crowd feeling rather like an interloper. Forbes, espying his friend and the state of his agitated face, called for silence.

"You have the look of a man with the devil after him," he said.

"Not the devil, not even his hobgoblins," Fisher replied. "I came as fast as I could to tell you of the news I have just received. It seems that elections were called, and the old Rump Parliament has been reinstated."

That caused a bout of cheering and loud chatter amongst the assembled townsfolk. Fisher held his hands up signalling that he was not finished.

"Not only that, but further news that I know will delight most of you gathered here. The first order of business was a motion to invite Charles Stuart back as king."

"And the result of that motion?" Forbes asked amidst a deathly silence.

"It was passed by a considerable majority!"

The first outburst was easily surpassed by the roar of cheering that greeted that bit of news.

"Tomorrow, it will not matter if the heavens open and we are drenched," Forbes laughed, tears streaming down his face. "That news will ensure the merriest May Day we have enjoyed these last many years!"

"But I do not want it pouring with rain," Rosie muttered to herself.

Rosie should not have concerned herself – May Day dawned with not a cloud in the sky. She was up very early, peering first through the window and offering a short prayer of thanks. Others, especially those concerned with the organisation of the pageant, did much the same. Rosie threw a robe over her nightdress and shot downstairs to start making the porridge for breakfast. Fresh bread was delivered shortly afterwards by the lad hired by John and Evelyn to make the morning round of regular customers.

Rosie hacked off a warm, crusty end of a loaf, smeared yellow butter from the dairy down on the Heath, and sat munching happily as she stirred the porridge. She was humming contentedly to herself when her young brother Jamie clattered down, hacked off the other, crusty end, and wandered out to tend the chickens. He was back some minutes later with a basket of eggs. These would be placed on the front step with a bowl to collect the coins left by those who regularly bought from them. He put four eggs on the table for Rosie to prepare to go along with the bread and porridge.

"Are you all prepared for a repeat performance?" Ella asked as she came down for her breakfast.

"Yes, mama – but I hope Reverend Forbes *does* tell everybody that I am only doing it as a favour. Otherwise, everyone will hate me!"

"Nobody in this town will ever hate you, my angel. Reverend will tell everyone – so will your dada and I; so will all the family – and nobody argues with your grandad Abel or your uncle Simon!"

"Not if they wish to keep their heads firmly attached to their necks!" Gill laughed as he sat down for his meal. "There will be no work done today by anyone – with the exception of the tavern, of course. They are going to be rushed off their feet."

"Might I offer to help them?" Jamie asked. "I am sure they could do with all the help they can get."

Gil and Ella exchanged a look of astonishment. Their son had indeed become a different person working part-time at the smithy and at the bakery, but they had never suspected him of any altruistic tendencies.

"I might earn a few pennies," Jamie went on to explain. "And I could give those to the poor woman whose husband died last week when he was gored by that horrible bull. She will not be able to stay at the farm and work it herself."

"That is a lovely thought," Ella was moved by her son's compassion. "But steward Barton will never allow the woman and her two little kiddies to starve!"

Rosie, having finished her breakfast chores, left Jamie to attend to the chickens, then walked smartly up to the church to get herself ready for the pageant. Already there were Evelyn Ramsey, her other grandmother, the two little girls from Parke, their mother May, and a small host of helpers. Standing at the gate was the flat wagon on which she and her two diminutive attendants would be paraded through the town.

Kitty and Poppy, respectively six and four, were already dressed in their white dresses. The sleeves were adorned with yellow ribbons and on their heads were garlands of cowslips, primroses, celandines, and wood anemones. As had been previously stated, they looked like little angels. May, who knew far better, wondered whether her two daughters would be able to refrain from their usual mischief – at least, until the pageant was over.

Rosie went with grandmother Evelyn into a small room and got into her own dress – a larger version of the smaller ones. She was handed her small staff of office and went back to join everyone else. By the time they had got to the front of the church, a crowd had gathered in the street. There came a few muttered words from the crowd until Reverend Forbes raised his hand for silence.

"My dear friends," he spoke in his loudest voice. "Here we are yet again to celebrate the coming of Spring by crowning our May Queen. Many of you will have noticed that Rosie is yet again our queen. The original choice was Imogen, but she has declined the role because she truly believes that what we are celebrating is the residue of a pagan ceremony. I for one, cannot but applaud her firmly held beliefs. She is not to be thought of as selfish but commended for sticking to her firmly held beliefs. We found this out only yesterday – far too late for anyone else to take up the role that she had not even rehearsed. We are lucky indeed that Rosie has agreed to do the honours again. She was very reluctant to do so, as she knew that it would be looked upon with some disquiet. But instead of being annoyed, we should all be very thankful that Rosie has slipped back into the role so as not to ruin our usual celebration. So, with no more ado, let us crown our May Queen and have the most wonderful day."

Evelyn came forward with a larger version of the flowered chaplet. Forbes placed it gently on Rosie's curls. "Hail Queen Rosie – our Queen of the May!" he roared.

An accompanying roar of applause dislodged any apprehension that Rosie had feared. She slowly went up the short steps and took her garlanded seat on the wagon, her two little attendants taking smaller chairs before her. Hob took up the leading rein and the procession through the streets began. Rosie and her little girls waved and smiled to everyone as they passed slowly through the small town. It was a spectacular success, so successful that Rosie completely forgot her earlier fears. She was regarded as a young heroine and basked in the adulation!

Jamie's offer of help was seized upon with glee. He spent ten hours shooting between rows of tables with foaming mugs of ale, returning fistfuls of empties, rinsing them, refilling them, then shooting back again. By nine in the evening, he was utterly exhausted, but revived somewhat when presented with a shilling by Dick Allen.

Rosie went to bed that night also in an exhausted state. In her case, she was exhausted by the constant smiling and waving – and being given winks and whistles by all the young lads. One in particular had sidled up to her as she sat in state outside the tavern. He was foolish enough to make some lewd remark to her in the hearing of her uncle Simon. He retired from the scene nursing a large bruise.

The last thing she remembered before being walked home to bed was a very drunk Simon Dingle, the town butcher, standing on a table and roaring, "God bless our King Charlie!"

But he is not king yet, Rosie thought as she fell into a deep sleep.

What she did not know about until the next day was what befell after she had been taken home. Cuthbert and Honor Hopkins had somehow managed to restrain themselves during the pageant itself. However, the roaring and laughter emanating from the tavern proved too much to bear. They donned black capes over their black attire and walked purposefully up the street. They managed to push their way through the crowd and enter the tavern's large taproom.

Abel Smith, head and shoulders above the rest, caught sight of the two. "Hold fast, my beauties," he roared. "Misery descends upon us!"

"Sod off, you miserable buggers!" Simon Dingle called out, waving a mug of ale in their direction. "We want none of your preaching here!"

"Such sin, such debauchery, will not be unnoticed by the Almighty!" Cuthbert retorted as a threatening silence descended upon the room. "If there were the slightest justice, you would all be struck dead by the wrath of God Himself!"

"Let's lynch the bastards and have done with it," Dingle suggested. "We believed that Hubert and Mercy were misery itself, but these two have them beaten into a cocked hat!"

"Aye, let us do that!" came another voice. "They shall not spoil our day!"

"We are the Lord's chosen, and you cannot harm us!" Honor screamed.

"Wrong!" yelled Dingle. "You are *our* chosen for a ducking in the horse trough, and then we will lynch you!"

Harry looked at Hob and decided that things had gone far enough. He went to the kitchen door and seized the large cudgel that Dick Allen used to quell disturbances. Hob armed himself with Sal's huge rolling pin and came back to stand at Harry's side.

"That is more than enough!" Harry shouted. "Nobody shall be lynched. You, Master and Mistress Hopkins, will leave and go to your home. Not another word from you – just go. However, Hob and I might be powerless to stop these good folk from ducking you in the horse trough before you are sent on your way!"

That was greeted with gales of laughter. The two were seized none too gently and hauled kicking and screaming towards the large trough. Standing and dripping water, the two were escorted to their home by an amused bailiff and his equally amused deputy. At the Hopkins' cottage, Harry added another warning.

"One more incident from either of you and I shall have you dumped into the town jail. Go inside and damned well stay there!"

The town jail was a highly insalubrious, little stone building that had a stout wooden door that was secured by large iron bars. Inside, it was very small, full of rotten straw, and smelled like a disgusting privy.

"We are not done with the Lord's work!" Cuthbert muttered.

"Just bear in mind my warning," Harry replied. "It is no idle threat!"

Little work was done the next day as far too many of the population were nursing sore heads as a result of imbibing vast quantities of Sal's renowned ale. Not all were in that condition – Avril and James were up early expecting many requests for hangover remedies. Rosie was also up early, dressed in a neat work dress with a white pinafore. It was to be her first day apprenticed to the apothecary. She was very excited at the prospect. Had she known how hectic that first day would be, she would not have been quite so keen.

She arrived at the shop just as James was opening the shutters to let in the early morning light into the interior. He gave Rosie a peremptory nod of welcome before scooting back into the room behind the shop where the pills and potions were prepared. Rosie stood in the shop looking a trifle lost until Avril espied her and came to give her a warm hug of welcome.

"Today is going to be a very busy day," she gave Rosie a warm smile to go along with the hug. "Yesterday, many people in the town drank far too much than is good for them. Within an hour, the shop will be crammed with them nursing sore heads and bilious stomachs – and they will expect us to cure them in five minutes!"

Rosie decided it was time that she aired her somewhat sparse knowledge.

"I have been reading about medicines," she said. "Is it not willow bark that is good for headaches?"

"Well, that is one thing we shall not have to teach you," Avril was very pleased that Rosie was taking it all very seriously. "Indeed, willow bark is excellent for all sorts of pain. Your first job will be to go into the back room and start preparing a lot of it – we are going to need a vast supply, or I am seriously mistaken!"

She followed Avril into the back room and knelt on a stool at one end of the sturdy table. Avril showed her how to use the special, curved herb chopper, rocking it backwards and forwards to slice and chop the thin pieces of bark into small fragments.

"This thing is correctly called a mezzaluna and has been used by Arabs for centuries. Nothing has ever been invented that beats it. But be very careful; always use both hands, never one. When you put it aside, make sure the blade is facing away from you as it is kept wickedly sharp. See how I use it and then have a go yourself. It does not matter how small you chop the bark – the smaller the better. Make a start on that pile and then I'll tell you how it should be used as a medicine."

Rosie gently picked up the tool and, spreading a few slivers of bark on the table, started rocking the blade back and forth, reducing it to very tiny pieces.

"That's excellent. I now have to go and start preparing arrowroot. Many coming in here will have sore stomachs – some will have severe diarrhoea as well."

"Is that what papa calls the squits?"

"Yes – and it is nasty whilst it lasts. Arrowroot is good for that as well."

James was whistling quietly to himself as he measured small amounts of various powders and grains into little paper packets, folded them neatly and applied a blob of sealing wax to hold them closed. When he had finished a batch, he took a quill and wrote a shorthand version of the contents on the packet.

Rosie paused in her chopping to see him pen a crude arrow on a packet. "That's a lot quicker than writing arrowroot," she muttered to herself. She glanced at the shelf above the table. It was stacked with little packets, giving her a mental exercise deciphering what was within them. 'WB' was obviously willow bark; she guessed that 'CF' might be comfrey; she was defeated by 'XXX'. She went back to her chopping.

And then the first 'patient' arrived with a tinkle of the doorbell. Avril went to answer it. Unsurprisingly, the man wanted something for a severe headache.

"Take this packet of willow bark," he was told. "Put half a mug of weak ale to warm with two large pinches of the bark. When it is just hot enough to dip your *clean* finger in it, take it from the heat and leave it for half an hour. Then drink it down. You can repeat the process every hour if necessary."

And so it went on. By ten that morning, there was a long queue at the door needing James to help Avril in the shop. One man came in with a gash in his head.

"Fell over the step at my door," he explained. "Head-butted the door frame."

James took him to a cubicle at one side of the shop where he cleansed the gash, applied a salve and then a linen bandage.

"I'm off the ale for a week!" the man said, thanking James for his ministrations before walking unsteadily up the street.

"Aye, and pigs may fly!" James grinned at the retreating figure.

"We shall have to take our dinner in relays," Avril grunted as yet another man staggered off up the road, alternately clutching his parcel of arrowroot and the seat of his breeches. Rosie volunteered to prepare a cold dinner as she had finished five piles of willow bark. The offer was very gratefully accepted.

By the time the distant church clock chimed six in the evening, James closed the shop with a sigh of relief. During the day, he had seen to two more gashes and had set a broken arm. Avril had examined a set of mashed toes and had bound them up after having tested to see whether any were broken. She had also removed a rusty nail from the arm of a woman who had absolutely no idea how it had got there. Rosie was utterly exhausted.

"For a first day, it has been quite an experience," Avril gave her a rueful grin. "But you have done a splendid job, and we are lucky to have you. Thank you for all your hard work. Tomorrow will not be anywhere near as bad, I promise! And Nell will be back from Newton to talk you through a host of other tasks."

Rosie went the short distance to her home and almost fell asleep over her supper. She was even unable to relate her experiences to her parents. She disappeared up to bed and slept for ten hours. Gil and Ella exchanged a grin.

"Our little girl has learned that life can be hard," Ella remarked. "Only an exhausting day could have kept her silent like that."

"Aye, silence is not her usual condition," Gil laughed.

CHAPTER XXI

By the twelfth day of May, everyone in the town had heard the news that Charles had started upon his journey back to England. Parliament had extended the expected invitation for him to come back and to take up the crown. However, everyone also knew of the promise he had made. From a meeting, there had come a statement known as the Declaration of Breda. Charles, with Edward Hyde and some other advisors had published it. It stated that there would be a general amnesty, that there would be liberty of conscience, an equitable settlement of land disputes, and that the army would receive full arrears of pay. What was not stated was that he would have to accept that he would be bound by the deliberations of Parliament. There was something for most people in the agreement.

Colonel Fisher, when he had heard of the terms of the Declaration, gave an explosive grunt. "General amnesty, my arse! How the devil can he be persuaded to grant a general amnesty to all those who signed his father's death warrant? There is no way on this earth that he will honour that."

His ancient housekeeper, busy peeling onions in the kitchen, heard that soliloquy – most people in the nearby houses probably heard it as well. Fisher's visitor, a messenger for Cornwall, often stopped by at Fisher's house to impart the latest news. The man knew full well that he would be fed and watered in style every time he called. He would also depart with some extra coins to fill his purse.

"Aye, Colonel. There are many in London and Westminster now feeling their necks and worrying for how much longer they will be able to do so."

"And what about this liberty of conscience, eh? Does that imply that each and every person will be able to exercise freedom of religious observation, free from let or hindrance? If so, it will sit very uneasily with the Puritans, the Catholics, and the Protestants – not to mention the myriad other sects that infest the country. Each believes in the rightness of his or her belief – and has shown no tendency towards toleration in the past. Why should now be any different, eh? Answer me that!"

"I cannot answer you that, Colonel," the man replied. He was very used to the rhetorical discourse of his host.

"Do you know, the only bit of this rigamarole that I sincerely believe? That the army will receive full arrears of pay! His father never had the means to pay his so-called army. Lambert found out the hard way when he failed to reimburse his army. At least Cromwell, Fairfax and Monck had the good sense to keep loyalty with proper payment. Young Charles may be all sorts of a scoundrel, but he is no fool. Aye – he will ensure that this part of the Declaration is honoured."

"You call him a scoundrel, Colonel?" the man faltered.

"How many illegitimate children so far, eh? Four, so far. James Crofts, Charles Fitzcharles, Catherine Fitzcharles, and Charlotte Fitzcharles – and those are the ones known about! I say scoundrel and I mean scoundrel! What is to stop him carrying on in the same vein? I am willing to bet that the mere placing of a crown on his head shall not deter him from his ways!"

Even after his visitor had left, Fisher continued to mutter to himself. He had been utterly devoted to Generals Cromwell and Fairfax. He was a staunch Protestant, although never going as far as Cromwell had in the slide towards Puritanism. He was a soldier – had been ever since the age of fifteen. He had never married – had never been in one place long enough to form a meaningful relationship. He was a stickler for duty, a rigid disciplinarian towards both his soldiers and himself. He viewed the coming of Charles the Second with many misgivings.

"Dissolute scoundrel," he muttered yet again as he sat down to mutton stew for his dinner.

It was about the same time that Hob rode up the town to call upon the barrel makers. He found them sweating in the Spring sunshine, struggling with a load of oaken staves recently removed from the steamer. They had to be bent to shape fairly quickly, or they would have to be re-steamed. Matt was pulling one end of a stave over the former, whilst Herb was anchoring the other end.

Hob watched fascinated as the final stave was bent, and the hoops hammered into position. Only then could the two men stand up and give attention to the young deputy bailiff.

"What brings you up here, Hob?" Matt enquired. "Come to see real men doing real work?"

"If I wanted to see that, I would have gone to the smithy!" Hob grinned. "Nay, I have news that might just raise a smile to your grimy faces."

"And what could that possibly be?" Herb grinned back. "We have been awarded a hundred pounds for services to barrel-making?"

"Hardly!" Hob replied. "It is of a far more serious nature than that. The man found setting light to your barn was tried yesterday at the Assize. Harry went there to give his evidence and was highly praised for his efforts. The man hardly uttered one word in his own defence. He seemed to relish his coming death. Anyway, he was hanged in the late afternoon, along with two highway robbers and an old woman guilty of poisoning her husband. You will not get any further trouble from that quarter."

Matt and Herb exchanged a look. Hob interpreted it almost immediately.

"If, by the merest chance, you *were* responsible for setting fire to his business, then you are just about the luckiest pair of men in Devon," he gave them an almost accusatory look.

"But we are innocent," Herb responded in his most earnest voice. He was, Hob noted, careful not to say of what they were innocent. "Anyway," Herb went on. "There was no evidence that made us guilty and now that the wretched man is dead, he cannot accuse us!"

"That is true," Hob acknowledged. "But what of the remainder of his family? He leaves behind a daughter, a son-in-law, and three grandchildren. Have you no worry that the daughter may carry on the fight?"

"Nay – the daughter and her family live far off near to Bristol. It is of no concern to them as they have their own business to care for. The man is concerned in shipping and has some new enterprise concerning a trade with the African continent," Matt offered.

"And how came you by that knowledge?" Hob asked. "It seems strange that you should have prised that information about a man whose business you swear you did not harm!"

"Aha!" Herb gave his mate a very warning look. "We were soldiers and quickly learned the lesson – know your enemy! We took pains to find out as much as we might about the man who falsely accused us."

That is a man who has an answer for everything, Hob said quietly to himself. And in this case, he is right – there is no proof against them.

Hob mounted his horse and went back to tell his boss that the message had been delivered – and about his misgivings. Hob's wife May gave a snort of laughter.

"Matt is not clever enough to have thought it through that astutely," she remarked. "I have known Matt ever since I was a little child. He is still what he always was – a simple soul. But I have no doubt that the two of them *did* set fire to that business."

"Aye, I agree," Harry nodded. "You say that Herb told you of a business concerning Africa. I have recently heard of that. Apparently, it concerns sending ships empty to the African coast, loading goods there, then transporting those goods all the way across the Atlantic to the islands. They offload there, then load spices and sugar to bring back here to Bristol and Liverpool. I hear that the entire trip may take up to one year!"

"What could possibly be of interest to them to go all the way to Africa?" Hob was puzzled. "I have not ever heard of goods from there being of any interest to anyone!"

"It must be something of value," Harry mused. "These merchants are hard-headed men of business and would not invest all that time and money for little or no reward. But as to what it might be, I have no idea."

The next day, being a Sunday, saw the arrival yet again of Adam from Newton Abbot. Nell, giving not one iota of care, rushed out to greet him with a fond kiss – much to the absolute disgust of Honor Hopkins who happened to be on her way past at that moment.

"Disgusting!" she growled. "Another year in Hell's fires awaits you!"

"Oh good," Adam gave her a broad grin. "I feel a trifle cold at present as the sun seems to have deserted us."

The two disappeared inside the shop before Honor could muster a reply to that quip. Avril had roasted a pork joint for dinner. That, along with turnips, cabbage, and parsnips, formed the main course. It was waiting on the table, as was a large jug of ale and another of a sweet, white wine.

"And now, the final debate on the wedding," Adam declared after he had heaped compliments on Avril for a wonderful meal.

"Debate, eh?" James smiled. "And what is there to debate? I was under the impression that Avril had planned every conceivable detail already."

"Oh, tush," his wife waved an admonitory knife at him. "There is *always* some little thing to debate."

"Indeed, there is," Nell agreed. "For example, how are the dresses for my attendants coming on?"

"Brilliantly!" Avril shot back. "Lou Crowley has only just finished embroidering the yellow and red roses on the skirts. And I may tell you, they are absolutely lovely."

"And what of your own dress?" Adam looked inquisitively at his bride to be.

"That is something you shall not see until the day itself!" Nell waved an equally admonitory finger. "Not only shall you not see it, we shall not discuss it either."

"In some aspects of life, we men are powerless," James gave a loud guffaw. "Learn that lesson *before* you wed and your life shall be that much more serene."

"So, anything else – any other matter that needs to be nailed down?" James almost pleaded for a negative answer.

"I do believe that everything is now fully settled," Nell admitted. "But to change the subject – young Rosie is doing exceptionally well, is she not."

"Aye, that she most definitely is," Avril nodded. "I would never have thought it possible when one remembers the little rebel of a year ago. Her skill at drawing and painting is truly remarkable. She has pinned a drawing of each herb and item above every section of the storage shelves. They are so accurate in every tiny detail. Along with that, she now insists on reciting her new knowledge every day before she departs."

"And it is very seldom that she makes even the smallest mistake," James added. "We were blessed with Mary, and then with you, Nell. It seems we are thrice blessed to have Rosie. But tell me, how is your own enterprise coming along?"

"Oh, my workroom is complete in every detail. I shall be able to start almost immediately after the wedding. I am very blessed with a quite wonderful husband to be."

"Indeed, you are!" Adam grinned at her. "There has never been such a wonderful husband to be!"

"And are you resigned to becoming a wife – and all that that entails?" Avril asked Nell privately before they went to bed.

"Aye – not only reconciled, but happy as well," Nell did not even blush – as she most certainly would have done only a month before.

Earlier that afternoon, Mary and Matthew Kent had been joined by Colonel Paul Larkin at the Brimley estate. Rather than sit inside on a fine spring day, Mary and Kent had chosen to have their meeting outside, on a large bench under the shade of a large horse chestnut tree. Its tall, spiky 'candles' of white flowers were just starting to droop and deposit now and again a tiny white petal that made it seem as if it was gently snowing. They had started to go through the written applications that had arrived from the lawyer they had engaged. There were four applications for purchase of the entire estate. And then they were joined by Paul Larkin, who started off with a fulsome apology for interrupting them.

"Please excuse my sudden appearance," he began. "But I heard that you were about to discuss the applications you had received for purchase of the estate."

"We had that intention," Mary gave him a polite smile and gestured towards a wooden seat opposite the bench. Kent sat down and realised that some further explanation was necessary.

"I would also like to express my interest in the sale."

"Then you are doubly welcome," Kent gave him a smile of his own. "But first, we must dutifully consider the written applications. Who is first?"

"That would be Sir Walter Strickland," Mary said, reading from the first letter. "He has expressed an interest because he wishes to turn the entire estate into a farm for the rearing of pigs. He has also offered an amount well below what we have valued the estate."

"How very fitting," Kent laughed. "Strickland is from the west of Dorset – or so I believe. He is also known for his lack of manners!"

"Could we in all conscience allow Violette's estate to become a piggery?" Mary snorted. "I for one do not believe we could!"

"And I for another second that. Who is next?"

"A certain Horace Dobworthy. He writes from Redruth in Cornwall saying that he has a small estate there and another on the Somerset coast. He desires yet a third somewhere in between the two. He also is offering well below the price we are asking."

"Have we overestimated the value?" Kent asked. "I do not believe we have."

"And neither do I," Mary shook her head. "So, the third comes from a Lord Walkden, and it is via his London lawyer. It is written in language that only a lawyer could have penned."

"And what does he offer?"

"Actually, he offers the price we are asking. But I have never heard of him, or what he does, or even what he intends for the estate. The lawyer is careful not to go into any detail about his client or his intentions."

"Er, pardon the interruption, but I have some information about Walkden that may have a bearing upon your decision," Larkin ventured. "Lord Walkden is a close associate of Master Andrew Scrope. Scrope was one of those who signed the death warrant of Charles' father. What may happen once his son is king I have no idea. But Scrope's future does not look promising - and maybe neither does the future of any of his close associates."

"We are indebted to you for that information," Kent gave him a nod of appreciation. "I doubt we should have any dealings with someone whose future is uncertain."

"And I agree," Mary said. "Well, three down and one to go. The last letter comes directly from a Gertrude Prince – or so I interpret the scrawled signature. The body of the letter is little better in penmanship. She, whoever she may be, would have been better advised to employ the services of a scrivener. However, she also offers the whole asking price but again makes no mention of her intentions for the estate."

Kent was silently rocking with mirth. And then, unable to stifle his merriment, gave vent to a bellow of laughter.

"And what, pray, causes that outburst?" Mary enquired.

Kent struggled to get his features into some semblance of order. "Gertrude Prince – from where does she write?"

"An address in Southwark," Mary scanned the top of the letter.

"Lady Violette would either be vastly amused or utterly horrified," Kent could not help another bout of laughter. "Gertrude Price of Southwark owns and runs one of the best known bordellos on the south bank of the Thames. I have little doubt that she would turn this estate into a country retreat for those who could afford a holiday in Devon, with the attentions of her very best courtesans for company."

"Dear Violette would turn in her grave if we even gave a moment's thought to that particular application," Mary also could not help a laugh at the very idea.

"Well, we are no further forward, are we? Four letters and all dismissed out of hand. But you mentioned an interest?" Kent looked directly at Larkin.

"Yes, I did, did I not. You would be right in supposing that the pay of a senior officer over the space of years would be insufficient to result in savings equal to the price you are asking. I am an only child. My mother died many years past. My father left only a small house that I sold. However, my uncle, my maternal uncle, died but recently and left his considerable fortune to his only living relative – me. I not only have more than sufficient funds to meet your price, but the wherewithal to maintain this estate for many years to come. It would be my dearest wish to own this place. And I give you my solemn word that it would be maintained in its present form, with security for any who live and work here."

That was met with a stunned silence. Mary was the first to respond.

"Speaking for myself, I cannot think of a better owner for Brimley. If what you are saying constitutes a firm offer of purchase, I would heartily endorse your application."

"And that goes for me, as well," Kent gave a huge grin at his fellow member of the Sane and Sensible. "May we assume that a firm offer has been made and accepted?"

"Yes, my offer is firm," Larkin replied.

"Then we shall proceed to the drafting of a contract," Mary was as delighted as the other two. "It should not take many days before we can proceed to a completion of the sale. I take it that you will want to live here?"

"Indeed, that would be my firm intention. But what of your father and mother-in-law? Are they not residents?"

"Yes, they occupy the largest of what used to be the guest bedrooms. Lady Violette's suite has never been occupied since her death."

"Please reassure them that their tenure is secure. I shall leave the day to day running of the estate to them – and to that excellent steward and his wife. I intend to spend a deal of time exploring the moor where I am informed there is money to be made extracting minerals and stone."

"Indeed, there is," Kent affirmed. "And as yet, there are few people taking advantage of the opportunity. You could well be ahead of the pack!"

"Well, an afternoon that started off with gloom and despondency has ended in glorious triumph," Mary beamed. "May I now suggest that we repair to the house to celebrate with a suitable wine?"

"That is a suggestion that I am glad to second!" Kent laughed.

"And I make it unanimous!" Larkin got to his feet. "Let us toast the future of Brimley."

CHAPTER XXII

To say that the rooms behind the apothecary were in turmoil would be exaggerating the case; there was what some would term fevered activity. Nell, bring the main actor in the drama, was the calmest of all, much to her own surprise. The 'fevered activity' was being acted out by Avril, Faith Smith, Evelyn Ramsey, and Lou Crowley. It was the evening of the twenty-fourth of May and the day before the wedding. James, being a prudent man, had invented an urgent visit to a patient in the town who was suffering from persistent boils. It was a visit that he was determined would take him all of the evening.

Adam and his father, along with Adam's cousin Alfred, were happily settled at a table in the tavern. They would stay the night there so as to be ready for their appearance at the church the next morning.

Nell gave a sigh of resignation as the dress was adjusted for the seventh time - Lou being dissatisfied with the hang of the sleeves. Avril was sitting at the table going once again over the menu that had been ordered for the wedding feast. The weather was hot rather than the comfortable warmth everyone expected for late May. Therefore, was a milk-based pudding a wise choice? Jamie. who had been 'borrowed' for the evening, sat outside in the shop. He was bored to distraction whilst awaiting the next message to be delivered. After a few more moments deliberation, he was sent up to the tavern to see Sal Allen with the message that the milk-based confection should be replaced by early fruits. Avril knew that this would cause the least disruption as there was an abundance of those early fruits available.

Evelyn had already baked and decorated a cake for the occasion. It was laden with dried fruit, covered in marchpane, then decorated with coloured sugar flowers. She was exceptionally proud of it. She had ordered John to safeguard it whilst she was down at Avril's house.

At long last, at nearly nine o'clock, Lou declared that she was at long last satisfied with the dress; Avril put away her lists, Nell heaved a deep sigh of relief; Jamie went home, released at last from his vigil. Peace descended on the apothecary as James made a belated appearance, first peeping through windows to see if the coast was clear.

The wedding would proceed with almost military precision – and Avril slept the sleep of the utterly content. Nell was both excited and still a trifle apprehensive. Nevertheless, she managed to sleep quite well.

Back at the bakery, Evelyn cast a last look at the cake, gave herself a metaphorical pat on the back, and went to bed. Adam, in his bed at the tavern, watched as the ceiling slowly stopped revolving. He and Alfred had imbibed fully if not prudently.

Colonel Paul Larkin also slept very well that night. Earlier in the day, he had arrived with his horse and a cart with his belongings. The contract for the sale of the Brimley estate had gone without a hitch; it had been completed only that morning.

He had arrived at just before eleven to find Peter and Laura Cove, Luke and Meg Farmer, plus all other 'inside' and 'outside' staff gathered to greet him. He dismounted, then climbed up the steps to the large front door, turned and gave them all a cheery wave.

"Be assured, nothing changes!" he assured them.

Peter and Laura joined him at table for dinner, a dinner that Meg had planned with scrupulous care and attention. A haunch of venison was accompanied by seven different platters of vegetables. The wine to accompany it had been specially chosen by Farmer – a deep, red from the south of France.

"Please assure me that we do not dine like this every day," Larkin said, laying down his knife with a grunt of satisfaction.

"Nay – Meg and Luke were determined to see that you were welcomed in style," Peter Cove laughed. "That simple word of assurance was music to the ears of every single member of the staff."

"I simply wanted them all to know that I intend for the estate to run as perfectly under my ownership as it did under Lady Violette's."

"Both Peter and I will continue to see that it does precisely that when you are away up on the moor," Laura gave him a sincere look. "May we ask what it is that you intend studying up there?"

"Oh, there is no secret to it," Larkin grinned. "There is much history up there. I have heard of the remains of stone dwellings, even stone and bronze implements being unearthed. I intend to study as much of the place that I can, and then write what I sincerely hope will be a detailed history of the moor. Some say that parts of it were inhabited as much as two thousand years ago."

"But surely that would put them there well before Our Lord himself walked the earth!" Laura exclaimed.

"And not that long after the Good Lord Himself created mankind!" Peter added.

Larkin sat and remained silent. He was not at all sure that the Creation, as written in the Bible, had happened in the manner described – nor that it had taken place when some scholars had determined. Did that make him guilty of heresy? He was not sure, so maintained his silence.

Peter and Laura noted that their new landlord had not responded to their observations but put it down to deep thought rather than a reluctance to speak.

"I have the rest of Spring, the coming Summer and Autumn to make a start," Larkin eventually continued the conversation. "I have the strangest feeling that I could well be about my studies for many a year before I am ready to commit pen to paper."

"You must be aware also of the varied nature of the weather up on the moor – especially the higher parts," Peter warned. "The mists can descend almost at a moment's notice. The rain, even the merest drizzle, can soak you through in minutes. There are bogs aplenty, pixie holes to catch the unwary, small rivulets that can turn in an instant into dangerous torrents. It is not a place where a prudent man may take liberties!"

"Surely a sensible man like you cannot believe in pixies?" Larkin smiled.

"Nay – most certainly not. But the holes exist – and some of them are precipitous and very deep. Nobody has ever explained their existence, but they most certainly *do* exist. Many a sheep has been lost down one, and so have a few unwary souls!"

"Then I shall have to be extra careful. Now, on the subject of the moor, do you happen to know of anyone who would be willing to accompany me there, to plot the various landmarks – in effect, help me to make an accurate map."

"There is much superstition where the moor is concerned," Laura observed. "But I am sure that some enterprising young man would be willing to undertake such a mission."

"I do not expect that he would be willing to do it just for the adventure," Larkin grunted. "He would be suitably recompensed. He might even, should the work be of a good enough standard, have his name appended to the eventual publication."

"I know for a fact that Hal – Luke's and Meg's son – would jump at such an adventure if he were old enough and not already apprenticed to Abel Smith," Laura thought aloud.

"On that score, so would Simon's son Jack. He is an adventurous lad but is still far too young – and also apprenticed to the smith." Peter Added.

"Have we overlooked Jamie?" Laura wondered. "He is either twelve already - or is approaching that age. I know for a fact that he has a very sharp mind and is always on the lookout for adventure."

"Why cannot you enlist one of your soldiers?" Peter asked. "Surely, they would not be unused to such a life."

"That would be the most obvious," Larkin agreed. "Were it not for the fact that few of them are able to read and write to any degree. I need someone who is literate and numerate, able to take bearings, gauge distances, who is reasonably familiar with the area. Young Jamie just might fit the bill in another one or two years hence. Correct me if I am wrong, but he is the son of Gil and Ella Ramsey, is he not?"

"Aye, and never one to be content with weeding and harvesting vegetables!" Peter grinned.

"Then I shall approach his parents and see what they have to say on the matter," Larkin nodded to himself. "It would be as well that I do *not* mention it to the young lad first – he might just take it into his head to do it anyway, despite whatever the feelings of his parents."

Nell woke up from a deep sleep and immediately leaped to the window to see clear sky and sunshine. She breathed a sigh of relief. At least the weather would smile upon her great day. And then she sat down on her bed again realising that, when that sun disappeared again, she would be Mistress Nell Clements, no longer Miss Nell Dawkins. She kept as silent as a mouse, fearful of waking James and Avril; she wanted a time to herself for some deep thinking.

First question, she posed to herself – do you love Adam? Answer – an unequivocal yes. Second question – do you love him enough to want to be with him for the rest of your life? That caused about two seconds of thought – yes, I do. Third question – are you happy with the life that is planned for you? Given that I shall have my own workshop, then yes, I am. Fourth and last question – do you want children? Immediate answer – yes, most certainly, but I'm still scared of giving birth. Listen, she lectured herself. You have been in the apothecary business for some years and have seen all manner of illnesses and problems. How many in all that time have died in childbirth? Well, only one – and she was very frail to start with! Stop now and get on with the day!

Nell went out of her room and hammered on the next bedroom door.

"James, Avril – the sun is shining, and it is my wedding day. I shall make breakfast and it shall be ready very soon. Get up!"

Rosie woke up but was nowhere near as tranquil as Nell – or as tranquil a state as Nell had talked herself into. For some days, Rosie had been using all her spare time in her bedroom putting the finishing touches to the wedding present she intended to hand to bride and groom at the wedding feast. It was a picture drawn in pen and ink on a large, rectangular piece of the finest paper. Nell and Adam were featured from the shoulders up, their heads almost touching, and gazing straight out of the paper towards the observer. The two heads were surrounded by drawings of roses, and Rosie was immensely proud of it. The previous evening, she had taken it to Gaston Bessant who, not only an expert on books, was also an accomplished carpenter. He had manufactured an oak frame for the picture. Rosie gave it one final look before she, like Nell, went downstairs to prepare breakfast.

To her annoyance, she found that brother Jamie was already there. Not only had he not started preparing the breakfast, he had not even made a start on feeding the large number of chickens – or collecting the eggs.

"Could you not, just once in your useless life, have helped? Have I to make breakfast *and* tend the hens?" she grated at him.

"But sister dear, you do it all so very competently!" Jamie gave his elder sister his cheekiest grin.

"Jamie!" came a shout from upstairs. "Go and tend the chickens, collect the eggs and just for once make yourself useful!"

"Er, yes, papa," Jamie knew better than to disobey his father. Gil came down as Jamie disappeared out of the back door carrying a sack of grain and a large basket.

"At least it gets him out from under your feet," Gil gave Rosie a pat on the shoulder and a big grin. "Tis a very big day for the town. You shall be very prominent, being right behind Nell."

"Aye, father, I know. I shall also have to keep the other little girls in order. May I ask yours and mama's opinion on something?"

"Of course," Gil sounded intrigued. "And what are we supposed to pass an opinion upon?"

Rosie dashed upstairs and came back down carrying the framed picture very carefully. She placed it on the table for Gil to inspect. Gil looked long and hard at it, then raised his voice."Ella, come down and look at this," he called.

Ella hurried down, believing that some minor catastrophe had happened. Gil pointed wordlessly to the picture.

"Dear Lord above," Ella gasped. "Is this what you have been doing every evening? It is simply beautiful!"

"Aye, beautiful it most certainly is. I take it you wish to present it to Nell and Adam today?"

"Aye, father. That is my intention. Do you think they will like it?"

"Like it? They will love it! It is something they will cherish all their lives."

"How can we have produced a daughter blessed with such a gift?" Ella gave her daughter a hug that almost crushed Rosie.

Jamie came back in with a basket piled high with eggs. He paused to inspect the picture.

"Nell needs a beard like Adam!" he laughed. His mother gave him a fierce glare.

"If you set so much as one finger on that picture, I shall personally tan the hide off you. To suggest defacing it is cruel and spiteful. You are a wicked boy to even suggest such a thing!"

"I was merely jesting, mama," Jamie blanched at the ferocity of the verbal assault from his usually placid mother. "I would not even touch it, I promise."

"Well, your humour is ill-placed," Ella seemed mollified by Jamie's assertion.

Rosie took the picture and put it safely on a high shelf where it would come to no harm. Gil found a piece of clean linen and covered it up to make assurance double sure. Rosie, heaving a sigh of relief, started making breakfast. Her brother went out again to feed and water the hens. Gil and Ella faced one another and shared a look of pride.

Over two hundred miles distant, three ships entered the small port of Dover. Many hands were ready for the mooring ropes as the first vessel rubbed against the jetty. Many more were raised in salutation as an elegant figure was seen ready to proceed down the gangplank. It was a tall figure dressed in the finest silks – silk stockings above silver buckled shoes, silk breeches disappearing beneath the skirts of a long coat embroidered with gold thread. Atop a full-bottomed wig perched a large hat decorated with a large feather. Beneath the hat, a face also decorated with a thin moustache, was looking sternly at a shore he had not seen in quite a few years. Charles Stuart had arrived on his home soil.

It had become common knowledge in the halls of Westminster that Charles would promote his chief advisor Edward Hyde to the office of Lord Chancellor. Hyde had been a roving ambassador in Paris and Madrid. Many were puzzled that Hyde had not travelled with his future king.

Following a very heated, and just as combative, debate, the Mayor of Dover had eventually claimed the right to be the first to speak. As Charles stepped from the gangplank to the jetty, the mayor sank to one knee.

"May I be the first to welcome you back to your rightful home, your majesty," he cried in ringing tones. Most of the rest of the assembled dignitaries also fell to one knee and a chorus of 'welcome' echoed off the cliffs.

Charles maintained a dignified face, managing to hide a smile of satisfaction. He had dreamed of this day ever since he had managed to evade being a witness to his father's execution.

"I thank you for your welcome," he replied in lofty tones. "I am returned to see justice properly done."

And with that, he swept past everyone, his own attendants following, into a rather splendid carriage.

"And what the hell was that supposed to mean?" one dignitary turned to his neighbours.

"I have the strangest feeling that it shall not be too long before we find out!" another grunted.

The church bell was ringing as Nell walked slowly up the street. Her right hand was tucked under the arm of James – who was aware that he was standing in for Nell's long-departed father. Nell wore the splendid dress that had been fussed over my Lou Crowley. On her head was a garland of flowers. Immediately behind her was Rosie, in another of Lou's creations. She held in her hands a small garland of flowers. Behind Rosie came the two little girls who had recently been her own attendants at the May Day pageant.

The street was lined with nearly every inhabitant who could be spared from the necessary labour. As the bridal party passed, they all fell in behind Avril who was furiously blinking back tears of happiness for the girl she had always regarded as her daughter.

"See – everyone is here to wish you well," James whispered as they walked sedately up the street. "I told you that they would."

Nell was tempted to wave at everyone - but held herself in check. She knew that she had to maintain a dignified silence and bestow only a smile as she and James slowly processed through the town. As they reached the church on the left, the small procession passed up the path and at long last Nell was able to see Adam with his father Josiah waiting at the porch. Reverend Forbes was standing behind them, ready to hear their vows.

The crowd behind them pressed forward to witness the exchange of vows and for that special moment when the Reverend pronounced them man and wife. They all fell silent, nobody willing even to scuff the ground with their feet in case they missed a single word. Nell came to stand facing Adam and they gave one another a smile of happiness.

"Dear friends," Forbes hardly had to raise his voice. "Here we are on this wonderful day, come to witness two young people being joined in holy matrimony. We have all known our Nell since she was – what? – four years of age and have watched her grown into a lovely young lady. We have seen for ourselves how she has dedicated herself to learning and the healing arts – and many here will be especially grateful for her ministrations in time of need. That she has followed in the footsteps of James and Avril is no surprise. Who could have wished for better teachers? Before her came Mary, and now comes Rosie – each one dedicated to help their fellow humans when illness or misfortune strike. So, before I may proceed further, I am obliged to ask if anyone here knows of any just impediment why these two may not be joined in holy matrimony?"

He paused, then smiled at the deafening silence that followed.

"As I thought!" he announced to some polite laughter. "And now we come to the meat of the business."

Both Adam and Nell took turns in declaring that they freely entered into marriage to one another. Then they declared their vows in the strict formula laid down. Following that, they declared that they took one another to be their lawful wives and husbands. Finally, wrapping a stole around their joined hands, Forbes declared them to be man and wife. A small ripple of applause slowly grew into a tumult of cheers as Nell and Adam grinned widely and rather self-consciously at the crowd.

And then everyone processed into the church for the service
– which was conducted in a respectful silence, punctuated now
and again by a small choir. And then it was time for the couple
to proceed down the aisle to rousing cheers – and down the street
to the tavern where a magnificent spread was awaiting them.
Rosie, resplendent in her dress and flowers, sped back home to
collect the picture which she carried carefully back to the feast.

Blushing a rather deep shade of pink, she approached the top
table and laid it before Adam and Nell. "This is my wedding
present to you," she stuttered.

The two gazed for a moment at the framed picture. Then Nell
stood up and went around the table to Rosie and enfolded her in
a hug. "It is just the loveliest present you could have thought of,"
she said. "We will treasure it always – and I know exactly where
it shall hang in our new home. Thank you so much. We both love
it."

With a deep sigh of relief, Rosie disentangled herself and
went to take her place where she immediately started to tuck into
slices of beef in a rich gravy. Everyone else was doing the same
and, for a while, all that could be heard was the chomping of teeth
and the grunts of appreciation. It was not customary for there to
be anything but a main course, cheeses, and a fruit dessert.
However, Evelyn – with the happy connivance of James and
Avril – came in with her special cake which she presented before
Nell and Adam. She was followed by John who held a massive
sword. He presented this, hilt foremost, to the couple so that they
could make a big show of cutting the first slice. Grinning like
idiots, the two held the sword between them and sliced it from
centre to edge without the slightest difficulty. Evelyn then took
it away to a massive cheer so that it could be divided into many
small pieces. Adam rose to his feet and waved for silence.

"My dearest new friends," he began. Nell was surprised to
hear that there was no hesitation in his delivery. "You see before
you a man blessed with every joy anyone could wish. Previously,
the happiest day of my life was when Nell agreed to be my wife
– and, I may say, she took some persuading! But that has been
eclipsed by today when she agreed to spend the remainder of her
life with me. I know that you all heard the vows we made to one

another – in the accepted form. But now, I would like to offer another to Nell."

He drew Nell up to stand beside her, then taking her hands in his, proceeded to speak directly to her.

"Nell, I vow on my life that I shall respect you, shall treat you as my equal in all matters, and shall love you more and more each and every day. You have my heart and my undying love. I shall care for you no matter what may befall us and will never give you cause to doubt me. I shall never betray you."

He then raised Nell's hands to his lips and kissed them.

"Some of you may have seen Rosie hand us a present," he held the picture aloft for all to see. "It is just the most perfect present and will be cherished in our home. I believe that Nell has already chosen a spot where it may hang. I am not one who decries the achievements of women and girls. God has chosen to grant Rosie with a very special gift and I for one am in awe of the results of that gift."

He sat down to a thunder of applause.

A little further down the table, Alfred, Adam's cousin, turned to Avril to was sitting on his right.

"Who is that rather lovely young lady sitting down there between that massive smith and his wife? He asked.

Avril said, almost without thinking. "Why, that is Maud. She is the sister of May who is married to Hob, the deputy bailiff."

"May I further ask why she seems to be unaccompanied?" Alfred persisted, aware that he well might be stepping onto someone's toes.

Sensing that something good may come from her conversation, Avril started to explain.

"May's and Maud's parents died a few years back. Maud was as good as betrothed to Zachary, the son of our hosts today – Dick and Sal. Zach was also taken by the same wretched disease. Since then, Maud has lived a rather solitary existence, despite the efforts of her sister May to introduce her to other young men. None has sparked the slightest interest. Poor Maud has, we all believe, settled for a life of loneliness and spinsterhood."

"That would be a terrible waste," Alfred stated. "She is far too lovely for that to happen. May I ask a cheeky favour? When the dancing commences, would you be kind enough to introduce me

to her. Believe me when I say that my intentions are as
honourable as those of my cousin Adam."

"Well, upon that assurance, I shall be only too pleased to do
as you ask. But a word of warning. Maud is shy and reserved.
She will need gently coaxing out of the shell that she has
constructed around her."

Alfred noted this carefully and started to think of words that
were both innocuous and interesting. He regarded Maud again
and knew that she would be a challenge but was determined that
he would win through somehow.

CHAPTER XXIII

Unbeknown to either Adam or Nell, Colonel Paul Larkin had arranged his own surprise for the couple. As soon as it appeared that the time was drawing near for the newlyweds to depart for their home, he mounted his horse and rode quickly back to Brimley. He changed into his old uniform and gathered six men from the estate. Luke Farmer had been a royalist soldier, whilst Sam Garvey and Robert Hook from Parke had been Parliamentary soldiers. These, plus three others strapped swords to their belts, mounted their horses and trotted back to wait quietly outside the tavern. Those who had not managed to get seats inside for the feast eyed this posse with some misgivings.

"Be not afraid, good folks," Larkin grinned at them. "This is simply an escort for the happy couple. Our swords shall be their protection."

Inside the tavern, people were dancing and making merry. A motley band of local musicians were doing their best with viols, sackbut and drums. Avril did as she had promised and steered Alfred to where Maud was sitting at the side.

"Maud, my dear – may I present Alfred Clements. He is cousin to Adam and has been his groomsman. He has asked me to effect an introduction. Alfred, may I introduce Maud Fletcher."

Maud looked up, a trifle startled. However, good manners took over almost immediately and she managed the ghost of a smile and extended her right hand.

Alfred managed a slight bow and took that hand gently in his. "Miss Fletcher, I am delighted to make your acquaintance. May I ask whether you would join me in a dance?"

Maud, ever ready to shun male company, realised that this was neither the time nor the place to be churlish. She again managed a tight smile, rose and joined Alfred at the edge of the floor. Alfred, giving Avril a grin of thanks, took Maud in his arms and, keeping a respectful distance between them, led her in a decorous dance.

"Avril tells me that you have a particular interest in the history of England," he opened the conversation as he steered her expertly through the throng. "And that your particular interest is that of the wars between Lancaster and York. It is mine also."

Maud was immediately suspicious that this was a mere ploy. "If that be the case, Master Clements, perhaps you would be so good as to tell me the relationship between the two Houses."

"You test my integrity? Well, in that, I would not blame you. However, to set your mind at rest, I shall regale you with my knowledge and interest. The House of Lancaster derived from John of Gaunt. The house of York derived from Edmund of York. Both were sons of Edward the third. His eldest son and heir, known as The Black Prince, died before his father, leaving *his* son to inherit the throne. The eventual war between Henry the sixth and Edward – who later became Edward the fourth, split England into savage wars."

"Either you have been doing some recent study, or you do indeed have an interest," Maud acknowledged. "I sincerely hope it is the latter, and not some ploy to worm your way into my affections."

"To prove my deep interest, may I list all the battles from the first conflict at Saint Albans, through the carnage of Tawton, up until the final battle fought at Bosworth – where York finally fell to Tudor."

"Then it would appear that you do indeed have a deep knowledge of the subject," Maud was surprised to find that she was pleased with that result.

"As we seem to share that interest, may I suggest that we ride out together to further our combined knowledge?"

Maud took some time answering that. She had ample excuse as they were threading their way through dancing couples who were steadily getting more and more merry. She used the time to cast surreptitious glances at her partner. All she saw was an earnest face and not a trace of deception.

"I should indeed be happy to do so," she replied.

"I shall, with your permission, call upon you next Sunday after church. I have more than one horse – one of which is a gentle mare."

"I shall look forward to that," Maud gave him a shy smile. She was doubly surprised to find that she really *was* looking forward to it.

May had not missed the dance, nor had she missed the smiles and the conversation between Alfred and her sister. She disengaged herself from her two little daughters with whom she had been dancing – well, sort of. She passed them hurriedly to the care of Lou Crowley, who passed them onto the care of ten-year-old Felix. As the lad was four years older than Kitty and six years older than Poppy, he was not best pleased with the arrangement as he had been looking forward to joining Jack. The two had planned an expedition beneath the tables where they had thought it would be a merry jape to tie people's shoelaces together.

May and Lou sought out Hob, who was downing a mug of spiced ale with Harry and Reverend Forbes.

"Have you seen Maud and Alfred," May blurted out. "They seem to have hit it off quite splendidly. I wonder if that means that my sister is at long last over the loss of Zachary?"

"If so, then tis long overdue," Hob's eyes wandered over the floor and gave a grin when he saw the two heads engaged in smiling conversation.

"What is known of Adam's cousin?" Harry asked. "Adam is a quite splendid fellow and will treat our Nell with care and kindness. But, what of Alfred?"

"That, I most certainly need to find out," May stated, her jaw set in the determined fashion that Hob knew only too well.

"My dear wife – you are not your sister's keeper," he warned.

"No, I am not. But Maud seems so helpless since she lost Zachary. I cannot help it, but I must see her safe!"

"And how do you propose going about it? You can hardly march up to the man and demand to know his intentions!"

"Yes, dearest husband. I know I cannot. But I can approach his cousin and make discreet enquiries. Failing that, his uncle Josiah seems a very nice man. I may approach him instead."

"I would heartily recommend the father first," Harry laughed. "After all, it *is* Adam's wedding day, and his mind is likely to be elsewhere."

May thought this was sound advice and wandered over to Josiah Clements who was sitting alone with a glass of wine, casting a smile over the dancing couples gyrating in front of him.

"Aha! A gentle lady come to take pity on an old man!" he gestured the seat beside him as May hovered. "Do they not make a lovely couple?" he gestured towards his son and Nell who were laughing together as they stepped in unison around the floor.

"Aye – they make a wonderful couple," May was very relieved to have the conversation opened on such an innocuous topic. "I see that my sister is dancing with your nephew," she went on, as if that were just a mere observation.

Josiah gave her a smile. "And you are wondering what sort of man is young Alfred, unless I am seriously mistaken."

"Oh dear, am I so transparent?" May had the grace to blush.

"I am afraid that, in this instance, you are. But cast all worries aside. You are naturally concerned for your sister – and that is something I can readily understand."

"Maud is rather vulnerable," May started to explain. "The young man to whom she was as good as betrothed died a few years past – and she has been almost a recluse since that tragic happening."

"Then your concern is doubly understandable. So, let me allay your fears. Alfred is an extremely studious young man. He is of a slightly Puritan turn of mind – but not to any extreme, I am glad to say. He is engaged in business with a firm of lawyers, not that far distant in Totnes. He studied for his law degree in Oxford and specialises in law as it pertains to farming. You may have no fear for your sister as Alfred is a quiet, well-mannered young man. He neither drinks to excess nor indulges in tobacco. His passion is the history of England. He states that his burning ambition is to write *the* definitive book upon the subject – from the Conqueror down to the Tudors. I have to confess that he can be somewhat boring upon the matter – when he is in the mood to deliver one of his lectures.”

May gave a little giggle. “Then he and Maud have a head start. She is also fascinated with history – the part concerning the wars between York and Lancaster in particular. I wonder if they might actually bore one another to death when the subject arises?”

“Please rest assured that your concern for your sister is fully understood – but also rest assured that it is groundless. She is safe with Alfred. It is probably more true to say that *he* is the more likely to be tongue-tied!”

May spent some time conversing with Josiah before returning to Hob to relay what she had learned.

“Then you can relax and enjoy the rest of the evening,” Hob gave her a playful poke in the ribs.

Dick Allen, self-appointed master of ceremonies, saw that the ‘musicians’ were getting tired and needed a break. He also knew that it was just about time that the happy couple were sent on their way. He made a careful approach to Adam and made the suggestion.

“Aye – that is well thought,” Adam nodded. “We need to make a start so that we can be sure to get to Newton before the sun sets. I do not intend starting life with Nell by finding our way home in the dark.”

Dick gave a chuckle. “On that score, you may have no concerns at all. There is a mounted and armed escort awaiting you.” He seized a large metal bowl and hammered on it with a ladle to get everyone’s attention.

“Tis the time for our newly-wed couple to travel to their home,” he bellowed. “Let us all form a guard of honour for them as they depart for their horses.”

There was a mad scramble as people fought first to get through the doors, and then to obtain the most advantageous places. Nell looked at Adam, gave him a shy smile and slipped her hand into his.

“I would crave just one small favour,” she almost whispered. “I have a call to make before we depart.”

Adam immediately knew what was in Nell's mind. As they passed through the lines of cheering people, they became aware of Larkin and his mounted escort in the street. Nell and Adam were somewhat startled but were immediately reassured by a cheery wave from Larkin.

"Your escort awaits," he called. Adam glanced at Nell and gave her hand a squeeze.

"I would be a fool indeed if I did not know where you need to be. Take all the time you need. I shall come with you to the gate and then wait patiently for you." He turned towards Larkin and explained that they would be only a short while, then went with Nell to the gate into the small cemetery.

Nell walked over to her father's grave and knelt at the side. Silently, she took off her flowered headdress and placed in on the grave.

"Hello, dada," she said quietly. "Here I am, a married woman. Did you fear this day would never come? Well, it has, and I have the perfect husband – so you may rest easy as your little girl shall come to no harm with him. I shall talk to you every day as I have always done and shall come to visit you as often as I am able. Please tell the mama I never knew that her daughter is very happy and content."

Rising, she blew the usual kiss towards the small headstone, turned and walked purposefully to her new life.

AUTHOR'S NOTE

So ends part 4 of the saga. I started in 1646 with the Battle of Bovey Heath. This part ends with the Restoration in 1660 – fourteen years of battles, despair of some, triumph of others, continued life in a small Devon town.

The experiment of the Commonwealth effectively ended when Cromwell himself died on the 3rd September 1658. Coincidentally, three hundred years after, to the exact day, I started my own, short military career! Cromwell's son Richard (Tumbledown Dick) was a well-meaning, totally ineffective replacement for his father, leading to all sorts of comings and goings.

John Lambert, a military commander of great experience, ousted the elected members of parliament and ran what was essentially a military dictatorship. Unfortunately for him, he neglected to pay his soldiers. So, when the time came to face an advance from Monck and Fairfax, these same soldiers melted away into the night. Back came the old Rump Parliament. It was called the 'Rump' because it was the remainder of the original, large, elected parliament that had been so disastrously ignored by Charles I. Monck recalled the Rump and almost its first order of business was to invite Charles Stuart back as king.

In the narrative, I make short reference to the Declaration of Breda. This was an agreement made by the exiled Charles II in the Netherlands town of Breda in early April 1660, six or seven weeks before he made his return to Dover in late May. In it, he agreed to a general amnesty of all enemies of his and of his late father *who acknowledged him to be rightful king*. It also went on to allow tolerance of religious belief, settlement of land disputes, and full arrears of pay to the army. No wonder some people in high places were somewhat concerned by the 'amnesty' clause!

He brought back with him Edward Hyde (Later 1st Earl of Clarendon and Lord Treasurer). He was Charles' principal advisor – and will take some part in the next episode – A Time Of Disillusion.

The period of this book – 1659-1660 – was indeed a time of change. There were many changes! Most of them made little difference to the lives of my Bovey inhabitants. They continued to have their own problems – the weather occasioned mainly by its proximity to Dartmoor – deaths due to 'winter fever' – hard work maintaining continuity of food supply. However, I have managed to inject a small measure of happiness to some, and general contentment to others. Whether any if this is actually justified, I leave to your determination.

9 781917 601443